Praise for

League of Love

The League of Love is a superb series by the very talented Ms. Gallagher. I absolutely love these characters and the men who are all hunky heroes... If you are no fan of footy then prepare to be tempted to go down under and see what it is all about.
~ *Coffee Time Romance*

I loved the overall plot of the story, and the message really hits home: you have to love yourself before you can love anyone else. Emily's Cowboy moved at a great pace... I will definitely be picking up the rest of the books in the series. ~ *Just Erotic Romance Reviews*

Totally Bound Publishing books by Donna Gallagher:

League of Love Volume One
Caitlin's Hero
Mandy's He-Man

League of Love Volume Two
Laura's Light
Pippa's Fantasy

LEAGUE OF LOVE
Volume Three

Emily's Cowboy

Sarah's Soldier

DONNA GALLAGHER

League of Love Volume Three
ISBN # 978-1-78184-681-0
©Copyright Donna Gallagher 2013
Cover Art by Posh Gosh ©Copyright 2013
Interior text design by Claire Siemaszkiewicz
Totally Bound Publishing

Published in 2014 by Totally Bound Publishing, Newland House, The Point, Weaver Road, Lincoln, LN6 3QN, United Kingdom.

EMILY'S
COWBOY

Dedication

To the lovely ladies of the Sydney branch of ARRA —
thank you for your support and friendship.
As always, hugs and thanks to my wonderful editor,
Amy.

Chapter One

They were going to kill him. The collective look in the men's eyes was one of pure animosity. Emily could see it clearly defined in their faces, could see the intent as they charged towards the man she loved — three huge men, covered in mud and perhaps even blood, judging by the russet-coloured liquid leaking from one of the men's bandaged head — and there was nothing she could do about it. She couldn't look away and sat frozen in the moment as she watched the horror unfold before her, silently praying that Gareth would survive the next few brutal seconds.

Then they were on him, two around his upper body, one knocking his legs out from beneath him as they picked him up and slammed him, back first, onto the hard ground. The four men wrestled together. He was caught beneath the onslaught from the three above him — she could see him struggling to get to his feet. It really only took a matter of seconds, but for Emily it was a lifetime. Her heart raced, her palms moistened and she could not get the air into her lungs to take her next breath, the fear he would be hurt was so overwhelming.

Just when Emily thought she could bear it no longer, the men stopped struggling. They broke away, stood and faced each other. Gareth reached down, put the ball under his foot and rolled it behind him. Emily drew a breath down deep into her oxygen-deprived lungs… The tackle was over.

Every game was the same for Emily. It didn't matter that for all intents and purposes Gareth was no longer hers, by her own choice. It would always be like that for her—the same fear, the same panic that overwhelmed her as she watched him play his beloved rugby league. It had started way back in the days of their childhood when she and Gareth had been joined at the hip, back when she would accompany his family to those junior rugby league matches. Emily always had the same reaction—horror and fear as she watched every tackle in a hypnotic trance, a panicked state, her breath trapped in her lungs until the moment she saw him back on his feet, healthy and unharmed despite the brutality of the sport he loved. She had never loved the game the way he did. Her only reason for watching was for reassurance that he remained uninjured, and had survived his time on the field without harm. She didn't care if the team won or lost. For Emily, it was just about Gareth.

Of course, her family—and even Gareth himself—had no idea her interest was so limited. They believed her a true fan of the sport. Why wouldn't they? She had been with Gareth for every local game he'd ever played. Well, apart from that time she had been in the hospital, but she would have been there watching if she could have.

As Emily tuned out, uninterested in the commentator's wrap up of the televised game, she absentmindedly rubbed at her scars, the puckering skin of her deformity, the unkind reminder of the day her world had changed. She was hardly aware of her unconscious movement—her focus was on her relief that the final siren had sounded, concluding yet another game her precious Gareth had remained unscathed.

"Chin up, Em. This is what you decided. No point second guessing or reminiscing. Gareth has moved on, his life is in the big city and you have chores to do." She spoke the words in an attempt to quell the usual sadness she felt, as her only link to Gareth ended with the conclusion of the television broadcast. Emily turned the seldom used television off, waited till the black screen was all that was left to see and walked from the room. Her posture was hunched, her gait slow as she headed to the barn to feed the horses and clean the stalls. The routine, mundane tasks would fill her mind enough that the pain that lanced her heart would eventually fade.

"Game finished? How'd he go? Did they win?"

Her father's deep voice breached her thoughts, bringing her back to the here and now, preventing any further painful memories from surfacing.

"Yep, they won. Gareth came through okay." Emily didn't want to discuss Gareth any more. It was better to push him from her mind for now, knowing full well that it would only be a week before once again she would sit white-knuckled in front of the television, riding every moment with him, feeling every knock he took as if it was her on the field. Why she could not just keep herself from this anguish week after week, she could not explain. It was just something she had to do.

She had sent him away, destroyed every plan they had ever made for their future—and they *had* planned and dreamt about what a perfect life they would have together, had talked of such things late into the night on many occasions. That was before she'd pushed him from her life, but she could not stop loving him, worrying for him. Emily knew this like she knew she would take another breath, and until that last breath she would love Gareth like no other.

But she'd had no choice. The accident had robbed her of that future, that destiny. Her deformity had changed all that. It was hard enough for *her* to live with it every day, and she could avoid the scarring if she stayed away from her own reflection. Those around her, forced to gaze upon her, had no such luxury—no, to their eyes the deformation was glaringly obvious, and Emily could not bear the looks of pity on the faces of the people she loved, and especially not on Gareth's.

Maybe once she had been good enough for him, but now there was no way. He deserved beauty in his life, not some hideous excuse for what she had once been. Gareth was loyal and Emily understood that he would have remained with her out of pity, a sense of duty to what they'd once had, the dreams they had once made, but she could not let that be the life for him. A life filled with the sight of her ugliness, when he woke each and every morning to see her as she was now. A life spent trying to ignore the whispered comments as she walked by, or the pointing, the looks of horror on the faces of innocent children scared by her appearance. Gareth deserved much more than that, and that was why Emily had sent him to the big city, told him to go and make a career playing rugby league, the way he was meant to. Despite all the plans they had made, she had told him, as her heart had broken, that she had changed her mind, hated the thought of living in a chaotic place full of cement buildings. She had told Gareth that she could not live without the fields and freedom of the countryside, told him she would not leave the family farm, would not make the move to the city with him as she had promised.

She had known that living without Gareth would be suffocating, nearly impossible to survive, but she had hidden those emotions from him, ignored his pleas. Ignored the distress she'd seen in his eyes, in his features as she had pushed him away, until finally, Gareth had done as she had asked, and left.

Taking away her sunshine.

Her heart.

Emily tried not to think of the hurt she had caused Gareth. She was doing the right thing for him, the only thing. He would see that eventually when he found someone new, someone whole to love. Emily just hoped that when that time came, she would be able to hold herself together, to survive seeing him happy with another woman, surrounded by children—his and his new love's. It would remind Emily of the plans they had made together, which had been robbed from her by the fire that had ruined her life.

"We really should use the quad bikes more, Em. Need to catch up with the other farms, but I just love the old ways, the feel of my horse beneath me. But I do get tired of the manure, that's for sure."

Her father made this same statement nearly every day, and Emily smiled at the comforting familiarity of the moment. She did love the farm and adored her father. Being with him was no hardship. His love would have to be enough for her. Her father was a hero to her. He loved her without hesitation, never one with the idea that men must guard their emotions or else be thought of as weak. Not Daniel Mackenzie. No—Mac, as he was known to his friends, was proud to show his affection for his only daughter. He had not hidden the tears on his face as he had waved goodbye to his son, Dylan, who was off fighting the war in Afghanistan, a member of the Australian contingent of serviceman sent to serve in that area.

"Dad, if I had a dollar for every time you said that, we could retire to some waterfront mansion on the Gold Coast." She laughed, her mood slightly better, her memories back under control, locked away in that safe place usually only opened late at night when she was alone in her room. "You do what you want, Dad. Use quads, stick with the horses...gee, buy a helicopter for all I care, as long as you are happy and we get the work done. It's your farm."

"Rubbish, Em. This is as much your farm as it is mine, especially now...with Gareth leaving you and all. I'll never understand that boy—so selfish..."

"Dad, *stop!* I've told you a million times it wasn't like that. I sent Gareth away. I just didn't want the same things as he did anymore. It was not his fault. You need to remember that. *It was me.*" Emily was shouting at her father, she knew she was, but she could not stop, could not lower her voice. Her emotions were out of control. It was too soon after the agony of watching him play—the teasing close-ups of his face had just added to her pain, reminding her of what she could not have.

"Okay, Emily, no need to shout. It's a father's right to place blame on everyone but his own children. I know you hurt. Hell, you miss him — a blind man could see that. You never leave the farm, never even talk to anyone but me and the workers. If what you say is true, and you sent him away, why haven't you moved on, girlie? I'm getting old, hoped to have some grandchildren to bounce on me knee someday. You're not going to break the dreams of your old man, are you, Em?"

Even though her father winked, spoke in a teasing manner, a barb struck directly into Emily's heart.

"Dreams are not always meant to come true, Dad. That's why they're dreams. Maybe you can harass Dyl. He's older than me, anyway, and I just don't think I'm cut out for motherhood."

Emily ignored the shocked look that had appeared on her father's usually smiling face. She took up a shovel and fiercely attacked the dirty hay in the stall she was in, hoping that her father would take the hint and leave the subjects of Gareth and grandchildren alone. Emily would not be bringing any children into this world — not now she wouldn't be sharing any with Gareth, and certainly not any that would have to deal with the embarrassment of having a monster for a mother.

Chapter Two

"Ooh... You're Gareth Andrews! You play for the Jets."

The high-pitched female voice screamed in his ear as the woman spilt her drink over his shirt. God, he hated groupies, wished they would just leave him be. Gareth tried a smile but only managed a grimace in the squealing woman's direction as he wiped at his wet shirt with the napkin he'd picked up from the bar he stood at. All he had wanted was to be served his beer, but now he had to deal with this.

"Yep, that'd be me. Nice to meet you, love, but I'm not looking for any company right now," he replied quickly, gruffly. He had found that directness was the best option when dealing with this sort of unwanted attention. After dropping the soggy paper towel back on the bar and retrieving his change from Mick the barman, Gareth grabbed his beer. He spun on his heel and made a quick retreat to the private area that Mitch 'Rook' Harris had set up in his nightclub, Jetstream, for his fellow Jets teammates.

Gareth could see that the area was full tonight after the team's—*his* team's—latest victory. All the usual suspects were in attendance. Coach Brodie James and his wife, Caitlin. Assistant coach Jon 'JT' Thomson, taking up a lot of space with his gigantic presence, and Mandy. Most of his fellow teammates—guys like Deano, Mark, Joseph, Josh and their significant others—all mingled about, enjoying themselves. Gareth greeted them all with a nod before quickly moving to join the one person in the city he felt closest to—the Jets' physiotherapist, Phillipa Rogers, Pippa to her friends.

"Hey, Cowboy! Caught some attention at the bar tonight, I see." Pippa's friendly teasing at his ordeal made him smile—a genuine smile. She understood his discomfort at the notoriety that came with playing first grade rugby league. She knew the story of his broken heart, his longing for the girl he had left behind, his Emily. It wasn't long ago that she had shared that connection with him, had had a longing of her own, but that was all sorted out now that she and Rook had officially become a couple, after years of secretly yearning for each other. They had even announced their engagement, started planning a wedding.

"Give it a rest, Pippa. It's your fault, you know. Before you and Rook patched things up I had you to protect me, keep me safe and out of the clutches of the marauding groupies. You left me defenceless, a poor country boy naïve to the demands of the forward city womenfolk."

"Oh, poor Gareth, my heart bleeds for you, mate." Gareth heard the familiar sound of Rook's voice behind him. "Men the world over would kill for your problems. Don't blame my woman for abandoning you. Find your own to save you from the groupies—this one's mine."

"Yeah, Rook, I know…first world problems. Still can't believe she picked you over me. You're getting on in years, buddy, and yet here I am still in the prime of my life. Maybe I'm still hoping to win her over for a bit of pity love."

Gareth gave Pippa a wink, letting her know he was only joking. Gareth was well aware that Pippa loved Rook, had for years, and there was no way in hell she was letting Rook go now she had him. Anyway, Gareth—even after three long, lonely years—had still not been able to push Emily from his heart. He had at one time, briefly, thought he could make a go of loving Pippa, but had only been kidding himself, mistaking friendship for something more. It had probably been more a case of trying to ease the hurt Pippa had been suffering over the whole Rook thing. That was in the past, just like his Em should be. Gareth did enjoy winding up his captain and Jets' halfback, though, and amusingly he nearly always got a jealous reaction from his friend. Gareth was not disappointed this time, either, as Rook glared at him.

"Fuck you, Gareth. Pippa's mine and you keep your bloody hands off her."

"Gareth, Mitch, stop it. Mitch, he is just getting a reaction from you. You know it's not like that between us. You will always be my fantasy man, Mitchell Harris, and you know it." Pippa pinched Gareth on the arm in retaliation for his teasing of her beloved fiancé.

"Ouch, that hurt, Pippa." It hadn't really, but Gareth played along with the conversation, enjoying the banter, the connection to those around him, in the hope that he could banish the loneliness that had haunted him since his move from the country to the big city.

He had given some thought to accepting the advances of one of his female fans just so he could feel some human comfort, block out those feelings of loneliness, but it never felt right. Gareth didn't feel comfortable using a woman that way, knowing that any lover he took to his bed would be just a poor substitute for the one he really wanted.

Gareth could hardly believe that he had been celibate for so long. It had to be over three years since he had last made love to Emily. That last memory was bittersweet in his mind. The pleasure of her body under his, the feel of her hot, moist pussy surrounding his cock, her skin soft to his touch, her breasts full, her nipples hard. The taste of her juices haunted him to this very day. He craved them, could still remember her flavour on his tongue, an addiction he could not cure, no matter how he tried.

The pointlessness in holding on to those memories of her was never far from his mind. She'd ripped out his heart by sending him away. Emily had tried to make him believe that she didn't love him anymore, didn't want him or the plans and dreams they had spoken of so often. But Gareth knew it hadn't been that—it had been her inability to face what had happened to her, to ignore the scars that marred her body, the marks that were a testament to her bravery. He had not seen them as she had. Gareth had hardly noticed the burns at all, but that was all Emily had seen. Even when she hadn't been looking in a mirror, she'd seen them in her mind, and even though Gareth loved her more than anything and everything on this earth, his love hadn't been enough for Emily. It hadn't been enough to convince her she was his. She was beautiful. She was allowed to be happy and have all the dreams that they had planned.

So instead of sharing the life they had planned together, both he and Emily remained alone and apart.

"Earth to Cowboy... Come in, Cowboy..."

"Eh, what? Did you say something, Pippa? I was miles away."

"Yeah, I got that impression...and I can guess where. Mitch has gone to the bar to get you another beer, said something about saving you from the attention of your adoring fans. Gareth, seriously, you need to do something about this whole Emily thing. Why don't you take the advice I was given by someone I love, and just tell her how you feel? What's the worst that can happen?"

Gareth was a bit shocked that Pippa was using that same advice he had given her right back at him, but he knew in this case, words would not help.

"Pippa, I have told her. Over and over again. I've begged and pleaded my case, but it didn't help...wasn't enough. The fire damaged more than her skin. It changed her, her spirit. My Emily is gone. She hides behind her scars, uses them to keep us apart. Who knows, maybe I've got it all wrong. Could be that deep down it's just an excuse I've dreamt up. Maybe she just doesn't feel the same way about me anymore. Maybe I need to face up to that. Move on."

Even saying the words cut deeply. Gareth would never be able to move on. He understood that. He had loved Emily for as long as he'd had memories, could not recall a time when he had not loved her in some way. Could not really remember a time that Emily had not been a part of his life. Their families were neighbours, albeit miles apart, but in the country that was the way it was. The Mackenzie house was the nearest home to the Andrews house. They had grown up together, he and Emily. They were the same age and they had played together, gone to school together. Gareth could even remember the exact moment his body had reacted to hers, male to female, and his feelings of brotherly love had become much, much more.

He recalled noticing over their early teenage years, without a great amount of interest on his part, that Emily's body was changing, but it was during their eighteenth year, that first time they had swum together after a long, cold winter, that he had really seen her as a temptation, as more than just a friend. The sun had finally been shining and the country heat had been rising with the return of spring, back towards the usual scorching temperatures that the northern areas of New South Wales achieved. They had spent the afternoon on horseback, riding together, checking fences between the two properties, when they'd reached one of the dams their neighbouring properties shared. The attraction of freshening their sweaty bodies in the cool water of the dam had been hard to resist. They had swum together many times, so when Emily had urged her horse in the direction of the water, yelling, "Last one in is a rotten egg!" over her shoulder as she'd taken off at full gallop, Gareth had followed suit. He had jumped from his horse before her and stripped down to his briefs quickly, as he had done many times before, and had raced to the water's edge, winning the race his only concern. He had thrown himself into the waist-deep water and as he'd broken the surface, then stood shaking his head to clear the water and hair from his eyes, he had caught sight of her.

She had been standing alongside his discarded clothing, had removed her boots and jeans and was clad in her girlie underwear. Her shirt, also removed, had been clutched before her, in front of her chest and she'd had a look of uncertainty about her, a shyness Gareth had never seen in her stance before. He'd stood still, had watched her as her eyes had locked onto his, had seen the slight movement of her hands as the shirt had dropped and fluttered to the ground.

Gareth's world had altered in that one movement. Altered for all time as his gaze had moved from her face to her body. Her very feminine body.

Emily, wearing just a bra and panties. He had taken in the picture she had presented him. Gone was the familiar, nondescript child's body he'd been used to seeing and in its place was a beauty he had never imagined. Emily's breasts had filled the bra, a roundness that reminded him of soft pillows, spilled from the top of each cup. His mouth had gone instantly dry as his thoughts had turned to images of touching the tempting swells, feeling the weight of each perfect, plump breast in his hands. He had been able to imagine how good that feeling would be, fingers and hands by his sides mimicking his thoughts, pumping and clasping at the water. But the vision had not ended there. Gareth, finally managing to drag his eyes from Emily's plump, round breasts, ran his gaze slowly over the rest of her nearly naked form. A hunger he had not ever felt before consumed him as he took in the sight of her. His Emily.

Her black hair had fallen around her breasts all the way down to her slightly flared hips, caressing her body, outlining her shape, framing her beauty. Gareth had just made out the black covering of hair on her pussy through her white underwear, had imagined that the feel of the covering would be velvety soft to touch. Her legs were long, toned, but still had a feminine softness about them, their shape he'd found for some reason enticing. Her skin had appeared silky and he'd had the urge to run his hands along that smoothness, to caress every inch of her. He'd felt his penis go hard, achingly so, and had been glad he'd stood waist deep in water to conceal his embarrassing new reaction to her. She was Emily, his childhood buddy. Gareth had wondered what was happening to him, why her new shape was making him react in such a way.

"Shit, Em, what happened to you?"

Gareth remembered those eloquent words to this day. He and Emily had laughed about them on many occasions. His lack of subtlety. The fact it had taken so long for him to notice how she had grown from child to woman. It was Emily's response to his question that had sealed their fate, her shy, timid question that had made his heart race and had him striding from the water to gather her into his arms.

"Do you like what you see Gareth? Please say you do. Put me out of my misery. I've prayed for you to notice the changes in me, hoped that you would want to kiss me as much as I dream of kissing you. Just looking at you, your broad shoulders, your long legs, how strong you have become, makes me crazy. I need to feel you touching me Gareth, kissing me. Please. I don't want to go insane. Help me."

And he had kissed her, tentatively at first, their lips joining lightly as they'd explored each other's taste. They'd caressed and touched places that until that moment in time had been private. But to him, Emily was an extension of himself. Touching her and kissing her had felt like the most natural thing in the world to him, and yet so incredibly pleasing. The feel of her breasts had been such a wondrous thing. There were no words that got close to describing the feel of her soft skin against his.

"Don't even try, Mitch. He's gone again, off in some dream world…"

Gareth crashed back to reality as Pippa's words to Rook about him broke through his thoughts. He was back in real time, back to the world where he now lived — the world without Emily.

"Sorry, guys, I'm finished dreaming. Where's that beer you promised, Rook?"

"It's the one that's gone warm sitting in front of you, mate."

"Yeah, right. It'll be fine. Thanks," Gareth said. He picked up the bottle and took a mouthful of the amber fluid, putting his memories back where they belonged — locked up tightly in his mind where they could not cause him any added pain.

"So what did I miss? What's the latest on the big day? Any new drama you need your Cowboy to wrangle back under control, Pippa?"

Gareth had been both delighted and horrified when Pippa had asked him to stand up for her as a pseudo-bridesmaid. She had wanted her best friend — Cassie — Riley Walters and Gareth to act as her side of the bridal party. Luckily for Gareth, Riley had been equally horrified at the idea, and so they had been saved from what sounded like an uncomfortable ordeal. Gareth really cherished his newfound friendship with Pippa, but really? Friendship only went so far…

"Huh, you're just still trying to get back into Pippa's good books after you refused to be her bridesmaid at our wedding." Gareth could not miss Rook's smug grin as he took a gulp of his beer.

It was always like that between Gareth and Rook these days—both trying to score points over one another where Pippa was concerned.

"Look, I just didn't want Riley to feel too bad over the whole thing, so I sided with the guy. What can I say? I'm sensitive that way."

The ensuing laughter over his comments helped Gareth banish any residual sorrow from his reminiscing over Emily, and for the rest of the night he kept his mind locked onto the present, enjoying the friendly banter with his friends but still refusing to acknowledge any attention from the female crowd at the popular nightspot.

Gareth was relieved that he and Rook were back to normal. Their friendship had hit a few rough spots during the whole Rook-and-Pippa drama. But they were solid again—even the perpetual teasing was just goodhearted fun. Gareth was thankful for his teammates being the stand-up guys they were, otherwise he would never have been able to deal with the life he now led, the constant training, travelling between each game and Gareth's biggest nightmare— public appearances.

He did love the fact that through his unasked for notoriety he could do some good in the community. Gareth enjoyed being able to bring some cheer to sick kids with his visits to children's hospitals, or to assist charities and other good causes with fundraising by lending his services, be it standing around looking stupid or donating some signed piece of memorabilia. That was the upside of his playing footy—that and actually being on the field. Playing rugby league was his life, being pitted against rival teams, revelling in his competitive nature, his desire to be the best. But with all that came the drawbacks—the press, the spotlight, the ever-present groupies and the pain of training.

Thoughts of training had him remembering the following day's recovery session. Thankfully, Brodie had set it for mid-morning and not the usual crack of dawn schedule that he usually favoured. That probably coincided with the fact Brodie was at the club with his stunning redheaded wife, which was not a usual occurrence of late, as Caitlin had recently given birth to the couple's second child. Both Brodie and JT were now proud fathers, with a boy and girl each. Gareth loved the days that the team spent surrounded by their kids and partners. They were an extended family of sorts, each member equally protective of the others. Gareth realised that it would be the closest he came to having children of his own. Being an adoptive uncle to the gaggle of children was all that he could hope for. The idea of a child that wasn't Emily's was not for consideration.

"I'm heading out, Pippa, Rook. The game's starting to catch up with me, need to go and grab some shut-eye before tomorrow's training." Gareth finished the last of his second beer, the fluid warm and flat, having sat on the table for so long. He was always vigilant about staying below the legal alcohol limit. He didn't want to chance driving impaired. Alcohol and driving were not a good mix, ever.

"Why, Cowboy? Are you feeling something serious now, something you need me to take a look at?"

Gareth could always count on the physiotherapist in Pippa to jump all over any statement he made about soreness after a game. It was her job, after all. He also knew that she worried about him as a person.

"No, Pippa, nothing to concern you with... Just a general tiredness."

"Good to know, Cowboy. Thought you were angling for a private massage or something. You know Pip's a sucker for a strained muscle. She likes to pay particular attention to my groin area, you know."

"Mitch..."

The blush that stole over Pippa's cheeks at Rook's sexual innuendo was a delight to Gareth.

"Yeah, Rook, I bet she does, or maybe she's just trying to strengthen the muscles. Maybe you're lacking in some stamina there, bud? Catch you all tomorrow." Gareth couldn't resist flinging the last sledge at Rook before he headed back through the throng of party-goers to the club's exit, looking forward to being away from the blaring noise of the music and relentless hub of the Jetstream. Deep down, Gareth was a country boy, a cowboy. He enjoyed the simple things in life—the quiet of the countryside, the wide open spaces—and even though he did love his footy, he looked forward to the day he could return to the peace and quiet of the land.

Chapter Three

"Son, it's your mother."

"Yeah, that was a given, Mum. Not many people call me 'son'! What's up? Has something happened? Is Dad okay?"

The phone had awakened Gareth from a dead sleep. Concern for his father was his immediate reaction—he was speaking to his mother, so she was obviously okay.

"No, Gareth, your father is fine. *I'm* fine. It's Mac. There has been a terrible accident...a tractor rolled. They are transporting him, by plane, to a hospital in Sydney. It's serious, son. I'm not exactly sure of all the details—all I know is that Emily is with him. I thought you would want to know. She might need a familiar face, some support. I know you two are not... Well... I know things are different. But I just wanted you to know...you know, in case."

"Which hospital, Mum?"

Gareth could tell his mother was worried, could understand her concern for the Mackenzie family, for Mac and Emily. They had been neighbours and friends forever—close friends, a friendship only those in the rural community could begin to understand. Gareth had appreciated the fact his parents had never made an issue of what had happened between him and Emily, had respected his privacy surrounding the events. But Gareth knew his mother was disappointed. Her heart had been set on he and Emily marrying some day, having her grandchildren, but she had tried to hide her disappointment from him, had been supportive of his decision to move to Sydney and sign with the Jets. And she had been right to call him about what had happened.

He pulled on the nearest clothing he could find, grabbed his keys and phone, then took off at a frantic pace for the hospital. He was thankful for the GPS system installed in his car as it showed him the way, and he arrived as the dawn's rays heralded the beginning of a new day. All Gareth's thoughts centred on finding Mac and Emily and being there for them, whatever they needed.

After enquiring at the hospital's reception and admissions desk in a not so polite or friendly way—more a demand to know where Mac was being cared for—Gareth took off all but running, trying to correctly navigate the maze of corridors and doors that would lead him to his destination. Only to be halted in his desperate undertaking at the last impediment—the entrance to the intensive care ward—by a stern, determined nurse.

"Only family members allowed at this stage, sir, I'm sorry. If you take a seat in the waiting room, I'll go and find out some information for you about the patient's welfare, although there is not much I can tell you without the consent of the patient or his family."

Gareth saw red, so angered by the obstinate nurse denying him entry that he could feel himself shaking.

"That's just bullshit. Mac is like family to me and his daughter is facing this on her own. They need me with them," he shouted, his words harsh as frustration joined with the anger he now felt. One set of doors was all that stood between him and Emily. All that was keeping him from her — and Mac — was one stubborn, autocratic hospital employee.

"Be that as it may, sir — and I must insist you refrain from using that type of language — I'm just doing my job, following hospital policy. The policy that states 'immediate family only'." The nurse pointed at the sign on the hospital wall that confirmed her stance, but Gareth was not appeased, and growled in frustration as he read the words. "Please, if you sit down and stop shouting at me I can go and get you some information."

She was right. Gareth had no right to speak to her in such a rude manner. It was just that he was worried sick.

"You're right. I apologise. Please, if you could go and check on Mac — I mean, Daniel Mackenzie from Gunnedah — I'd be very grateful for your help. Tell them Gareth Andrews is here, if you can."

Gareth noticed the flicker of recognition in the nurse's eyes at the mention of his name, and the way she gave him another subtle once-over. But he was relieved she didn't waste time acknowledging the fact as she hurried off behind those doors, those grey impediments keeping him from getting what he wanted.

* * * *

What on earth was taking so long? Emily could not stand it any longer—the waiting, the not knowing.

Her father, Mac—the larger than life, most important person in her world—was in surgery. Battling for survival. For how long was anyone's guess. No one had been out to see her for hours. She should have gone searching for him sooner, should have known something had been wrong. Emily was going out of her mind as she replayed the afternoon's horrible events over and over.

The sight of him lying under the fallen tractor, so still, so pale…if she lived to be a hundred, she would never forget that sight. Her sense of panic, not knowing what she should do first, or if her dad was still alive. Then the utter hopelessness at her inability to free his unconscious, barely breathing body from under the weight of the tractor pinning him to the ground. Her fear she would not be fast enough as she had ridden her horse, without mercy, to the Andrews farm to get help, terrified that he would die out there all alone because she hadn't got help to him in time.

The call to the emergency services, as she had tried to explain what had happened coherently, was a blur. Emily had thanked the Lord for the help from Malcolm and Gail Andrews, for her neighbours' aid in not only directing the emergency services to the correct location, but Malcolm's insistence on returning with her to her father's side to wait. It had taken an excruciating length of time for the paramedics to reach the paddock her father had lain broken in. Then there had been the wait for the helicopter to land, to airlift her father to the aircraft that would make the flight to Sydney, to the surgeons who were needed to repair her father's damaged body.

There had been so much waiting, and there was just so much that she hadn't managed to do. It was all adding up in her brain. She still had not contacted her brother directly. The number Dylan had given her to use in an emergency — and Emily could not think of any worse kind of emergency — had not proven very helpful. The person recording her near hysterical version of events had remained quite emotionless and unable to tell Emily, with any certainty, when Dylan would get her message. He had only said that it would be as soon as possible. What the hell did that mean? As soon as possible — what sort of time frame did that involve? What if her father didn't pull through surgery before Dyl was informed? What if her brother never had the chance to see their Dad alive again? She should have tried harder, been more demanding, insisted on speaking to someone in authority. But she had just been holding it together as it was, reaching a breaking point, not sure she could stand another second of the torment of not knowing.

The lights and smells of the hospital were making her sick, making her head throb, and even that made her feel guilty. How could she be caring about her own problems when her father was in who knew what condition, what amount of agony? So she continued pacing, her agitation growing with every second.

* * * *

It seemed like hours had passed since the doors had closed behind the nurse with a resounding click. He had already decided that he would just break the doors down if he had to wait much longer. He'd envisioned shoulder-charging them as he would an opponent during a game — after all, it was something he was renowned for. Why not make use of that talent when it could aid him in his quest? He needed to make sure his friends would be okay. Or maybe he just needed to be with them.

When she finally reappeared, Gareth could read nothing in the nurse's features, nothing that would tell him either way what was happening. He rushed to her.

"Well, what can you tell me? Is Mac going to be okay? Is his daughter with him?" Gareth fired the questions at the nurse one after the other, not leaving her any time for a response.

"Mr Mackenzie is already in surgery. They took him straight there on arrival. He actually hasn't been to ICU yet, but he has been pre-admitted and will be here after the surgery."

Gareth was crushed. He had wasted precious time waiting to be told he needed to be somewhere else in the godforsaken maze of the hospital.

"How do I get there?" he asked, frustration choking the words he spoke.

"I'll show you. Calm down. If what you say is true and the patient's daughter is alone, the last thing she needs is for you to start a riot in the hospital. Your friend is not the only patient here and while I can see you are clearly distraught for the family's welfare, I need you to calm down. C'mon, Gareth. Follow me. I know a shortcut—staff only access. It will be quicker."

Again, Gareth could not fail to acknowledge how correct the nurse was in her assessment. He wasn't sure if she was helping him because she'd recognised him, or if she was just being helpful and had a good memory for names. Either way, Gareth appreciated the lengths she was going to for him.

He followed in her silent footsteps, the sound of his heavy boots on the hospital's hard floor like claps of thunder echoing against the bleak, plain walls of the endless corridors she was leading him along. Then, as he trailed after his guide like some mindless sheep around one more corner, he saw Emily.

She looked pale and grief-stricken, twisting her fingers through each other as she paced the room like a caged animal. Though it should have been the last thing he noticed, the last thought going through his mind at such a terrible time, Gareth could not stop himself from appreciating her beauty. Her long, black hair was dishevelled, her clothes crumpled, her dirty jeans hugging her like a second skin, and still she was the most breathtaking sight Gareth had ever seen. God, he had missed just looking at her. He stood there like a cement pillar, soaking up the sight, committing the image of her to his memories.

"Ahem, excuse me — Miss Mackenzie, is it? Sorry to disturb you, but I have a friend of the family who is keen to see you."

At first, Gareth could have killed the nurse for making their presence known. He had been so pleased to be able to see Emily in the flesh, forgetting his original purpose, the reason they were all here. Now, due to the nurse alerting Emily to his presence, he was afraid that she might refuse to speak with him, was faced with the only too real possibility that she might send him away again. The thought of it terrified him. If he could just feel her in his arms again, just once more… *My God, I'm so fucking in love with her it's beyond endurance.* The thought was like a knife piecing his chest.

Gareth stood still, holding his breath, unable to resume even the simple task of filling his lungs until he saw her reaction to him being at the hospital, to him being so close. Until she accepted him and the fact he was here with her, for her, and would always *be* there for her.

Chapter Four

When Emily heard her name being called, she assumed it was someone coming to update her on her father's condition. The last person she expected to see standing there was Gareth Andrews.

Instinct took over and she found herself in his arms, his steel-strong embrace holding her, his arms wrapped around her, and Emily had never been so grateful, so incredibly thankful for his existence, for Gareth, for that comforting, familiar feel of him as he held her, for the smell of him as she buried her face into his chest. His hard, muscular chest.

"Gareth!" She sobbed, unable to say more. She was so overcome with emotion, with relief at not being alone anymore.

"I'm here, Em. Everything will be okay. I'm here."

His soothing voice repeated the same words in her ear. The feel of him stroking her back, her hair, did manage to calm her, even though she knew his words were just hopeful, soothing utterances voiced in an attempt to alleviate her fears, her pain. The chance her father would not survive and that everything would *not* be fine at all was very clear in her mind.

Emily stood clinging to Gareth for an eternity, soaking up his warmth, letting him hold her to him. She remembered the sensation of safety that being in his embrace had always evoked in her in the past, before the fire. It was like a maelstrom of emotion churned throughout her body, mind and soul. All the memories, the horrific events of the day, the impending sense of doom and her guilt at not being able to do enough were all overshadowed by this new, powerful emotion that filled her — this all-consuming, overpowering jolt to her already fractured emotions.

Gareth had come to her when she needed him the most. And Emily needed him — that was the understatement of the century. He, Gareth, had always been the one she turned to. He had saved her from the bullies at school, had soothed her bruises and tended to her grazes when as a small child she had fallen, had talked her through any concerns. He had always protected her, had been her first and only love. Gareth had even pretended not to see, pretended to ignore the ugly disfigurement the fire had delivered to her body and face. And he was here again, even though she had pushed him from her life, had told him she didn't want him or love him anymore. Lied to him.

* * * *

"Em, baby, wake up. The doctor is here."

Groggily, Emily shook herself awake, felt the warmth surrounding her, blinked against the harsh florescent hospital lighting. She could not believe that she had fallen asleep on Gareth's lap, managed to rest

35

while her father fought his battle, but Gareth's words about the doctor had her struggling to her feet.

"My dad...?"

"He's in recovery, Miss Mackenzie. He lost a lot of blood at the accident site before anyone was able to stabilise him. It put enormous amounts of pressure on his heart, but there was no significant damage as a result. There are just a few things that we will need to monitor closely for the next few days. We also feel confident that we have managed to save his leg. We have reattached the tendons, nerves and blood supply, and are hoping for a positive outcome."

Emily nearly crumpled to the floor with relief, Gareth's grip on her arms all that was holding her upright. The doctor's comments about blood loss had nearly destroyed her—she was to blame, she knew that. She should have thought of that, should have stemmed the flow before running for help. Thankfully, the doctors had been able to repair the damage she had done, and they'd saved her father.

"When can Emily see Mac?"

Yes, she wanted to see her dad. Gareth at least had the presence of mind to be asking the questions she should, Emily thought, once again doubting her own ability to cope with any of the most important concerns. *The doctor must think me a fool,* she chastised herself.

"Soon, just as soon as he is settled, but only for a short time. He needs his rest. Once he is in the ICU, you can stay with him longer, and perhaps other visitors can also see him, but you will have to check with ICU staff on that one."

"Thanks, doc. I'm sure that they will let us know. They seem pretty up to date with hospital policy."

She didn't understand what Gareth was saying and watched him shake hands with the doctor, then offered her own hand too late for him to notice. It was all just too much. Emily felt as if she was in some nightmare state, unable to make the smallest decision competently. She just needed to see her dad, make sure he was okay, was alive.

"Won't be long, Em. Someone will come for you soon and take you to see Mac, so you can see for yourself that he is fine. Come sit back down. You look like you're about to drop."

He was right and Emily managed to find the energy, the willpower to sit back down in the hard, white plastic seat behind her. It was not nearly as comfortable as being on Gareth's lap, held in his arms. She sat there numbly, waiting again, until the sound of a phone ringing made her jump, startled her with its loudness in the deathly quiet room. The sound was so close and Emily finally realised, as she watched Gareth pull the mobile from his pocket, that it was his phone ringing.

"Andrews." His voice was so deep, so hypnotic to her. She could listen to him forever, Emily thought, momentarily distracted from her worries.

"Sorry, I didn't realise the time... Yep, I know I should have, but there's been a family emergency... No, not my folks. It's Emily. I'm at the hospital with Em... No, not her, her father. A tractor accident... Yeah, flew him in by plane... Last night... Out of surgery, just waiting to go to ICU... No, not today, if that's okay with Brodie... Yeah, I'll give him a call. And Pippa? Thanks. You will be the first person I call. Promise... Yeah, love you too."

The one-sided conversation was pretty easy for Emily to follow. Between what Gareth was saying and the extended silences where the caller was obviously speaking, it was clear to her that Gareth had missed being somewhere, probably training, because of her. But it was the last three words of his conversation that stung, ripped her heart from her chest. Caused such unimaginable pain she thought she would scream from it. She had heard correctly, there was no doubt about what he had said.

'Love you too'.

And Emily had also heard the name of the person Gareth had been speaking to. A female name — Pippa.

Gareth had told another female that he loved her, and he had done it right in front of Emily. He had told this *Pippa* person that he loved her.

Emily didn't have a chance to question Gareth about his phone call, because just as he disconnected from it the nurse came to take her to her father.

Chapter Five

Gareth had completely forgotten about training until Pippa had called, and honestly, he wouldn't have left Emily even if he had remembered. He was more than likely facing some sort of disciplinary action, probably a fine, but he didn't care. Any fine would be worth it. Hearing Mac was going to be fine had been such a relief, and just the memory of Emily in his arms, the feel of her in his lap as he'd watched her sleep, was worth any monetary fine coming his way. Gareth was amazed that even with his continued tormented memories of Emily, he had forgotten how good it was to hold her, how perfect she felt and how just having her in his arms brought him such peace. Even with the unsettling events unfolding around them.

The relief on Emily's face had been unmistakeable at the doctor's assurances that Mac would pull through the surgery, and even though she had still looked a little shell-shocked and upset as the nurse took her in to see her father, Gareth was sure that just the sight of Mac would settle her fears. Waiting was such a hard task, and imagining the worst was easy to do. Gareth had started to feel a bit panicked at the length of time Mac had been in surgery, as well. The man had been like an uncle to him, and the thought of Emily losing her father was just impossible to imagine. Emily…alone.

I wonder if Dylan knows. Gareth pondered the question for a while, but with no answer. He didn't have Emily's brother's contact details, had not seen Dylan Mackenzie in over a year. The last time had been at a Jets game, when Dyl had contacted him to hook him and a few of his army buddies up with tickets to the game. Their conversation had been tense back then. Neither of them had wanted to mention Emily, or the fact Gareth had left her at home while he had headed off to the city. Dyl had probably had his own guilt at leaving the family to run the farm alone.

It had been a rough couple of years for the Mackenzies, what with Emily's mum passing away suddenly. An aneurism or something had just exploded in Sally Mackenzie's brain, and she had fallen dead to the floor in the middle of the family kitchen—no warning, just dead. It had been, at the time, the worst moment of Gareth's life. Emily had been shattered, as could be expected, and she had turned to him in her time of grief. He'd been so helpless, unable to make her better. He had only been able to hold her and console her, just as he had done tonight.

He made a few calls while he was waiting for Emily to return. He rang Brodie and apologised for his no-show at training, explaining the situation to his sympathetic coach. Brodie had given Gareth a few days leave from the training paddock, but wanted his assurance that Gareth would be available for the next game. Thankfully, that was not until Sunday afternoon and was a home game, so there'd be no travelling. That gave Gareth the rest of the week to care for Emily and Mac.

Gareth also rang his mum to update her on Mac's condition, repeating what the doctor had told him. He could hear the weariness in his mother's voice—the worry was taking its toll on everyone. She promised to try to find Dylan Mackenzie's contact number for him, not able to confirm either way if Emily's brother had been informed of his father's accident.

Gareth tried to think of all the details that might need to be taken care of so he could assist Emily in any way. All the while, he waited for her to reappear through the doors the nurse had led her past. Quite a length of time had gone by since Emily had left to check on her father, and Gareth was beginning to worry that Mac might have taken a turn for the worse.

Hospitals truly sucked—the smell, the sense of helplessness… Even when he'd visited the sick kids in the children's hospital, Gareth had always felt uncomfortable, and even sorrier for the poor tykes forced to remain when he left. The colourful bedding and the decorations on the walls of the kids' wards still failed to cover up the fact that hospitals sucked.

Just when Gareth had made the decision to go looking for Emily again, the doors swung open and she came staggering back to him, her face deathly pale. But she didn't come back into his arms. Emily stopped a few feet from him, her shoulders drooping, weariness etched in her pale face, the scarred tissue that marred one side of her cheek and neck. The pink and brownish, damaged skin was more prominent than usual. There were dark shadows under her eyes, and her fidgeting and reluctance to meet his gaze alerted him that something was wrong.

"Em, what is it? What's wrong? Did you see your Dad? You were gone so long I started to get worried. Is Mac okay?" He reached for her, but she pulled away before he could touch her.

"Dad's asleep, tubes and wires jutting out of him everyplace. I was too afraid to touch him. They're moving him to ICU now, said to give them ten minutes to get him settled. You didn't need to stay, Gareth. I thought you might have gone already—just came back to get my jacket. I left it on the chair over there."

Emily was pointing to a chair in the far corner of the stark, cold room, still refusing to look him in the eye. Gareth could not believe that she had really thought he would leave. What had she been thinking? He wouldn't leave her to deal with something so terrible alone. Never. But something had changed in her. His Emily was gone again, and the new Emily was back. The one who had pushed him away.

But not this time. This time Gareth was going to fight harder, fight to stay with her.

"Of course I wouldn't leave. I want to see Mac for myself. God, Mum and Dad are both worried sick. I want to be able to tell them I've seen him and that he's okay. They both wanted to come to Sydney, but they need to stay in Gunnedah. They're looking after both farms now, at least until Mac gets better. Mac is my friend too, you know, Em, and so are you. I would never leave you to deal with this alone. I can't believe you think I would."

"I just thought, after the phone call and all, that you might be needed elsewhere. I don't want to interfere in your life. I'm guessing you have training and stuff, people to be with…"

Gareth didn't know whether to be angry with Emily or just drag her into his arms. She looked so lost, so confused, so tired, and she was saying such stupid things. Did she not know him at all?

"I don't have anywhere to be but here with you and Mac. The coach has given me the next few days off. There are no people who are more important to me than the Mackenzies. Well, maybe Mum and Dad as well—but Em, I'm here for you, baby."

Gareth watched as Emily's gaze slowly rose to meet his. He could tell that there was something else, some flicker of doubt left in her pretty little head, but he would remove it eventually. This time, he was not giving her any chance to push him anywhere. He was staying.

"C'mon, let's grab some coffee. When did you last eat, baby?"

"I don't remember. Yesterday, sometime," she said, waving her hand as if it were of no concern. "Don't think I could eat anyway."

"Well, let's just find the cafeteria and see what happens. I could use a strong coffee about now, anyway."

Gareth was pleased that it didn't take much coercion on his part to get Emily to eat some food. Getting her to sit still while she ate it—well, that was another matter. She was terrified to be away from her father, worried that something would happen in the ten minutes it took her to wolf down a dried up ham sandwich. He grabbed an unappetising-looking roll with some indistinguishable piece of curled up meat on it—which he thought could be roast beef, but tasted more like cardboard—and forced it down. He collected the coffees as soon as they had been made, and with a skittish Emily's hand in his, he went in search of the Intensive Care Unit. Gareth wondered whether Nurse Ratched would still be guarding the door.

Chapter Six

Emily knew she shouldn't lean on Gareth, but old habits died hard. She was exhausted. Her face and neck ached, felt tight and hot, probably due to her overwhelming, bone-deep tiredness. Seeing her father lying in the hospital bed was awful. He looked as if he had shrunk overnight, as if the hospital bed had sucked his size from his body through those horrible tubes and cables attached to him, draining fluid build-up and pus, checking his vitals.

The monotonous beeps, the perpetual noises all the machines made were deafening in their regularity. *Beep... Beep... Beep... Wheeze... Beep...* The noise was maddening against the silence of the room—so impersonal.

Her dad was naked, with one thin sheet between him and the world, with all those tubes everywhere. Emily knew he would just hate it—the fussing, the continual scrutiny from the nurses. God, she needed him to get through this, to come back to her. She couldn't bear the thought of losing him, her father...her dad. Tears slipped from her eyes. She had given up trying to brush them away. The motion was ineffectual, since they just kept coming.

But through it all Gareth sat by her, hour after hour.

"Babe, why don't we take a minute, get something to eat? Nothing has changed in the last two hours, and you need to keep up your strength. Mac will need you more then, when he is awake. You have to be ready for that."

Emily looked into Gareth's penetrating blue eyes, fell into them. She loved those eyes, their unique colour reminding her of sun-filled country skies, and in them the concern for her showed unreservedly. Emily could always judge Gareth's mood, his emotions, by looking into his eyes, as if they opened a door to his soul for her.

His blond hair, a little darker now since he wasn't spending time working on the farm under the bleaching, harsh rays of the Australian sun, was mussed, the curls falling over his brow. *He needs a haircut.* It seemed like a strange thought to have under these circumstances. Emily could not resist touching his hair, brushing it from his face, remembering the familiar texture. She ran her finger down over his high cheekbones, caressing his face, his lips with her fingertip. She felt the stubble on his strong jaw — prickly, masculine.

"I've missed you so much." The words slipped from her lips before she had a chance to censor them. But they were true. She had missed Gareth with a ferocity that had made her weep, night after night, at the loss.

"I've missed you too, Em. But I'm here now, and that won't change. Let's go for a walk, get some air."

It was a good idea. Emily needed some air, needed to get her emotions back under control. She loved Gareth — always had, always would — but her reasons for pushing him away had not changed. He deserved someone better than her. Someone he could be seen in public with, be proud to have on his arm. Maybe this Pippa woman was the answer? Emily understood that, but it still hurt. She couldn't lose her resolve when it came to Gareth. She loved him enough to see that, and as much as it would destroy her she would push him away again—but later. She needed his strength to get her through this, as selfish as that motive was. He had said he was worried for Mac as well, wanted to be there for her father, so she would let him for the time being.

After checking in with the ICU nurse, giving Gareth's phone number and extracting a promise that they would call her if her father's condition changed, Emily let Gareth lead her from the ward. *I must look a wreck.* Deep in thought, she mentally listed the items she could purchase at the hospital shop for herself and her father. *Toothbrush, hairbrush... I'd kill for a change of clothes. Wonder where the nearest shopping centre is?* She was so caught up in her mental list-making that she didn't realise until too late that Gareth was greeting someone.

"Rook, Pippa—what are you two doing here?"

As soon as she heard that one name, that same name he had used before—*Pippa*—her heart became a leaden weight in her chest. *Oh, my god.* Gareth's girlfriend, the one he'd told he loved over the phone, had come for him. She tried to spin from his grasp, turn back to the door of the ICU, tried to find the call button to gain admittance, but Gareth would not let go of her. His grip on her hand was painfully tight, allowing her no chance of escaping the nightmare that was about to unfold, no chance of ignoring the woman who stood in front of them. The woman with the beautiful, unblemished face. Emily wished the ground would open up and swallow her, and fought the pressure that was building behind her already tear-swollen eyes.

"Em, these are my best friends, Mitchell Harris—but everyone calls him Rook, so feel free to call him that too—and his fiancée, Pippa Rogers. Pippa is the Jets physio. Rook, Pippa, this is my Emily."

Emily didn't know which part of Gareth's introduction to be more shocked at. Her head spun with the details she had just heard, still trying to make sense of the new information. Pippa was engaged to Rook. Emily knew of Rook, had watched enough Jets games to recognise him as the star halfback and captain of Gareth's team...and Rook was engaged to Pippa. She, Pippa, was Gareth's friend. A friend he *loved*. Emily could have wept with relief at the knowledge, if not for the next part of Gareth's introduction. Her heart had restarted, and was beating rapidly with his claim. He had introduced her to his friends as his—'my Emily'. What did that mean?

"Emily, it's so nice to finally meet you. Gareth has told us so much about you," Pippa said, her voice warm and friendly.

"God, talks of nothing else," Rook said, butting into the conversation, the comment taking Emily by surprise. It was all a bit too much to take in at once.

"Mitch, shut up, darling. You're not helping," Pippa replied. She reached out and took Emily's hand in hers. "Ignore him, Emily. I'm so sorry to hear about your father. How is he?"

Emily was lost for words. Pippa was pleased to meet her. Gareth had talked about her—and from what Rook had blurted out before Pippa had stopped him he'd talked about her often. What did he say? What sort of things did Gareth tell people about her? How she had broken his heart? Pushed him from her life, destroyed their plans for the future? God, she hoped not. But she needed to pull herself together, answer the enquiry about her father, acknowledge Gareth's friends.

"Nice to meet you, Pippa, Rook. I haven't met any of Gareth's city friends before. Dad is doing as well as can be expected. It's been a long twenty-four hours." She managed to pull the words from her chaotic mind, managed to string coherent sentences together even though she was reeling with her own questions.

"I had a thought this afternoon, after I talked to Gareth and he said you had been flown to the hospital, that maybe you wouldn't have had time to grab any personal items. I hope you don't mind, but I grabbed you a few things I thought you might need. Some toiletries, a change of clothes—I didn't know your size and was hoping you might fit into one of my tracksuits. Now I've seen you, I can see that we're almost the same size, so the clothes should fit okay."

Pippa thrust the small sports bag she was holding into Emily's hand. Emily was again at a loss for words at the kindness and thoughtfulness of this stranger. Okay, she was Gareth's friend, but still… Emily was so touched by the act. The caring. She knew that she and Pippa had the possibility of becoming good friends just because of that one act of generosity. Emily could tell Pippa had a good soul, and was a close friend of Gareth's.

"This is so kind of you, Pippa. You're so right, I didn't have a chance to grab anything. I was mentally making a list of necessities in my head when Gareth saw you. I was miles away, didn't even notice you at first, I'm sorry. I'd love to change my clothes—I feel so dirty. Thank you for your kindness. It will be heaven to get out of these filthy jeans."

"You are more than welcome, Emily. I want you to know that Rook and I are here for you, anything you need. Just let me know, and I mean really—let us know, don't just say yes because you think it's polite, but with no intention of ever asking. Okay?" The smile Pippa gave her was so warm that Emily was captured by it, drawn to the brightness of the friendship it offered. "Were you two heading somewhere before we interrupted?"

"Yeah, Pippa, we needed some air and I need to feed Em. We were heading to the cafeteria. Why don't you both join us? The food is something to experience, let me tell you."

She wasn't sure she felt up to socialising, but after the couple's genuine concern and thoughtfulness, Emily didn't think she could refuse. It would be rude of her to do so.

She was surprised to find that the added company was refreshing, helped clear her mind of dark thoughts as she listened to Rook and Gareth discuss the training session Gareth had missed. They joked at some of the antics of the younger players and laughed at the gossip surrounding Gareth's no-show.

"Ah, so quickly discarded," Gareth said, following up with a loud, theatrical sigh, then laughed when Rook retold one of the stories circulating—that Gareth had been cut from the team for a reason that was as ridiculous as it was implausible. The sound of Gareth's rumbling laughter was a soothing balm to her tense body.

"Yeah, was a bit confused myself though, Cowboy, when you didn't show, and as you can imagine, Pippa was worried sick. Thought maybe the soreness you'd been complaining of last night was more serious. I think she'd imagined you unable to drag your poor broken body from your bed. And thinking about you in bed is something I don't want Pippa doing."

"Mitchell, give it a rest."

Pippa gave her fiancé a look that said more than enough. It was distinct, cautioning, given to end that line of conversation. Emily was now more than a little curious to find out the whole story between Gareth and Pippa. It was obvious from Rook's comments that something had happened between them, and Emily could not stop the jealous reaction that stole her breath. Her stomach clenched and rolled at the thought of the man she loved with the perfect, friendly, lovely dark-haired woman sitting opposite her.

"Yeah, go on, Rook…whatever! Because hey, Pippa hasn't loved you since she was fifteen or anything. Although I must admit I'm a pretty awesome sight first thing in the morning. Aren't I, Em?"

Emily's face burst into heat at Gareth's question in front of his friends. He was an awesome sight, he was right. She had spent many early mornings just soaking in the image of Gareth sleeping next to her, memorising every nuance of his face, his hair, his skin. She knew exactly where every freckle sat on his handsome face, had counted them—all of them—more than once, loved each and every one of the spattering of dusky, adorable spots. But she was not buying into this conversation, that was for sure. Her embarrassment grew tenfold. So instead, she decided it was time to flee.

"I should get back to Dad. I might see if I can grab a shower and change now that I have something else to wear," Emily said, pushing her chair back. She stood, willing her feet to move, and even as she spoke the next words she felt the heaviness in her heart. She wished she didn't feel the need to say them, but knew she had to. "Gareth, stay with your friends, don't let me keep you. Pippa, it was lovely to meet you, and thank you again for the clothes and stuff. Rook, nice to meet you too, and good luck with the rest of the season. That was a great try you scored last week. Can't believe you managed to put the ball down before you went over the dead ball line. It was amazing. Anyway, thanks again."

"Stop it, Em. Stop trying to run away from me. I told you I'm staying, so just get on board with the idea."

"Well, look at you, Cowboy—acting all dominant. Don't worry, Emily, it's not like he has anywhere to go anyway. Usually he just mopes around between games and training sessions. He's a bit antisocial, is the old Cowboy."

"*Oh, my God*, Mitch! Will you just be quiet? Seriously, think before putting that mouth into gear for once, will you?"

"*What*? What did I say?"

While Pippa and Rook were distracted by their own conversation—the sight of Pippa taking Rook to task one more time amusing Emily—Gareth pulled her to his side, locking his arm into place around her, connecting her to him. He seemed determined to prove that he was serious in his promise to stay with her. Emily's sense of relief that Gareth had not taken the chance she'd offered him to leave was immeasurable.

"C'mon, baby, let's leave these two to their squabbles," Gareth said as he turned towards the exit, back in the direction of the ICU. "Hey, guys, we're heading back. Thanks for coming. I'll keep you posted."

"Sure thing, Cowboy. Let us know if you need anything."

After all the teasing and ribbing, it was quite a shock to see the solemn change in Rook as he made the offer to Gareth. In fact, Emily nearly tripped over Gareth's feet as he spun back towards his friends quickly, pumping Rook's hand in his before he dragged Pippa into his arms for a hug.

It was clear to Emily that Gareth had made a good life for himself in the city, made close friends, no matter how Rook had teased him about being antisocial. Emily found that she genuinely liked these people, liked the fact they were so close to Gareth. They would be there for him when she left, returned home. Not only that, but Emily had not once thought about her scars until now, neither Rook nor Pippa commenting or even paying any undue attention to them. Gareth must have told them all about the fire and her sensitivity to the ugly mess on her face. *They did a good job ignoring it*, she thought as she made her way back to sit by her father, the warmth of Gareth noticeable at her side.

Chapter Seven

It had taken a monumental effort on Gareth's part to convince Emily to come home with him and get some rest at his apartment. Actually, the efforts of Gareth, a now conscious Mac and Nurse Ratched—who had turned out to be a friendly and caring nurse—plus the incredibly gracious offer from Rook and Pippa to keep Mac company. Finally, Emily had conceded to Gareth's request and agreed to leave her father's bedside.

He had still had to drag her away, leaving Mac and Rook deep in discussion about the changes in the modern game compared to those of yesteryear. Mac's communication had been stilted by pain, but he'd been doing an admirable job of disguising it. Mac had seemed to enjoy this change in conversation from that of the continual worried concerns over the past two days of his overly attentive daughter. Emily had almost nagged the poor man back into a coma with all her fussing. Gareth smirked at the idea. Emily was a very good fusser.

Now, having achieved his goal of getting Emily away from the hospital for a few hours, Gareth had the tormented pleasure of imagining Emily in his shower. Naked in his shower. He could visualise the water sluicing down her nude body, and he had the rock-hard boner to attest to his vivid imagination.

Fuck, man, get it under wraps. The last thing Emily wants or needs, is you trying to get in her pants, Gareth scolded his lust-filled mind. *Not that she's wearing any at the moment,* his ever helpful mind added, making him groan even more as that train of thought rampantly took hold.

He was trapped, unable to move, standing outside his own bathroom door. He could hear the sound of the water running, but could not for the life of him take a step away, although he was terrified that at any moment, Emily would open the door and see him standing there stupidly, sporting a boner hard enough to hammer nails into wood.

"Yeah, that would be awesome. She'd appreciate it, I'm sure," he murmured, his feet still refusing to move. Then he heard it—soft sobs coming from behind the closed door. Emily was crying, and Gareth could not stop himself, was unable to ignore the sounds of the woman he loved in despair. He opened the door and, disregarding the fact he was fully clothed—cowboy boots and all—he stepped into the shower stall. The sight of her crumpled to the floor with her hands over her eyes as she wept was heartbreaking, and he gathered her into his arms.

"Oh, baby… Shhh… Don't cry. Mac will be fine. He is going to be fine. The worst is over."

Gareth held her to his chest, stroked the length of her wet hair, felt her chest, her breasts rise against him as her sobs racked her body. Emily's tears had more power to bring him to his knees than any opposition player's tackle. The fact that she was naked in his arms was but a distant observation. He hated seeing her in pain, in distress. Would do anything to stop her tears. He didn't care that he was now completely soaked, his clothes heavy with water. Consoling his Emily was Gareth's only concern.

Then he felt her lips on the skin of his neck, their warmth as she kissed him there, and her arms as she reached around behind his head, drawing him down so his mouth was tantalising close to hers. Like a lightning bolt hitting him, awakening his body, Emily's naked form came back to the forefront of his mind. Like a heavy hit lined up and delivered perfectly from an opposing forward, his need for her slammed into him, robbing him of any previous gallant intentions. He needed Emily, needed to feel her skin. Needed to feel himself buried deep, balls-deep, inside her.

"Love me, Gareth. I need to feel something other than the guilt that's eating me alive. I should have done more, should have reacted quicker, found Dad sooner... Distract me. Make it go away. Make me think of only you, even if it's just for a while... "

"Emily, you did all you could. You probably saved your father's life, got him help, did all the right things. Stop it. Stop trying to take the blame for everything that happens, every time life deals a blow that's unfair. Mac's accident is just one of those things. Working the land comes with its dangers. You know that."

Gareth was not a saint, and he was not going to give up the opportunity of showing Emily how much he still loved her. If she wanted him to make love to her, distract her, he was going to do that…and more, until she had no doubt of his love.

He took her mouth with his as he steadied her head in his hands, drawing her body hard against his own. He turned her face gently to gain a better angle, a better connection. Their faces mashed up against each other, he devoured her, his tongue demanding as he laved every part of her mouth hungrily, eagerly. The sounds of her sighs — muffled by his mouth, but still audible — sent him into a sexual frenzy. He needed more. Needed to feel her orgasm, needed to be the one that brought his Emily fulfilment. Only him. Always him.

"More, I need more. I need you naked, to run my hands over your chest, Gareth, need to have that experience again," she begged when she dragged her lips from his.

He had fought her attempt to break from the kiss, but with her words he responded to her plea. Fighting to disrobe from the sodden clothing was difficult, endlessly time consuming, when what he wanted was to be touching her again. In frustration, he ripped his shirt open. Buttons flew and the sound of material ripping echoed around the bathroom, but Gareth didn't care. He needed to be naked. As he fought to undo the button on his jeans his fingers felt like thumbs. The simple task of undoing the metal fastening — something he did a million times a day — was an impossible assignment when his mind was full of Emily, fixated on her naked body.

"Here, let me."

And before he could blink, there was Emily, his Emily, on her knees in front of him, one of her hands gently grasping his balls as the other stroked his rock-hard cock through the soaked fabric of his jeans. He feared he would come from just the touch of her hand, even with the jeans shielding him from the feel of her delicate skin wrapped around his cock. He needed them off now, wished he held some magical power so that one sweep of his hand could make the jeans and his boots disappear. Remove the barrier that stood between him and ramming his cock home in the sweet haven of her pussy.

"Oh, Em, I don't think I'll last. I want you so much."

Gareth groaned the words, his voice conveying both his agony and his complete need for her. If she felt the same as him—the overpowering longing that had robbed Gareth of the ability to relay from his brain the instructions to successfully unclasp the metal fastening—then she hid it well. It only took Emily a moment before she was pushing his jeans down past the swollen head of his cock, which—now relieved of the pressure of being strangled by the constraining denim—was standing fully erect, brushing against her cheek. She managed to get his jeans past his hips but stopped at his knees. Gareth's boots, now full of water, were an impassable impediment.

But his Emily was not to be deterred from her apparent goal. She gave up on the task of removing his jeans, instead focusing her attentions and her precious hands on his hard length. Gareth audibly groaned at the first touch of her hand. Her grasp was firm as she stroked his shaft, just as she knew he liked. With an anticipation that all but killed him, he waited for that sensation, that first lick of her tongue around the rimmed head of his cock. He knew that was what he would feel, remembered it, hungered for it…then it was there. The mind-blowing, cock-exploding feel of that warm, wet tongue on him, so fucking familiar, so fucking good that Gareth's sanity was teetering on the edge. It was all he could do not to grab her head and slam her mouth onto him, until his head reached the back of her throat.

Gareth felt the tightness of his balls as they drew up, so tight and so high they were almost forced inside his body. He was holding on by a hair's breadth as Emily's mouth rode him in perfect rhythm, swallowing him, worshipping him. The sight of her—his cock inside her mouth, in and out, rubbing against her lips, the stretch of her mouth around his girth—was pure heaven, but it was what Gareth saw unmistakeably in her eyes that finally did him in. Emily's eyes conveyed her emotion, and it wasn't just need, or an attempt to put sadness from her mind. In Emily's eyes was love. Gareth could not misinterpret, could not imagine or perhaps just project what he wanted to see, because it was too clear. Too honest. There before him.

Emily loved him. And for Gareth, that vision, that emotion her eyes betrayed no matter what her words had told him, was the most wondrous sight he had ever seen. He could not, would not come in her mouth—not this time. This first climax would only happen once he had made her see that he loved her just as much in return, after he had Emily screaming his name, begging for her release over and over. Until he could convince her of his need for her to be with him. Forever. Until then, he would not find his own release. It would be his reward.

He pulled her up from her knees, gathered her in his arms, ignoring her protests. He forced her to meet his gaze, trapped her face in his hands and kissed her thoroughly, trying to portray all his emotions. He didn't allow her to breathe, making her share his oxygen, share his breath, as he wanted her to share her life with him.

When he finally dragged his lips from Emily's kiss-swollen mouth, he was shaking, trembling under the force of something so strong, so elemental, that Gareth found it almost too hard to comprehend. He hadn't thought it was possible to love her this much. She was his.

"Mine. You have always been mine, Emily. Don't fight me on this — you won't win."

Gareth's tone was arrogant, dominating, but he didn't care. As he shut off the water still running from the shower, he twisted the taps with such force it was a wonder they did not crack under it. Gareth grabbed the towel within his reach and wrapped it around Emily's shivering body, hoping that it was desire that had her quivering and not cold but needing to make sure, needing to do everything for her, to protect her and cherish her.

Emily stood still, her eyes wide, staring at him, clutching the towel around her. Gareth removed his boots, shucked his jeans the rest of the way from his body. His brain was clearer now his mind was set — he was able to take charge of the moment. He was confident that with that clarity he would be able to send Emily so high, make her desire him, crave him, want him so much, so wholly that she would not — *could* not — walk away from him again.

He swept her, towel and all, into his arms and strode towards his room. He placed her gently onto the centre of his bed. He peeled the towel from her grasp, tossed it over his shoulder as he looked at her. Emily, naked, spread out on his bed — the bed that he had spent many a sleepless night tossing and turning in over the burning need for her. It was now perfect with the addition of her sexy form. Her hair was still wet, soaking into his mattress, his pillow. He didn't worry about any of that—all Gareth cared about was Emily. He knew that his face was not portraying gentleness— his expression was probably hard, showed off his intention, his determination to prove to Emily that they were meant to be together. But she showed no sign of fear in response to that lack of softness in his gaze.

Gareth lifted Emily's left foot, held it to his lips and gently kissed each of her toes, sucked them into his mouth as he began his journey, his mind focused on her and on making love to every part of her. He was unprepared to leave even one speck of her body overlooked or unloved. He kissed the length of one leg, licking behind her knee, raining kisses over her as she squirmed, her body arching into his touch, her need building as she tried to gain purchase on him with her hands, to expedite his long, slow journey. But Gareth would not be halted or hurried.

He could smell the aroma of Emily's desire, her pussy calling him to her, enticing him. When he finally reached the sacred spot between her legs, his own hunger was rampant. He nuzzled against the velvet-soft covering of her cunt, breathed the scent of her deep into his lungs. Her fragrance was more potent than any expensive, designer perfume to Gareth's nose. Nothing compared to her.

He attempted to reinforce his weakening composure, his longing for her nearly overwhelming. Gareth tasted her, prepared—yet unprepared as well—for the gut-wrenching reaction his body had to the sweet taste of her arousal. He lost himself in the pleasure of her taste, licking, imbibing her juices like some starving animal. Screams tore from her, pleasurable screams that satisfied his male ego as he continued his loving assault on her. He drove her hard with the force of his stabbing tongue, his eager lips as he pushed her towards climax, then refused to give her what she needed, refused to allow Emily to tumble into the abyss.

Gareth was waiting for her to cry out his name, to beg him, to promise not to leave him again.

His cock was so hard, the pain as much a stimulant as a reminder of his promised reward, and it pushed Gareth harder. He thrust two fingers into her pussy, finger-fucked her hard, ruthlessly, as he continued to tease her clit with his tongue, first with soft, feathery touches, then hard, firm pressure, before sucking the unhooded nub between his teeth, nipping, squeezing the ignition to her climax. Then she was begging, pleading words like, "Enough!" and "More!" and "Stop!" and "Don't stop!" contradicting herself with her breathless pleas.

They weren't enough. Gareth needed more from Emily. And finally he succeeded — he heard the declaration he had longed for her to utter, and the sound of it, those simple words, were more melodious to his ears than any piece of music in the world.

"I love you, Gareth. I need you… Please!"

This time when he felt the walls of Emily's pussy contract, felt the tension in her body as she strained to reach that peak, he let her fall. He sucked so hard on her clit and stabbed his fingers so fast into the tight folds of her sheath that he gave her no choice but to orgasm. As the quivering of Emily's body changed into rigidity he felt her come, and tasted it as her sweet cream coated his face.

Not giving her a chance to recover, Gareth climbed over her and buried his rigid, throbbing cock in her warm, wet pussy, still pulsating from the strength of her orgasm. He pushed through any resistance from her inner walls, seating himself fully into her depths.

He was home at last. "Fucking home, Em. I'm home."

He gave her pussy a moment to adjust to him, then Gareth gave in to his need. He thrust and pumped into Emily like a man possessed—and he *was* possessed, the desire palpable, alive in the room. He took her with him again as he reached his own release, sent her spiralling over the edge as he joined her. They were connected, sharing the bliss that their coupling had achieved, had always achieved.

Chapter Eight

I shouldn't be out here — it's too dangerous, stupid. The roaring in my ears is deafening, like a freight train hurtling towards me, and it's so dark. It's supposed to be the middle of the afternoon and yet I can't see thirty feet in front of me. I'm stumbling around in near darkness, hearing the cries, the continual scurrying around me of animals desperate to flee the monster bearing down on them, on me...but I have to find the horses. The mothers and their babies, the ones I turned out into the paddock, thinking it would be safe. Until the wind changed direction.

Panic is making me stumble, distracting me in these vital moments. I spin around helplessly, trying to gain my bearings, trying to hear the whinnying sound of my beautiful horses again. I need some way of finding them. It was so distressing to discover the emptiness of the paddock, to see the crumpled fencing they had torn through in their panic. Without thought I've come in search of them, to find them, to lead them to safety.

Where are they, my three chestnut fillies and their babies, all born in the spring? They'll perish on this summer's day if I fail. The idea of discovering their charred, broken bodies is a nightmare too heartbreaking to contemplate, but it spurs me on. I can't let that happen. No matter what.

The smoke is everywhere, and heat – it's like a furnace. The day's temperatures were already scorching without the added heat from the monster growing ahead, rampaging through the dry bushland, decimating, ravaging the lands, blackening the ground, leaving the earth looking like a vision straight from hell. The fire has been burning for most of the day, but I thought – we thought, Dad, Gareth and I – that it was headed in the other direction.

My thoughts, my fears will not be silent as I race around, ignoring the maelstrom of the ember storm as the fiery missiles hit my arms. The smoke is suffocating me. I'm straining to breathe through the material covering my mouth. Clean oxygen is long gone.

Then I see them, see my Sierra standing in front of her colt, throwing her head from side to side as if she can't make up her mind which way to run, her nostrils flaring. I think of how much the smoke must be hurting her, filling her lungs even before the fire has a chance to consume her. Her eyes are wide, fearful, crazy as she rears on her hind legs, looking as if she is trying to protect her foal, her baby, ready to fight the cruel tentacles reaching out with burning fury from the fire's belly. I hear the loud screech of my whistle before I realise I have called to her, and her ears prick up. She hears me! She is leading her foal.

Now I see the other two horses, but I don't see the remaining foal. I scan the area, obscured by the billowing, dense smoke, but find no sign of the small, defenceless animal. But at least I have found these ones. I need to lead them out of the fire's path – and quickly. The tremble of the forest floor is telling me there is not much time.

I run, looking over my shoulder, making sure the horses are with me. I can just make out the tree line, where the giant eucalyptus and gum trees end and our paddocks and fields begin. The horses rush past me. I can still hear

*thunderous sounds behind me, but it is not horse hooves —
it's the fire's approach. It's chasing me, catching me. Sparks
and embers are all around. The heat, the smoke, the smell of
singed hair filling my burning nostrils... My eyes are
running, my breathing laboured.*

*Then there's a loud crack, like a whip or a thunder clap,
and I'm on the ground. The pain is intense — my face, my
neck. I can hear screaming, the piercing human sound of
horrendous distress, someone in pure agony, but I can't find
the source of the screams...*

"Emily. *Emily...* Wake up, baby. You're having a
nightmare. Come back to me."

Emily had relived this nightmare over and over. As
she was pulled back to reality—awoken from her
dream state to Gareth's face hovering over her, filled
with concern—she swore she could smell the burning
bushland, hear the screaming—*her* screaming as the
burning branch had crashed down on her, leaving
behind the gruesome reminder of that time, branded
into her skin. She could not stop the reflex action of
moving her hand to her face, feeling the knotted,
damaged flesh under her fingertips, reminding her
constantly of her pain.

It had been Gareth who had come for her, saved her,
known she would be looking to the welfare of her
horses first and foremost. She remembered the
torturous, unrelenting agony of the burns, her flesh
withered and dead from the flames. The treatment of
the burns had been nearly worse than the injuries
themselves, as her bandages had been repeatedly
changed and rotten skin scraped away. After
surviving the ordeal, she had been left with hideously
disfigured skin. She was a freak. A monster.

"Are you still dreaming of the fire, Em?" Gareth said
in tender tones as he drew her into his arms.

"Not so much these days, but I guess the stress has fired them up again." She squirmed at her terrible choice of words, a pun that held no amusement.

"Oh, Emily, I don't know what to say. But, baby, you need to let go of it, let go of that awful time. The fire is still burning inside you, still causing you pain. Let me help you extinguish the fire, help you put it behind you."

"How can you expect me to put it behind me when I live with it every day? Just brushing my teeth or hair in front of a mirror brings it all rushing back. Look at my face, Gareth... *Look at me.*"

Emily was screaming at him as she dragged his face closer, refusing to let him pull away from the sight of her. She needed to remind him of what she was. Remind him why they had no future. How could she expect him to live with looking at her every day? She couldn't stand it.

"Do you know what I see when I look at you? I see the face of the woman I love. The woman I have loved all my life. My best friend. My childhood accomplice. My lover. The woman who turns me on with just a glimpse of her or a thought of her. The burns can't change that for me. I honestly don't even notice them when I look at you. They are irrelevant. My love for you is not conditional on how you look. My love is comprehensive—it's for Emily the person, and I will love you the same way when I am wrinkly and old, probably a cripple from footy injuries. Are you saying that if it had been me in that fire, you would not love me anymore? Is that what you're saying, Em? Because that is what you are deciding for me. Is that how shallow you think my love for you is?"

Emily had never seen Gareth look so angry. Her heart was racing, the terror of her dream and the words Gareth spoke both fighting for space in her mind. Fighting for dominance. Of course she would still love Gareth—she loved his good looks, his handsome face, but it was Gareth's soul she loved, his caring. The fact that he had always felt like an extension of her, a part of her.

She had never thought about it in those terms. She knew no scar, injury or illness would stop her love for Gareth. But what about the rest of the world—the looks of horror in the faces of strangers as they caught sight of her? Could he live with that?

"I pushed you away because you deserve more than this." She wept as she placed his hand against her puckered flesh, making him see and feel her scars. "More than the whispers that follow behind me when I go out in public. More than the knowledge that our children will have to live with the fact their mother is a monster, with their friends too scared to come over and play because of the sight of me."

Emily was trying to make Gareth see, trying to show him that she was doing this for him, because she loved him. She was shocked by the callousness of his reply.

"That's just bullshit, Emily. So you have a fucking few scars on your face, boo hoo. Get over yourself. Stop with this whole pity party that you continue to be the only guest at. Move on. Shit happens, and not just to you or because of something you did or didn't do. The fire was fucked up, destroyed crops and houses. You survived. Yes, you are scarred from it, but believe me, I have seen worse. Much worse. You have no idea of the suffering that goes on in the world. Just take a trip to the children's hospital with me. Kids with burns all over their tiny bodies, kids dying from terrible illnesses. The ones who are lucky enough to beat the diseases have done so by filling their bodies with poisons that make them so ill, so fucking sick that it is heartbreaking. But you know what, Em? These poor little tykes, they smile, they laugh, and when they're strong enough they play with each other. They don't give up. They don't hide away from the world and shun the ones who love them through some self-righteous fucking notion of doing the right thing. They are just fucking happy to be alive."

Chapter Nine

He hadn't been able to stop the words tumbling from his mouth. The hurt and frustration of the last three years, of Emily pushing him and everyone away, out of her life, had just kept coming, growing in momentum until he'd been shouting at her. He could see that he was hurting her, imagined that he had just destroyed any real chance of keeping her with him, of having the life he wanted. They had at one time wanted it together, before the fire had consumed more than just the bushland, animals and houses on its indiscriminate path of destruction, and had ultimately robbed him of his future.

The saddest part of it all was that the land had recovered, the fire but a distant memory, the once charred trees and burnt grasses regrowing, regenerating. It had only taken a few days for Mother Nature to fight back, small green shoots of life sprouting from the blackened landscape. But for Emily — inside Emily — the fire still burnt strong.

He needed space, needed to get away from her before it was too late, if that moment had not already sailed past. He pushed her away with hands that had been roughly gripping her, shaking her as his fury built and his words flew at her like barbs. He couldn't stand the pain of it anymore. The futility of loving her. It wasn't enough…she would never let it be enough.

Gareth grabbed the first clothing he saw — tracksuit pants, runners and a shirt — and dressed on the run as he fled his room, with just enough presence of mind to pick up his keys as he raced out of the door. Down the stairs he ran until he was in his car, heading he didn't know where, just away. He had just destroyed his life. He cried no tears. He felt nothing. Hollow, empty. Directionless.

Then the pain hit, sledgehammer-hard, right in the guts, followed by soul-wrenching sorrow and frustration, anger and finally regret. The full gamut of emotions bombarded him as he struggled to survive the onslaught. He'd known it was coming, had had to be away from Emily before it hit, thus his speedy escape. He did not want her to share this with him. If she could push him away, he could do it to her in return.

"What the fuck have you done?" he screamed, banging his fists on the steering wheel. "What the fuck have you done?"

It took a few minutes, parked safely beside the road, for Gareth to calm down enough to continue driving, and he headed for the only place he had left. He headed to the Jets' training ground, to the gym, hoping that maybe if he worked out until his body was in physical pain, it would outweigh the emotional agony ripping him apart.

Chapter Ten

Emily had waited for Gareth to return for hours, but he hadn't appeared. At first she had been furious with him, at the way he had spoken to her, accusing her of just feeling sorry for herself, making light of the terrible scars on her as if they didn't matter, as if she could just forget that they were there. But then his other words began to rattle around her head, the descriptions of the children, and Emily began to see. Began to realise that he was right—she was hiding. The fire that had failed in its attempt to kill her with flames was close to victory nonetheless, because of her own actions.

She had stared at her reflection, using Gareth's mirror—stared at it for a long time. It was bad, ugly, but not quite the grotesque vision she had let herself believe. Turning to view her profile one way, Emily could not see any disfigurement at all, no trace of the fire's wrath. She spun around to view the damaged side of her face and neck. Yes, it was damaged, but it was still her face under the scar tissue—still Emily. Gareth's Emily. He hadn't been repulsed by the sight of her—that had been her own reaction. If he could still love her, what more was there? Why did anyone else's reaction matter? Emily groaned as the full impact of her actions over the last few years sank in. She had been an idiot.

"I have to get him back, have to prove to him how much I love him, how much I want us, all the plans we made…the dreams. I have to show him they're possible," Emily sternly told her reflection, not allowing her damaged side to contradict her. She refused to acknowledge that warning voice in her mind that whispered, *If it's not too late already.*

Emily dressed, called a taxi to collect her and left Gareth's home. She visited with her father, relieved to find him resting comfortably. Self-pity and anger were not consuming *his* every thought. Mac was too busy being happy and thankful that he was alive and relatively in one piece.

They talked long into the afternoon and early evening. Emily told her father how she had pushed Gareth away and why. She admitted she still loved him and feared she had finally pushed one too many times and succeeded in driving him away, even though she now wished with all her heart she hadn't.

Mac listened sympathetically to Emily's sorrowful tale, a captive audience, shaking his head and tutting in all the right places. Finally, he spoke.

"Em, honey, you need to show him. You need to put yourself out there for Gareth and prove to him you are ready for him and to return to the world, no matter what the result is. Gareth loves you, Em. It has been pretty darn obvious to all of us around you both, and I might just add that as a father, that was not an easy thing to see, to watch blossom, that love between you. There were times I wanted to take a shotgun to him—

all those nights you crept into the house, looking dishevelled. A blind man would have known what Gareth and you were up to. But you know why I didn't shoot him in his young backside, Em? Because Gareth is a good man, and more importantly, because he loves you. What more could a father ask for than that?"

"Oh, Dad..." Emily's voice was choked with emotion in response to her father's heartfelt and wise words. "And there I was, thinking I was pulling the wool over your eyes all this time, and you knew! Bit embarrassing really, and really quite uncomfortable... Ewww... Let's not talk about this again, okay?"

Despite the fact that her Dad had known she was having sex, and specifically when, Emily ignored the embarrassment this new information brought. "What shall I do, Dad? Any ideas? Seeing as you are all-knowing, apparently." Emily smiled at the father she loved so much. She was so relieved he was going to be okay, still around to give her advice and love her unconditionally, despite her flaws.

"Go to a game, sit with his friends. Show Gareth with actions, not words, that you can face what will be a moment of scrutiny, and the inevitable questions that will follow. For him. Rook's number...he left it in the bedside cupboard. Find it, call him. Ask him and his fiancée to help you."

Mac was right. Her dad had come up with the perfect way for her to show Gareth she wanted to be with him, part of his life. Emily found Rook's number and placed the call.

* * * *

In what was probably a much better result in the long run, Pippa had answered Rook's phone. It had been so much easier for Emily to talk with Pippa, another female — to tell her all her fears, her desires and her mistakes. A deluge of words and emotions had rushed from Emily's mouth like water spewing through the open floodgates of Warragamba Dam. Pippa had then insisted on coming to the hospital so that they could continue their conversation in person.

Pippa had listened and understood what Emily wanted to achieve, agreed with the plan, and had offered to help, to introduce her to some of the wives and girlfriends of other Jets players and have Emily seated with them for company. They'd both agreed that they would keep Gareth in the dark about the plan, that Emily would just be there at the end of the game, amongst the other partners waiting at the door as the men left the changing room.

Pippa had even been outraged on Emily's behalf that Gareth had spoken so brutally, but conceded the fact his intentions had been in Emily's best interest, even if delivered perhaps too harshly. Pippa had tenderly inspected her scar tissue, so professional and yet caring at the same time that Emily had not thought to turn away from her light touch. Pippa had promised Emily that it was not as bad as she imagined — yes, noticeable, but not the monstrous face Emily had portrayed it to be. She'd offered advice on new lotions and medicated ointments that would help relieve some of the discomfort Emily felt in the damaged tissue when she was overtired or stressed.

Emily had stayed with Pippa and Rook for the rest of the week, visiting her father during the days and spending the evenings getting to know her gracious hosts better. Clearly Pippa and Gareth were very

Donna Gallagher

close, so Emily was enjoying the fact that Pippa was in her corner on this—her mission to get Gareth back, or as Rook liked to joke, 'corralling the Cowboy'. Emily felt a bond growing with Rook and Pippa, one she wanted to explore. They were good people. Rook was quick with a lighthearted remark when things got too heavy or sad, and Pippa was so nice, so genuine. If it hadn't been for Mac being still in hospital and everything hanging over her head with regards to Gareth, Emily would have felt as if she were on holiday, hanging out with friends. The idea of Gareth beside her while she spent time with Pippa and Rook was even more appealing.

Gareth had not contacted her at all. He had phoned Mac at the hospital, spoken to him at length, but not visited in person. Emily could only assume he did not want to run into her, and the thought that she might be too late haunted her.

But Rook confided in her, broke Gareth's confidence in an attempt to ease her worry.

"Cowboy is miserable without you, hon. He's been grouching around not talking to anyone...even more than usual." Rook smirked, putting his arm around her as a show of support, one Emily was truly grateful for. "Haven't even had to make up an excuse to keep him away—that in itself is quite the insight into how low he's feeling. Usually he runs to Pippa at the drop of a hat. Those two are very tight, and even though I tease them about it—and don't you dare tell either of them—I love the fact they are so close. Gareth's a good buddy, a top bloke. A friend you can count on and trust. I've never seen him with another woman. He hates the groupies and now I understand why. Why would he want another woman when he has someone as beautiful as you in his life? He's a lucky man."

The endorsement from Rook of her beauty and his confirmation of Gareth's fidelity were just what Emily had needed to hear. She could tell that Rook wasn't the type to wax lyrical just to make someone feel better. He was a straight shooter. Genuine. And his words made her stronger, solidified her strength to fight for Gareth.

"Thanks so much, Rook. I really appreciate what you and Pippa have done for me, and how you care for Gareth. I'm going to try. I want Gareth in my life, was an idiot to have taken this long to realise."

"You're not the first one to not see what was staring you in the face, Emily, and you won't be the last. God, took me years before I finally realised Pippa was the only woman for me, and I tell you I'm never letting her go." Love for his fiancée lit up Rook's face and it gladdened Emily's heart to know these two wonderful people had found each other. She listened as Rook continued, "I've already got plan B in mind if Gareth doesn't get it when you show up at the game. I figured between me and the boys we can drag him to Jetstream, fill his belly full of whisky, then you can use some of your cowgirl ropes to tie him to his bed. You do have ropes, don'tcha, Cowgirl?" he added with a grin. "Just don't untie him until he gives in."

Laughing at Rook's idea, Emily could see the possibilities in having Gareth tied to his bed and at her mercy. Thoughts of all the things she could do to his muscular, gorgeous body filled her mind. She could spend hours just exploring him, tasting him, and she thought of her mouth filled with his hard cock as she teased and drove him wild with need, but held him back just on the edge. She could almost taste him, feel the length of him, so hard, yet smooth at the same time. Taste the saltiness of the pre-cum as it leaked from the head of his shaft. She would lap the fluid up greedily, lick and lave his length, gently nip the sensitive flesh over the blue vein that would be pulsating along his swollen cock. Drive his desire higher and further than she ever had before, until his cum filled her mouth. Spurt after warm spurt, she would drink him in, drink him dry.

Then, just to torment him some more, she would pleasure herself before his hungry eyes. She could see them now in her mind—his blue eyes a shade darker, filled with passion for her as he watched her bring herself to orgasm without being able to touch her. She imagined that it would not take her long to achieve a climax after having spent so much time pleasuring him—she would be wet and needy and ready to explode—but she would draw it out for him. She'd manipulate her own nipples with her fingertips, pinch and roll them, maybe lean in near his lips so that he could have a quick taste of the protruding red nubs, but only a short taste, just enough to leave him wanting, ready to forgive her. To trust her again to love him forever.

"Hellooo...? Emily, you still in there, Cowgirl? I'm thinking by the look on your face you have a few ideas how to help 'ole Cowboy on the road to recovery then. That's a hell of a wicked grin you're sporting. Almost feel sorry for the guy."

Emily's face was burning and it had nothing to do with her scars—it was from the heat of her embarrassment over Rook's accurate observation of her thoughts. She loved the fact that Rook had taken to calling her Cowgirl, especially as it was a fitting match for his name for Gareth—Cowboy.

"Yep, busted. I do have a few interesting ideas rolling around in my head. Ideas I think might be quite persuasive." She giggled, a sound she had forgotten she could make. It sounded strange, girlish. Carefree. The attention Rook was giving her, the look on his face, was hysterical.

"Rook… Stop looking at me like that." Emily grinned, rubbing her hands together in wicked delight over her plans. "Your buddy will be safe in my hands…I promise. It just may take him a while to recover."

"Well, I seem to have missed out on something big, by the look of you two. 'Thick as thieves', I think the saying goes." Pippa joined them, a large bowl of bolognese in her hands, her eyes twinkling. She was clearly amused at the sight of Rook's and Emily's mirth. "You two aren't thinking up any nasty scenarios for my good friend, now, are you? I won't feed you—either of you—if you have anything too wicked in mind. Poor Gareth."

The laughter, hers and Rook's, mingled together even louder at Pippa's lighthearted threats, and for Emily it was so welcome, such a tonic to her soul that she was beginning to believe that everything *would* work out fine.

How could it not, with so many people in her corner? Gareth didn't stand a chance. All she had to do was meet a few people, and if they were anything like Rook and Pippa, how hard could it be? She would answer the questions about her face, give the details of the fire, get it all out in the open, ignore the stares, and her life would be perfect.

Chapter Eleven

It had taken all of Gareth's resolve not to go, on bended knee, and beg Emily to forgive him, to forget what he had said, to give him another chance, but he had stayed strong.

Strong and abjectly miserable.

Training had not helped, had not lessened the pain. Not wanting to be around anyone or to have to explain his mood, Gareth had kept a low profile. He had gone straight home after training, hidden out in his cave of misery, pretended it would be all right, that he would eventually feel better, get over Emily. He especially had not wanted to be around Pippa. Not only would she have picked up on his misery immediately, but her life was so happy now. She and Rook were always giving each other loving glances, cuddling and kissing, and had their hands on each other constantly. Gareth hadn't thought he could take it, the constant reminder of how things should be with him and Emily.

So he was looking forward to the day's game — couldn't wait to take the field, wanted to pour out his frustrations on the opposition. He could already imagine the feel of running the ball up into a wall of defence, craved the pain that would be inflicted on his body under the punishing demands of the full-body contact sport. Any other type of pain would be better than the one that had taken up residence in his heart and mind.

As he entered the team room to prepare for the game, Gareth tried to fully focus on the task ahead of him. He needed to have his head completely in the game—a distraction of any kind on the field could result in injury. He had to know where to place his body, in what position to have his head when he went in for a tackle. Hit a guy's hip or knee the wrong way, and he could find himself stretchered off the field with cartoon birds buzzing around his melon.

One of the first things he noticed was the cold shoulder he was getting from Pippa. Normally she would be at him the second he entered the changing room, wanting to strap his hamstrings or tape his ankles, but today she was flitting around well out of his reach. He actually had to go looking for her to get his pre-match preps done.

"Hey, Pippa, got time for me yet?" Gareth had tried to make the comment sound easy-going, a lighthearted request, but it had come out more like a grumble. He really had to get his act together, stop being so down.

"Oh, Gareth, you're here. Yeah, I'll get you done next. Grab the empty table."

It really wasn't his imagination—Pippa was acting strange, distracted. Gareth hoped it had nothing to do with Rook, hoped she was just put out that he hadn't been around.

"Everything all right, Pippa? You and Rook all good?" He tried to make conversation, but Pippa wouldn't meet his eyes, kept her head down busily while she worked on his ankle tape.

"Yep."

Her one-word reply really unnerved him. *It must be because I've ignored her*, Gareth thought.

"Look, Pippa, I'm sorry for not being around much this week. It's just—"

"Gareth, I'm fine. Just a bit busy. Can we leave this conversation till after the game? I'll have a big catch-up with you then, okay?"

Well, that was just great. His misery now extended to losing his best friend as well. Apparently he was becoming quite the expert at upsetting the women he cared for.

"Was thinking of missing the after-game shindig, maybe going in to check on Mac." Which was a bald-faced lie—there was no chance he was going to risk running into Emily just yet. He didn't think he'd be strong enough. "But I'll turn up for a little while and we can catch up then."

"Goodo, it's a deal. Great news about Mac moving out of ICU…"

Pippa stopped talking abruptly and rushed off, muttering something about more tape, leaving Gareth to ponder how she'd known that Mac was moving wards. He wondered if she had been to see him, whether she had spoken to Emily. He really wanted to chase after Pippa—to ask her what she knew, how Emily had seemed if they had crossed paths—but quickly realised there was no point in knowing. He was only making it worse for himself. He needed to cut all ties with Em.

Distracted by his internal monologue, Gareth missed Rook walking up to stand in front of him.

"Cowboy. Ready for a big one?"

At the sound of Rook's voice, Gareth closed the door on all thoughts of Emily and Pippa. "Yep, looking forward to it, itching for it. Should be tough. That Kiwi halfback's a slippery customer. If he gets past the first line of defence he can run. Gotta make sure we shut him down." It felt good to talk footy, to think about footy. That was what he did. That was who he was.

"Yeah, Brodie's already mentioned it at least a dozen times. I'm more worried about the beast of a winger. Seen the size of him? Don't want give to him a chance to wind up and get some momentum behind those tree-trunk legs."

This was the normal range of conversation between Rook and Gareth before a game, and the routine helped Gareth focus. He and Rook discussed a few more tactics as Pippa returned from wherever she'd taken off to and finished his rub-down, loosening and warming his muscles in readiness. He had no chance to question her or talk any further. Rook monopolised his time until Brodie called the team together for last-minute instructions, then they ran out and down the tunnel amidst the cheers and boos from the fans for the kick-off.

As Gareth homed in for the first tackle of the game, he felt sorry for his opponent—he was going to hit the guy with everything he had. All of his pent-up emotion was going into this shoulder charge. It had been the thought of this moment that had kept him sane all week. Gareth didn't disappoint himself. He set his sights on the player holding the ball, a prominent member of the opposition's forward pack, and charged at him, his shoulder connecting at the perfect position to send the opponent flying backwards, losing his grip on the football. Gareth scooped up the lost ball, passed it quickly out wide through the hands of the Jets backline and watched in satisfaction as Josh, playing on the wing, raced over the try line and scored under the posts.

The crowd went wild. The Jets had scored in less than thirty seconds from the kick-off siren, against the run of play. While Rook set up for the attempted goal conversion, Gareth and the rest of the team walked back down the field to take up their usual starting positions. The opposition would return the ball to the Jets, to resume play from a kick off, the try-scoring team retaining the advantage of possession. Gareth grinned as Rook easily converted the try to give them a six-nil lead, then gave him a high-five as he ran past.

"Way to go, Cowboy! What's got you all fired up? Anyone would think you had someone special in the crowd, someone to impress."

"Yeah, if only, Rook. No, that hit was just for me. A reward."

Chapter Twelve

The day had started off unbelievably well for Emily. She had been nervous, a little apprehensive. Thoughts of facing what was expected to be a big crowd, and of meeting Gareth's friends, had her wiping her perspiring hands repeatedly on her jeans. She had thought long and hard on what to wear, and had finally taken Pippa's advice — she had just worn an outfit she would be comfortable in. And that, for Emily, was denim jeans, newly purchased cowboy boots and a shirt. She had wrapped a Jets supporter's scarf around her neck to hide some of the scars, but there was nothing she could do to camouflage the ravages on her face.

Pippa had, as she'd promised, introduced her to a bunch of women. Emily had been convinced she would never remember any of their names, especially with her belly full of marauding butterflies, but she had been delighted to find herself wedged tightly between the coaches' wives, Caitlin James and Mandy Thomson. The women were so friendly and funny — they'd had her in stitches with their tales of their husbands, and Rook, and even some stories about Gareth. Emily had found she was really enjoying herself, right up until Gareth had run into the playing arena and the siren sounded for the game to begin.

She had nearly swallowed her tongue when Gareth had made that first tackle, charged in with no sense of self preservation. Even the women around her had gasped in shock at the ferocity of the hit.

"Brodie's going to love that one," she'd heard Caitlin say.

"Yeah, but JT is going to take all the praise, being forward coach and all," Mandy had added, laughing, the sound a little forced to Emily's ears.

"Looks like Gareth's not the only one making a statement." Emily hadn't seen Pippa sit down, and couldn't help but clasp her accomplice's hand.

"Heya, Pip. What you doing up here visiting us civvies?"

Emily wasn't sure whether it was Caitlin or Mandy speaking to Pippa. She was so focused on the game — on Gareth in particular — but when she heard her name mentioned she turned to find out what she had missed.

"How are you doing, Emily? Everything good? Caitlin and Mandy haven't been telling stories about me again have they? Gotta tell ya, it's tough when your bosses' wives know all your teenage secrets." Pippa didn't seem to be worried at all, in Emily's opinion.

"Who doesn't know your big secret? Oh, Pipsqueak's in love with Rookie..."

The adolescent voice Caitlin had used to tease Pippa was so funny that Emily found herself joining in with the merriment, forgetting the tension she had been experiencing while watching Gareth on the field.

"Huh, funny lady..." Pippa replied, her voice deadpan but her smile giving herself away and assuring everyone in earshot that she was just as amused at Caitlin's antics as they were. "Anyway, I'm not here to entertain the riffraff, I just came up to give Emily a bit of news."

Emily gave Pippa her full attention, worried that the plan might have a flaw, until Pippa set her mind at ease as she whispered, "Just thought you might want to know, Gareth hadn't planned on coming back to the club, but I changed his mind."

"Unless after he sees me, he changes his mind back," Emily grumbled.

"No, I don't think that will happen. I think Gareth will be very glad to set eyes on you. It was so hard not to tell him you were here—Go, Rook! That's the way, baby, give it to them!"

Emily's eardrum nearly burst as Pippa screamed her approval at Rook's run, and Emily joined in enthusiastically, cheering Rook on as he intercepted a floating pass from the Lions' attacking play and raced the length of the field to score a try. Pippa's comment that Rook's legs would be shot after having to run so fast, considering his age, had the crowd of women giggling in response.

Pippa left shortly after Rook's solo try and conversion, to prepare for half-time, promising to return to Emily as soon as possible after the game, to show her support. Caitlin and Mandy reassured Pippa and Emily that they would take care of her in the meantime, even offering their assistance to get Gareth and Emily back on the right path. Both Caitlin and Mandy gushed about how much they loved a happy ending, and how much they liked Gareth, and said that he needed a good woman in his life.

Emily felt such a strong connection with the women that she filled them in on all the drama of the last few days and the previous years. It was then that Emily realised none of the people she had met that day had even mentioned her face. She had forgotten about it.

Soon enough, the game was over and Emily was faced with the reality of what she was about to do — she was going to ambush Gareth and put him on the spot.

What if he really doesn't want to see me? The worst scenarios played out in her head, all negative images of Gareth shunning her. *He might be embarrassed, feel pressured into talking to me, not wanting to seem rude in front of his friends. He might be angry that I involved them. I never thought of that. What if I damage his friendships with Pippa and Rook? Maybe I should just leave, before it's too late.*

Her thoughts were spinning. Trepidation and the fear of Gareth's rejection swelled into a chilling sense of doom that left her frozen. She couldn't face it, couldn't face knowing that Gareth didn't love her anymore because of how she'd acted. It was unthinkable. She was trembling, her body reacting to the fear, her mind fighting hard to keep a grip on reality. How could she face the prospect of life without Gareth? How had she ever thought she could?

* * * *

The time before the players started to slowly drift through the doors played out like hours in Emily's mind. She hovered nervously behind the other women, her eyes fixed on any movement that heralded the arrival of a clean player, dressed in street clothes. God, what was taking so long? Had Gareth got wind of her and slipped out another way? Surely Pippa would let her know? Maybe she didn't want to relay the unhappy news to her, didn't want to be the bringer of bad news. What would she do? Should she go to Rook's nightclub and try again?

Emily was so caught up in her pessimistic thoughts that she missed Gareth walking out through the door, Rook and Pippa by his side. It was Pippa who gained her attention, waving frantically at her behind Gareth's back. Emily heard Caitlin whisper in her ear as she was shoved unceremoniously forward.

"Go get him."

So she did. With her head held high and a silent prayer, Emily walked towards her man. He hadn't noticed her—his momentum only halted when Rook stopped moving. He wasn't looking in her direction, was deep in conversation with Rook. Emily could see when Rook spotted her, caught the encouraging smile he sent her way.

"That was quite a game, Gareth. You really showed the Lions what for." She couldn't think of anything more appropriate to say. She wanted to beg for his forgiveness, plead for it, but now was certainly not the time for that. Not with the television crews and newspaper reporters hanging around. It would have to do.

It was like watching a slow motion movie. She could tell the moment it registered in Gareth's brain that it was her voice. Her heart skipped with fear as she waited for his reaction. It seemed to take a lifetime for him to turn to face her.

Chapter Thirteen

The rest of the game had played out the way the first few seconds had. The Lions hadn't had a chance—the Jets had never let them into the game. The slippery halfback had been ineffectual without the support of his forward pack, and the Jets had just punished them. In return, the Jets' speedy backline had carved them up, and the end score must have been an embarrassment for the visiting Lions. But Gareth had revelled in it—every tackle, every hit up, he had played like a man possessed.

And he was possessed. He was trying to exorcise a demon—his obsession. His love for Emily.

* * * *

Gareth was starting to get really pissed off. Every time he had gone to leave the room and make a run for it, to try to get past the fans and reporters, Rook had stopped him, asked him a question or got him to do some irrelevant task. He was reaching boiling point. He wanted to get to the club, fulfil his responsibilities and go home, but Rook had been stalling him at every turn. Finally they had been ready, and Rook and Pippa had followed him, talking nonstop as they'd exited the changing rooms.

Gareth was beginning to feel a bit wary at their strange behaviour. Before the game Pippa had given him the impression she didn't want to talk. Now she was prattling on like an idiot. Then he'd heard the voice, congratulating him on the game.

For a second he thought it sounded like Emily, but that was impossible. There was no chance Emily would show her face—literally—amongst this throng of people.

But it had really sounded like her. Rook was grinning like a fool and Pippa was sporting this dreamy expression, and they were both looking over his shoulder at someone standing behind him.

He sensed her then, knew it to be true as the hairs on his arms and neck responded to her. He was almost afraid to turn around in case it was his imagination, in case he was just projecting his desire. His hope.

But if it was Emily... God, that would mean she had reached out to him, put herself out there, faced her terror of public scrutiny. He so wanted that to be the case, desperately wanted it to be Emily standing behind him, and there was only one way to find out. He had to turn around.

And he did.

Slowly.

Emily was standing there with a hesitant smile and a hint of fear in her eyes. She had done this for him. He knew it. She was proving that she loved him enough to face her fears. It took only one stride for him to be within reach of her, and Gareth didn't hesitate, dragging her to him, lowering his mouth to take possession of hers. One touch of her lips to his and he was lost for all time. He slid his tongue along the seam of her mouth, begging for entry, and as she opened her lips slightly, he thrust his tongue inside.

It was a pure slice of heaven, a moment to remember forever. Gareth had almost forgotten he was standing in the shadow of a football stadium, surrounded by teammates, friends and complete strangers. All he could think of was how perfect it was to have Emily in his arms, the absolute joy in the simple act of holding the woman he loved in his arms.

"*Ahem...* Hey, Cowboy... Unless you want this to be front page in tomorrow's newspapers, I think you need to cool it."

Crap, that would be the very last thing Emily would want. Gareth had the urge to kill Rook where he stood for even mentioning the possibility. He felt Emily stiffen in his arms, and waited for her to go into full panic mode.

"Rook's just teasing, Em. It won't happen."

"Aw, shit, Cowgirl, I didn't mean to worry you, hon. Pippa, why'd you let me say something like that? Anyhow, what would it matter? You guys aren't doing anything wrong. What's not to like? A couple of good-looking country cow-folk doing bit of tongue wrestling—makes a better story than some of the shit that gets printed."

Emily was laughing. Gareth could hardly believe his ears, and that thought of killing Rook quickly morphed into a wish to hug the man—an equally disturbing thought for Gareth as he remembered the press corps still in attendance. Pippa was laughing, Rook was laughing, the place had gone mad and Gareth was overjoyed.

"Okay, you lot, get your backsides to the club. The quicker we can get that out of the way, the quicker we can all get over to Jetstream and really let our hair down."

It was the most ridiculous thing Gareth had ever heard Brodie James say. Everyone knew Coach didn't know the meaning of the words 'let your hair down'. He was the most serious, most responsible man Gareth had ever met. Just the thought of Brodie letting loose and having fun was enough to make Gareth laugh. "If this is a dream, I hope I never wake up," he murmured.

* * * *

The drive to the Jets' club, in Gareth's car, was perfect. Emily sat sideways the whole way, just looking at Gareth's profile. Every so often he would look in her direction and a broad smile would light up his features. Emily felt the love he held for her and it washed away all her fears and doubts that she had lost him. She couldn't believe how easy it had been to gain Gareth's forgiveness after having put him through so much over the last few years. He had not given up on her no matter how hard she had made it for him, how often she had given him reason. She loved him so much.

She watched his large, masculine hands on the steering wheel and wished they were on her body. His face, his hands, his bulging biceps all made her melt just at the sight of them, making her heart race, her pussy moist and her breasts heavy. Emily reached between Gareth's massive thighs and stroked his jeans-covered cock, cupped it, massaged it gently and felt it harden under her touch.

"Shit, Em, that feels fucking awesome, but it's making it...*really*...hard to concentrate on driving. Making everything really hard."

She laughed at the sight of Gareth squirming in his seat to find more space for his growing erection, at the pained look on his face and the hunger for her in his eyes.

"You're such a spoilsport. I was actually contemplating unzipping your jeans, taking that hard, beautiful cock of yours out, wrapping my lips around it and blowing you right here in your car...but if it would be too much of a distraction for you, Cowboy..."

"Em...I wouldn't survive it. My God, the thought of it alone — your head bent over my lap, your lips on my cock — is nearly making me blow. But if you look in the rear-view mirror you might recognise the people in the cars behind us."

Emily had forgotten all about the other Jets players and wives, all making their way to the club. She started giggling at the thought of what they would see — her leaning over Gareth, her head bobbing up and down. There'd be no way of misunderstanding what she was doing.

"Oops, forgot about them."

"Yeah, and as much as I love your idea, pretty sure the guys would guess straight away what was happening...although I'm game if you are."

Gareth put his hand on her head, gently directing it towards his lap and Emily wasn't sure if he was serious or not. She had just been teasing him, wouldn't have dreamt of being so brash or doing anything so explicit in public — not to mention the danger of distracting Gareth whilst he was driving.

"Um...maybe we should put a rain check on my idea. Another time, a darker road and without a convoy of your friends and teammates behind us."

Gareth continued to pull her head towards him, but just to kiss her quickly on the lips.

"I'll hold you to that, Em. One of these days I'm going to get you to make good on that idea. Now I'm going to try and get this hard-on back under control. You wicked woman, what will my groupies think if I walk into the club sporting a woody?"

"Your groupies will think that some woman — me — turned you on and that they have no chance in having you... That's what your groupies will think, and if they don't I'll be sure to point it out to them."

She knew Gareth was teasing her, but it did bring back some fear. These women who wanted Gareth would see her scars. What would they think? Would they think Gareth was with her only through some sense of pity?

"Stop thinking, I can see it written all over your face. I love you, Em, no woman holds a candle to you. I'm sorry. I shouldn't have teased you."

"It's okay, Gareth, I need to work through this. I love you too. Oh, and by the way, I was having a heart to heart with Dad and guess what? All those times I snuck out to meet you, so we could hump like bunnies in the dark, he knew what we were doing. He was tempted to fill your arse with buckshot. How's that for embarrassing?"

The horrified look on Gareth's face was priceless.

"Mac knew? Fuck."

"Yep! Exactly that!" Emily laughed, the sound loud and carefree. "So I'm guessing your folks were clued in as well."

"Dad never said anything if he did. Surprised Mum didn't haul me over the coals, though. She really loves you, Em, wouldn't have wanted me taking advantage of you. Although, as I remember it, you seduced *me* that day at the dam…tempted me with that sinful, blossoming body of yours. I was only human, after all, couldn't resist that sort of temptation."

"Yeah, yeah, we've been over this before, Cowboy. I'm a wicked, wicked woman."

"My woman, Emily Mackenzie. Thank God you've finally woken up to it." The serious tone of Gareth's voice sent shivers down her spine. Emily loved the sound of those words. She truly was Gareth's woman, and he was her man.

They pulled into the club's car park and as Gareth shut down the engine of his car, Emily noticed the others parking next to them. Pippa bounced out of the vehicle nearest them and pulled open Emily's door.

"C'mon, Emily, let's go have some fun. Looking forward to some bubbles tonight. Told Rook I was having a few drinks so he should be prepared for some hot, uninhibited lovin' later. Judging by the smile on his face, I think he liked the plan."

Emily giggled at Pippa's outrageous statement as she watched Rook get out of his car.

"Hey, Cowgirl. What's not to like, I say. My woman, hot for me."

"Sounded more like Pippa needs some alcohol in her system before she gets down and dirty with ya, Rook…but hey, that's just my read on it."

Emily was laughing so hard over Rook and Gareth's sledging that she nearly stumbled when Pippa put her arm through hers and started dragging her towards the club's entrance.

"It's always like that between them. You get used to it after a while."

"Pippa, thank you. I haven't had this much fun in years—meeting you and Rook, having Gareth back in my life, Dad on the mend. I've got a lot of celebrating to do... I see bubbles and lots of them in my near future."

Emily and Pippa, arm in arm, headed into the function room and found a table to sit at. Caitlin and Mandy followed, both women clutching a child in their arms. Then came Gareth and Rook. Brodie and JT, each man also holding onto a child, joined the table as well. There were people everywhere, the room packed with Jets supporters all eager to talk with their heroes and celebrate the recent victory. Emily was truthfully a little shell-shocked, had not expected such a large group of people. Her anxiety was rising.

"It's going to be okay, baby, I'm not going anywhere. I'm staying right by your side tonight." Gareth held her hand to his lips as he stared her right in the eyes.

She would be okay. She was surrounded by new friends, protected by Gareth.

"I can do this."

Chapter Fourteen

Gareth almost wished they had lost today's game. Then the club would not have been so packed — supporters were sometimes fickle, and didn't show up after a loss. But it was chockers tonight. *Just my luck that Emily's first night would be this busy*, he thought. She was doing okay, though, he noticed. His friends had welcomed her into their inner circle — Caitlin, Mandy and Pippa had taken Emily under their wings, sitting her amongst them all. It was the sight Gareth had always dreamt of — his Emily sitting amongst his friends and their kids, being part of his life. It was a perfect moment. He stood behind her chair, resting his hand on Emily's shoulder just to prove to himself it was real, that he was not dreaming.

There had been a moment when Emily had first entered the function room and seen the crowd filling the room that Gareth had thought she would run. He'd seen the flicker of unease on her face, but she had quickly recovered, staunchly lifting her head and walking beside Pippa to the table reserved for the players and family. Everyone had come back to the club—all the boys and their partners. There were kids everywhere.

Brodie handed him a beer, and Gareth noticed Rook had produced a bottle of champagne and was filling the women's glasses.

"Cheers, Gareth. You played one hell of a game today. Reckon it will put you in the sights of the New South Wales selectors, for sure."

"Thanks, Brodie. I really enjoyed the game. Don't know about a shot at rep footy, but wouldn't knock it back if I got the call-up," he replied, thinking that life was getting better and better by the second.

Then, at the sound of one innocent question behind him, his heart fell to his feet.

"Hello. What happened to your face?"

Emily had not been able to believe the amount of people who had crowded into the room. She was surrounded by Jets players, recognised most of them from the games she had watched on the television back in Gunnedah. Wives and girlfriends sat around her, and kids were everywhere.

"Footy players sure can breed," she'd whispered to Pippa, who had taken a seat to her left and had been handing out glasses of champagne, poured expertly by Rook, to the table of women.

"Got that right, Em. Macho men and macho sperm…"

Emily had taken a sip of the bubbles and had felt herself begin to relax. The heat from Gareth's hand on her shoulder that'd seeped into her tense body and the cool, bubbly drink had both done their part. As she'd leant forward to place her glass back onto the table she'd noticed a little dark-haired girl approach, but had not been prepared for the question she'd asked in such a tiny voice. The girl's saucer-sized brown eyes had been full of innocent enquiry, her small hand reaching out towards Emily's face, possibly to touch her scars.

Emily could not help but flinch out of the girl's reach, couldn't bear the thought of that delicate little hand touching her ugly, marred skin.

"Elaina, *no!*"

The voice boomed through the club, scaring Emily half to death with its ferocity. It nearly had her jumping from her chair in response. The club—well, at least those in the vicinity of the table—went deathly silent in response. The little girl beside her gasped, pulled her hand away from Emily's face, and tears welled up in the poor little thing's big, brown eyes. The girl's bottom lip started to quiver, then she began to cry, but before she could react, Mandy had her arm wrapped around the girl's shoulders, hugging the little girl to her side.

"There, there, Elaina. Don't cry. Daddy didn't mean to shout so loud. But you know, it's not polite to be a nosy parker."

"I d-d-didn't m-mean to make Da-a-d-d-y-y angwy..." Mandy and JT's daughter sobbed. Emily watched a torrent of fat tears roll down Elaina's sad little face as her mother tried to console her. All the kids around her were now crying, their mothers and fathers doing their best to quiet their offspring. Emily wasn't sure whether JT's booming voice had started off the waterworks or if Elaina's tears were infectious. "I j-j-just wanted to ask the pretty lady what happened to her face...and if it hurt..."

Emily's heart broke for Elaina. The girl was so upset that her father had shouted at her, yet those three little words were the most monumental, most world-changing words Emily had ever heard. Elaina had called her 'the pretty lady' — the slip of a girl had not cared about her scars, but had seen her as pretty. All the fears of children thinking her a monster were swept away. If this little girl could see past the ugliness, then it was high time she did too.

"Oh, Elaina — is that your name, darling? Stop crying, honey. You didn't do anything wrong. I'm sure your daddy didn't mean to shout so loud. I'll tell you a secret…your daddy was so loud I nearly fell off my chair."

Those big brown eyes turned sheepishly towards her. The hesitant smile on the young girl's face melted Emily's heart even more.

"My daddy is vewy loud."

"Yes, Elaina, your daddy *is* very loud, but I'm sure he didn't mean to make you and every other child in the room cry," Mandy said pointedly, as she sent what could only be described as a death stare towards her husband. "Isn't that right, *Daddy*?"

Emily looked on as an apologetic-looking JT tried to make peace with his wife and daughter. The room had come back to life. Conversations had resumed now the drama had passed, but Emily wanted to answer Elaina's question, wanted to show the sweet little girl that no harm had been done and she was not in any trouble.

"Elaina, do you still want to know about my face?" She was overjoyed when Elaina moved to stand in front of her, her eyes again like saucers. The solemn look she was giving Emily was so adorable, it was hard for Emily not to just sweep the girl into her arms and squeeze her to within an inch of her life.

"Well, a few years ago I got trapped in a bushfire. A tree fell on me and burned my skin."

"Oooh..." Elaina's mouth gaped open. Then Emily watched, transfixed, as the information registered in the young girl's brain, and saw the flickering in her eyes. Emily waited to hear what the first question would be—people always wanted to know more about the gory details surrounding the fire and her scars—so was taken aback when the words were nothing like she'd imagined them to be.

"I burned my finger once, touched a really hot plate. It really hurt. I cried and cried...and my little brother Jay, he told me I was a sooky lah-lah. You must have cried a lot."

"Yes, I did cry a lot, Elaina, and for too long. But I'm okay now. How about you, is your finger better?"

Such innocence shone from Elaina's brown eyes—no fear or revulsion apparent, just concern. Children seemed to be becoming a great source of learning for Emily. After Gareth's description of the children in the hospitals he'd visited, and now faced with this little girl standing in front of her, she had definitely finished feeling sorry for herself.

She had all but forgotten Gareth was standing behind her, so was surprised when he spoke to Elaina. "Hey, sweet-pea. So you've met my friend Emily, then?"

"Hi, Uncle Gawef. Is she your friend? She's pretty. Are you going to get married like Uncle Mitch and Aunty Pippa? She got burned on her face just like me on my finger, did you know that?"

Emily's head was swimming at the way Elaina had just pumped out the questions one after the other, but she loved the fact the child had called Gareth 'uncle'— it was so sweet. She listened with amused curiosity for how Gareth would answer.

"Yep, sweet-pea, my Emily is the prettiest girl around. Well, maybe next to you, that is. And just between you and me, I hope she *will* marry me one day."

Elaina's giggles and shy smile at Gareth's saying she was pretty was too cute for words, especially when Gareth ruffled Elaina's riotous brown curls. Emily was enjoying watching the interaction between them—Gareth was so easy-going, a natural when dealing with children, and Emily could see that Elaina was enjoying the attention.

"Do you want to know how my Emily got hurt by the bushfire, sweet-pea?"

"It won't make me a nosy parker, will it, Uncle Gawef?" It was such a serious little voice that both Emily and Gareth started laughing. Considering Gareth was about to talk about the bushfire that had almost destroyed her life, Emily was surprised at her own reaction.

"No, sweet-pea, it won't. My Emily is so brave. When the bushfire was burning close to her farm—she comes from the country just like me, in fact her farm is right next to mine—anyway, the fire was big and mean, burning all the trees and grass for miles…"

Everyone around Emily had gone quiet, all listening to the story Gareth was narrating. He looked like the Pied Piper, she thought, as she watched all the children gather around her man. By her quick count, ten sets of eyes, opened wide on little faces, gazed up at Gareth as though he was about to tell some fantastical tale. It looked so surreal. Emily had locked away all visions of Gareth and children, but seeing him surrounded and so at ease with the small folk, about to tell her sorry tale, was quite unbelievable—a place and time she'd never thought she would experience. She felt goosebumps on her arms as she awaited the response from those around her.

"Emily and I have lots of animals on our farms. Cows, dogs and cats and chickens and horses—big, beautiful brown horses that have long manes that flow in the wind when we ride them at full gallop. When our parents heard about the bushfire, they told Emily to put her horses in one of the paddocks away from the fire, thinking it would be safe. Emily did what she was told and moved her horses. Two of Emily's horses had just had babies. Baby horses are called foals. Emily put both foals into the paddock as well so they could be with their mummies."

As Gareth spoke Emily lived the day again in her mind, remembered every move she had made. Everyone else around their table, it seemed, was listening.

"Well, sweet-pea, a little while later the wind changed direction, started blowing the fire another way, towards the horses."

The little gasps from the children as they imagined what was about to happen caused Emily to worry. She didn't want Gareth to upset their tender little minds, worried how the children's parents would react. Caitlin and Mandy might not want their children traumatised by the events of that day. But when Emily looked at the women to judge their reactions to the story, they both smiled at her—smiles that told Emily that it was okay, not to worry. Before she could speak up and ask Gareth to stop, Elaina spoke.

"What happened to the horses, Uncle Gawef? Did the fire burn them too?"

"No, sweet-pea, that's just it. Emily saved the horses. She went searching for them. In their fright the horses had broken through the fence and actually headed towards the fire. The horses were so scared. But not Emily. She ran through the bush, all the trees and long grass, not scared of the fire burning around her, or all the thick smoke making it hard for her to breathe. She didn't give up until she found them. Emily led the horses away from the fire. Only just after the horses had galloped past her, all headed safely away from the path of the fire, a big tree branch crashed down onto Emily. The branch was on fire and it fell on her pretty face. I found Emily and lifted the branch off her, but the fire had already hurt her."

"Emily saved the horses from the fire!" Elaina squealed in excitement. The other children around Gareth were all smiles and cheers, as well.

Elaina turned towards Emily. "You're so-o-o...brave," she said as she threw her arms around Emily's neck. "I want to be as brave as Emily when I grow up and save horses too," she added as she turned towards her mother, Mandy, looking for approval. "I love horses. Do you think Daddy will buy me a horse? He did make me cry..."

"I don't think we could fit one in our backyard, darling, and Daddy making you cry is not a good enough reason, Miss. And anyway, I thought you wanted to be like Aunty Pippa when you grow up, so you could work with Daddy?"

"I've changed my mind. Aunty Pippa has to touch boys all the time...yuck!" Elaina's grimace at the thought of touching boys was quickly replaced with the best pleading look Emily had ever seen as she turned it full force on her mother. *Talk about puppy dog eyes – the girl was born to be on the stage!*

"Oh, Mummy, ple-e-ease can I have a horsey?"

"Maybe one day Aunty Emily might take you for a ride on one of her horses, if you're a good girl."

The choruses of "Me too!" and "I want to ride with Emily!" from all the children—probably listening in to see if Elaina would get her wish for a horse—truly surprised Emily, brought tears to her eyes, tears of joy. There were children climbing all over her, all begging for her to take them on a horse. None of them cared one iota about her scarred face, and were certainly not terrorised by it. Emily could hardly breathe from a mixture of being smothered by the rambunctious gaggle of small people, from having been referred to as Aunty Emily by Mandy and from the knowledge that she was being accepted by all of Gareth's friends, young and old.

It took both Gareth and JT to wrangle the children from her lap, but Emily didn't mind that she had been crushed. Just having the children clamouring for her attention had been such a gift. She promised to see what she could do about giving them all a ride with her on a horse, explaining that her horses were a long way away from the city, so it could be a bit tricky.

"I say we have a Jets excursion to a horse-riding ranch." Caitlin laughed. "Wouldn't mind seeing all you boys on horseback. I reckon it would be quite a sight."

"Settle down, Cate. Last thing I need is a team full of injured players from falling off horses. Don't think it would go down too well with the hierarchy," Brodie added quickly.

"Geez, Brodes, if Gareth can ride a horse there can't be much too it," Rook said, butting into the conversation between the coach and his wife. Emily shook her head at Rook's continued sledging of Gareth.

* * * *

As the night progressed, people introduced themselves to Emily, congratulated her, commented on her bravery. They told her how nice it was to meet her, but it was when they mentioned how nice it was to see Gareth's smile, his obvious happiness that she had made it to a game, that really made her heart burst. She had really made a mess of her life, and Gareth's, but was determined to make things right again.

The night flew by. Brodie and Rook made a few speeches, thanking everyone for their continued support. A raffle was drawn, the lucky supporter winning an autographed football jersey. The first part of the night was winding down, and it had been a pleasant experience for Emily—chatting to the other wives and girlfriends, and all the children. She still couldn't get over the fact the children looked at her like she was some sort of superhero, all vying for her attention. Elaina had stolen her heart. The vivacious child was full of stories about everyone, and there was not a shy bone in her body, Emily had decided. But it was the point when Elaina's grandfather—JT's father—arrived to collect both JT's and Brodie's children that really broke Emily up.

"That's my Pa over there." The little girl pointed to a man who, in Emily's opinion, was unmistakeably JT's father. His size alone matched that of his son. "He babysits us while Mummy and Daddy go to Uncle Mitch's club. I'm not a baby, but I am too little to go to a club, Mummy says. It's okay though, 'cause I don't really want to go to a noisy adults place, and I know a secret…"

Emily was still finding it difficult to keep up with Elaina's rapid-fire changes in conversation, but the way Elaina had whispered the last comment had her intrigued.

"A secret, you say. Is it a good secret?" Emily watched, amused, as Elaina moved her lips up close to Emily's ear.

"My Pa has a girlfriend. She makes us all hot chocolate with marshmallows in it. Mmmm...they get all mushy and gooey, it's s-o-o-o yummy. Sometimes when they think none of us kids are looking they kiss...just like my mummy and daddy do...on the lips."

Emily could not stop herself. She burst out laughing. "Oh, Elaina, I think you and I are going to be very good friends. Yes, that is a good secret. You go with your Pa and have a good night. I promise I will see you again very soon." Emily deflected the questioning look from Mandy, just shook her head, mouthing the word, "Later." She didn't want Elaina to think she was tattling on her to her mother. She couldn't wait to tell Gareth what Elaina had said, and looked forward to Mandy and JT's reactions as well.

Chapter Fifteen

The first half of the night had been a resounding success, Gareth's version of Em's fire horror winning her hearts young and old. He was so proud of how Emily had reacted, how well she had fitted in amongst his football family. Elaina had fallen in love with Em straight away, and had hardly left her side throughout the night. Gareth could see that Emily was enjoying herself. She had spoken to her father using Gareth's mobile, her voice full of happiness as she'd told Mac how much fun she was having.

Now, seeing her at Rook's nightclub, Jetstream, just added to his dream-come-true evening.

Gareth had spent so many nights in the club, surrounded by his friends, spending time with Pippa, but having his Emily with him was beyond words. He couldn't keep his eyes off her or the smile from his face. This was what it was meant to be like. This was how he had planned his future—playing rugby league, knowing Emily was watching him, cheering him on, then celebrating with her by his side.

"You know, Cowboy, I hardly recognise you tonight. That thing on your face, you know, that way you're holding your mouth... Who knew you could smile for that long?"

"Just never had the right company before. Just your ugly mug to look at, day and night—not much to smile about with that, Rook."

"Remind me to pass that information on to Pippa. Good to know she wasn't worth a smile or two. But then again, I guess knowing you had no chance with her because she was under the ole Rook's spell probably was hard to take."

"Ha ha, you're a laugh a minute, mate. Guess it's my shout. Wanna beer?"

"Thought you'd never ask, Cowboy. Better get the girls some more bubbly—they seem to be hitting it hard tonight." Rook smiled as he glanced in Pippa and Emily's direction. "Think those two are going to give us some trouble—thick as thieves already."

"Yep, think you're spot on, Rook, and I love everything about the thought." Gareth took in the sight of Pippa and Emily deep in conversation, heads bent towards each other. The sound of laughter filtered back to him, making him grin even more.

"Cowgirl's a good one—she's been staying with Pippa and me the last few nights and I gotta say I like her. Way too good for you, though. Lucky I've got Pippa in my life, Cowboy, or I'd be taking her off your hands. It would be sad to take another woman from you, buddy, but hey, no-one can resist my charming ways."

It was always the same between Rook and Gareth— the good-natured banter—but normally it was Gareth giving Rook grief, so he couldn't help the tinge of jealousy over Rook's teasing.

"Keep your hands off my woman, Rook," Gareth growled before he could stop himself.

"Ha, love it! Feels different when the shoe is on the other foot, hey, Cowboy? Cowgirl and I had a few chats about you—she's head over heels for you mate, got nothing to worry about there. Shame you forgave her so quick, though. Plan B was a belter."

The smirk on Rook's face intrigued Gareth. He tried to persuade Rook to go into more detail, but the man wouldn't be swayed, refusing any more information until Gareth had returned from the bar with another round of drinks. Gareth took off like a shot—the quicker he bought the drinks, the quicker he would hear the story that had caused the smirk.

Gareth excused himself through the crowded club and found a space at the bar, hoping to gain the attention of the bar manager, Mick, and receive some preferential service—he was, after all, buying the club owner a drink! Gareth didn't notice the women around him—that was normal; he never did—but he was furious when he heard snippets of the conversation next to him.

"If my face was that ugly I'd never leave my house. She looks like something out of a zombie movie."

"I know what you mean. You would think she could at least put some makeup or something over all the gross skin. God, makes me wanna puke just looking at it. Must be some charity case for the Jets team. Can't think how else she got into the VIP area."

Gareth stood there with his mouth gaping open. He could not believe the viciousness of the women's words. Fuck, what if Emily had heard them? They had summed up all her fears, had spoken them aloud. How dare they discuss his Emily so hatefully? He saw red.

The two women had been speaking so loudly that a few other heads had turned towards the Jets VIP area to gawk. All Gareth knew was that he was close to erupting. He had never hit a woman, had never even thought about it before, but he was close now. At hearing his Emily disrespected—by a couple of bitter groupies, no less—he was close to losing control. This was what she'd had to put up with. This was exactly what she had been afraid of, why she had pushed him away. There was no way Gareth was about to let this go, no way he was letting this type of inhumane person get away with treating the woman he loved so rudely...but if he made a scene, Emily would want to know why.

Gareth weighed the outcomes up in his head. Emily didn't deserve to be placed at the centre of attention by him or the women. If he took them to task about their behaviour, it could just escalate the attention focused on his Emily. But Gareth just couldn't let them get away with it. He was in a quandary. He almost missed Mick's question the first time around.

"G'day, Gareth. Same again, is it—one for you, Rook and some bubbly for the babes? Great game today—would it have anything to do with that gorgeous woman you walked in with tonight?"

Gareth caught the wink Mick sent his way as he placed the tray in front of him. He also heard the women beside him gasp at Mick's question, felt them swing around to stare at him.

"Gotta know it, Mick, finally got my woman down to the city. Took me a while to convince her to come. She doesn't think much of city folk, thinks them rude. I've been trying to convince her that not all you city slickers are bad, but it's a hard call, especially when so many of the city women are nothing but bitter sluts."

Gareth turned his angry stare full force on the women beside him, their eyes now wide, mouths gaping unattractively at his comments.

"Know what you mean, mate, but not all city women are like these two," Mick said as he pointed directly at the women. "In fact, they are not the sort of clientele we're looking for at Jetstream—brings down the whole ambience of the place," Gareth watched as Mick removed the drinks from in front of the startled pair.

"Hey, you can't do that..." one of the women shrieked.

"Guess what, doll? That's exactly what I can do, and more. Hey, Jerome..." Mick shouted to the doorman. Gareth watched as the gigantic Polynesian-born doorman sauntered towards the bar manager.

"Whassup, Bru? Got a job for me?" the doorman said, his Pacific Islander accent heavy, his size dwarfing most of the men standing at the bar. Jerome's sleeves were rolled partway up his arms, the tribal tattoos encircling his massive forearms clear to see, adding to the menacing look of the man Gareth knew to be friendly and easy-going in reality.

"Sure do, Jerome. Escort these two pieces of work out, and don't ever let me see them in here again. We don't want the likes of these in our club, mate— vicious, bitter and twisted types. Don't want to get a reputation for encouraging lowlifes in the club. Our patrons deserve better. Don't you agree, Gareth?"

Gareth could not respond to Mick, he was so choked up with emotion. Having friends—people who looked out for you and those you loved—was what it was all about.

The patrons seated at the bar had all gone quiet, listening in and watching as Jerome handed the two women their bags and pointed towards the exit. Both women were shouting and swearing like sailors at the treatment they were receiving, calling the club a shithole and various other derogatory names as they were ushered unceremoniously out of the door.

Gareth finally found his voice. "Thanks for that, mate," he said to Mick, and noticed the knowing smiles from the patrons around him—smiles that confirmed they agreed with Mick's description of the two evicted women.

"No problems, Gareth, they deserved it. Take your drinks back, enjoy the night, let me do my job and keep the riff-raff away."

"Cheers, Mick."

Gareth picked up the tray and headed back to Emily and the others. The smile on his face was not as genuine as before, as the reality of Emily's life and what she'd had to put up with every day became more apparent to him.

"What took ya so long, Cowboy? My stomach thinks my throat's been cut!" Rook greeted Gareth as he returned.

"Mick got distracted dealing with some rubbish removal. He's one hell of a bar manager," Gareth replied. "Here, take the beers while I deliver the bubbles to our girls."

Gareth took the bottle of champagne and headed towards Emily and Pippa. The smile Emily rewarded him with did wonders to lift his spirits, and he couldn't refrain from delivering to her smiling lips a possessive, hungry kiss, to a background chorus of, "Get a room, Cowboy!"

"Wow, what was that for, Gareth?" a breathless Emily responded when he'd ended their embrace.

"Because I love you, sweetheart."

Pippa's slightly intoxicated sounding giggles at his admission and Emily's dreamy-looking smile removed the disturbing overheard conversation from his mind.

"Hey, Cowboy, don't you want to hear my story?" Rook said as he squeezed past Gareth to take a seat next to his giggling fiancée. "Hey, sugar, I need a piece of that action too. Can't have Cowboy showing us up. Plant those sweet lips on mine."

Pippa climbed onto Rook's lap and, throwing her arms around his neck, she smothered Rook's mouth with hers. While Rook and Pippa were lip-locked, Gareth took the opportunity to sit down next to Emily and drag her onto his own lap, then he filled up both empty champagne glasses, balancing Emily on his legs with no effort at all.

When Rook and Pippa finally separated, both flushed in the face from their kiss, Gareth reminded Rook of his promise to expand on their earlier conversation. The smirk returned to Rook's face before he spoke.

"Well, it's like this, Cowboy. Cowgirl and I had devised a plan B, if you needed more encouragement towards the whole getting back together. Plan B involved me and the boys filling your belly with whisky and tying you to your bed. It's a shame you didn't play harder to get, my man, because I gotta say, the wicked look that Emily got at the idea of having you bound and at her mercy led me to believe she had thought up some truly torturous measures of getting you to see it her way."

Gareth's stomach quivered as he imagined himself tied up and at Emily's mercy. The thought also had his cock coming to life, encouraged along by the wiggling movements of Emily's bottom, positioned on his lap. Her sexy giggle just added to his growing discomfort.

Gareth was reminded of a time years ago when he and Emily had experimented with ropes. Both had found enjoyment in the experience, and it had been one of Gareth's most often-recalled memories in the years he and Emily had been apart.

They'd been sharing a picnic lunch. Seeing Emily sprawled out on the blanket, her arms above her head, had given Gareth the idea. He'd convinced Em to take off her clothes and let him tie her up. It hadn't taken much cajoling on his behalf—they had always been keen to try new experiences, and eager to take advantage of any situation where they were unlikely to be disturbed. After wrapping some of their clothing around the skin of her wrists and ankles to protect it, he had bound her using his lasso and the ropes from his saddle, so that her arms and legs were spread and secured between two bushland trees. It had given him complete, unhindered access to her body.

Taking his time, he'd closely examined and admired every inch of her. Using a branch from a eucalypt tree, he'd tickled her body, watching Emily squirm and struggle, unable to get free, held completely captive by the ropes and at his mercy. Gareth had been captivated by the sight of her pretty pussy spread before him like a banquet to rival no other. Using his thumbs, he'd gently opened her glistening folds so he could take his fill of her inner wet, pink beauty.

Emily had been shy at first, saying that she was embarrassed to be on display and so vulnerable, but it had not taken long before Gareth had had her begging him to bring her to orgasm. He hadn't at first, refusing to let her peak, enjoying both the playful torment of bringing her close to release and the power he had over her fulfilment.

Gareth remembered how wet Emily's pussy had become, her fragrant juices dripping from her slit, filling his mouth with her essence. He had lapped up the evidence of her arousal greedily, gently nipped at her clit, tapped at the sensitive nub with his tongue. He had let his lips travel along her prone and secured body, delivering kisses upon her heated skin, journeying up until he'd reached her breast. Sucking one hard and protruding nipple deep into his mouth, he'd finger-fucked her tight channel slowly, then with more vigour. He had thrust one finger, two fingers inside her, stretching her in readiness for his aching, rock-hard cock, exploring all of her pussy, her body, leaving nothing untouched or unloved by either his greedy mouth or his hands.

"I want to try the other way, Gareth."

He remembered those words exactly. Her voice had sounded hesitant, a hint of insecurity in the tone, but there had been a look of complete and utter trust on her face as she'd spoken them. Gareth had wanted to sink his cock into her rosy, puckered hole from the second he'd first set eyes on it. The thought of his dick rubbing in between her creamy buttocks as he thrust into the virgin hole had been a delight of which he could only dream. It had felt a little wrong, a bit kinky, to want such a thing. He and Emily had spoken of the idea and had agreed to try it, maybe one day in the future. So Gareth had certainly not been going to refuse her request. He'd quickly freed her from the makeshift restraints, then rubbed the skin on her wrists and ankles to make sure he had not caused her any harm. Then Gareth had repositioned Emily on her on her hands and knees in front of him. Her arse had stuck out before him like a tempting feast.

"Baby, are you sure you about this? I gotta tell ya, just seeing your sexy bottom in front of me like that has me half out of my mind with lust. I don't want to cause you any pain."

"I'm sure, Gareth. Please, touch me now."

Emily's reply had been music to Gareth's ears, but he had still worried that he would not be able to control himself. He'd needed to make sure Emily was ready for him. Gareth had remembered the lotion that Emily had always carried in her saddlebag to protect her skin from the harsh climate.

"Em, do you still carry that cream in your saddlebag?"

Just squeezing the generous dollops of moisturiser into the palms of his hands, to help lubricate the tight opening of her puckered hole, had caused fluid to leak from his eager cock. Taking his time, Gareth had stretched the tight ring of muscles in her anus.

Emily had groaned and panted in response, the noises she'd made confirming her thorough enjoyment. Gareth had also used the juices that had streamed from her weeping pussy to help lubricate his dick. He had taken his time, breaching her slowly, trying to be gentle. But her cries of desire had filled his ears. His cock had grown hard and thick at the erotic picture before him, and at the sound of his Emily pleading for him to fuck her.

Sweat beads had rolled down his back and off his brow, as he'd finally managed to seat himself fully inside her. All the while, he'd repeated phrases like, "Easy, Em..." and "Are you okay, baby?" both in his mind and out loud.

The pleasure he'd felt had been so extreme, so mind-blowing, that Gareth had known it would only take the slightest movement for him to explode, his seed filling her anal passage for the first time.

It had been a truly heady moment—the scent of their arousal mixed with their perspiration and the fragrant bushland surroundings had filled his nostrils. He had been almost out of his mind with the desire to thrust into that sinful tightness that squeezed at his cock like a satin glove. He'd leaned his torso forward over her back, his knees digging into the land beneath them, his groin hard against her soft cheeks as his cock had throbbed inside her, leaking his essence into her. He had felt the movement of her chest as she'd taken each heavy breath, felt the heat of passion emanating from their joined bodies. It had been a fantasy, heaven and a sensuous savagery all mixed into one. He'd felt so dominant with Emily on her knees under him, her head cushioned against her folded arms on the ground. So submissive. Her trust in him unwavering.

He'd used one arm to balance, pushing against the blanket to keep him upright while he'd wrapped the other arm around Emily's waist, his free hand placed against her pussy. He'd found her clit with his finger and had rubbed. He'd needed Emily to orgasm quickly—he hadn't been able to last very long and her satisfaction had been paramount. Because of what she had given him—this remarkable gift of her body—he'd had to be worthy, had to bring her the pleasure she was bringing him, or at least try. As he'd continued to strum her clit Emily had started to shake, her body pushing back onto his cock wildly, her pussy and back passage clenching around his hand and cock.

Emily had screamed her release and Gareth had come so hard he had wondered if it had damaged his cock forever, but he hadn't cared. The knowledge that he had taken Emily's virginity in every way possible had been worth any price to him. He'd loved her without reservation. Emily had been his everything. Still was.

They had played with ropes more than once, shared the pleasures of anal sex again, but nothing had rivalled that particular moment for Gareth. Being in the bush, surrounded by nature and taking her in an almost animalistic fashion for the first time had all added to the perfection.

"Um…Gare-e-eth, hello…? He's done this before, you know, Emily. Seems to be a recurring problem for him, drifting off into who knows where, but judging by the happy look on his face, I'd say he's thinking about something pretty good."

"Is that right, Pippa? Do you think it has something to do with my plans to tie him up and seduce him?"

Gareth had heard enough. Emily's amused comment had been last straw—his cock was so hard it was a wonder it hadn't torn through the zipper of his jeans. Without another word he stood, taking Emily from his lap and lifting her in his arms, ignoring her surprised gasp, and strode with her through the club towards the exit. He was taking Emily home and he was going to fuck her until she couldn't walk. Gareth ignored the knowing smile and "Giddy-up, Cowboy!" from Mick the barman, and the white-toothed grin from Jerome, who opened the door for him. All Gareth cared about was having Emily naked and in his arms where she belonged, and being buried balls-deep in her pussy.

Chapter Sixteen

As Gareth tore the clothes from Emily's body he had no memory of the car trip home. The only thing on his mind was getting her naked and prone on his bed so he could ram his aching cock into her, the recollections of the past making him nearly insane with lust.

"I need to be inside you, Em, need to feel your pussy wrapped around me. I want you so badly, need you so badly," he groaned as he spread her now naked legs apart and settled himself between them. The clothes they had discarded now left a trail from the front door to the foot of the bed.

"You're so wet for me, baby."

"Oh, Gareth, make love to me. I need you too."

The sound of Emily's voice, sensual and husky, was almost too much for Gareth. He was so close to shooting his wad that it took all of his determination to hold on. Emily had to orgasm first—there was no way he would leave the woman he loved unsatisfied, even if it killed him, and Gareth believed that it just might.

He buried his face in her mound, drew her scent deep into his flared nostrils, hunger and desperation so close to the surface. He licked the length of Emily's wet heat, savouring her taste, drinking it in, revelling in it. Emily was the only woman who could get under Gareth's skin, make him lose control. Everything about her made him crazy, like a starved sex addict. He palmed her fleshy cheeks and lifted her, trying to get closer to her, his mouth and nose firmly planted against her heat, his tongue stabbing at her clit.

"Yes, yes, don't stop... I'm so close..." Emily's cries were music to his ears. Her body was tense but unable to move from the onslaught of his greedy mouth. Gareth ate at her hungrily, wanting to taste every bit of moisture her cunt created, wanting her to come on his face. As her body shuddered he felt the walls of her pussy clench, felt her release as she screamed his name. But it was not enough. Gareth continued to stimulate her clit, replacing his tongue with his fingers as he crawled up over her thighs to suck on her protruding nipples. She grabbed at his hair, her nails scoring his scalp as she rode his fingers, striving to reach another climatic peak.

With a satisfied whimper, Emily let go of the death grip she'd had on Gareth's hair, hoping that she hadn't ripped any from his scalp during her need to anchor herself to him for fear she might just float away on the pleasure he had delivered her. Now it was her time, her chance to reward him and send him hurtling into space as he had just done for her. But first she needed to catch her breath, enjoy the high she was only just coming down from.

"On your back, Cowboy. Now it's my turn." Emily pushed at Gareth's muscled chest, indicating her intention. "Now, I forgot to bring my ropes, Cowboy, but I think I can make do...if I take this scarf..." Emily reached out to grab the discarded supporter's scarf she had been wearing earlier. Using two fingers to imitate a pistol, pointing them in Gareth's direction, Emily—using the huskiest voice she could manage—said, "Stick 'em up, Cowboy. Hands above your head."

At first Gareth didn't move. Emily was getting worried that maybe she had pushed too hard, acted too forward, but to her relief a wicked grin grew on Gareth's handsome face and ever so slowly, he stretched his arms up to the head of the bed, biceps bulging, muscles rippling as he grasped his hands together.

"Be gentle with me, Cowgirl. I'm just a poor ole country boy—I'm not used to you rough and tough outlaw types."

"Now, where's the fun in that?" Emily giggled. "I intend to use you ruthlessly to quench my sexual needs, country boy. I shall be heartless, show you no mercy."

"Is that right? No mercy, you say? My virtue will be ruined," Gareth drawled, his voice not the only part of him conveying his responsiveness to her threats.

Emily loved the fact that Gareth was playing along with her, and she was determined to blow his mind. She secured the scarf around his thick wrists and wound the ends through Gareth's metal headboard, fastening the best knot she could. There was no way that the restraint would hold Gareth if he really wanted to be free, but it was the symbolism of Emily being in control that had her juices flowing. Her man was spread out before her, under her, and he was at her mercy.

Emily took her fill of him, admiring the man she so adored, the man she'd so stupidly believed she could live without. His sexy as sin body, from his fingertips to his toes, was all man. She could have spent all day with her legs astride his wide hips, just looking at him, but Gareth had other ideas. He started to rock and buck beneath her, lifting her up and down. Emily squeezed her thigh muscles, gripping Gareth's hips more firmly. She felt as if she were trying to break in a rogue stallion.

"I don't think this is going to take long, baby. I'm on a hair-trigger as it is." The desperation in Gareth's deep voice caused Emily to smile wickedly.

At first, she ignored Gareth's plea. She caressed the length of his arms, palming the bulging muscles, feeling his strength in her hands, massaging and kneading his warm skin. She ran her hands over his broad shoulders, making sure to keep just out of reach of his eager mouth. She moved on, trailed her hands down his chest, felt his heart beating wildly. She played with his nipples, drawing imaginary circles round and round the hard buds, relishing the sound of every groan and curse Gareth uttered. She continued on her path, travelling down towards his firm stomach. She stroked every rib, drew a line over every ridge. Emily gently tugged at the line of dusky blond hair that ran from his belly button down towards his very erect penis. Finally, she responded to Gareth's supplication.

"That so, Cowboy? Well, I'll just have to take it slow, then…really slow," she teased as she stroked the length of his rock-hard shaft with a featherlight touch of her fingertip. "Mmmm…maybe just a quick taste of this little drop here…" she said, and lightly licked the pre-cum from the head of Gareth's cock. "Oooh…

Look, he's bobbing up to greet me." She laughed as Gareth's engorged cock jerked when she swirled the tip of her tongue over it and the salty taste of the fluid transferred to her taste buds.

"You're killing me, Em. Goddamn it, do something," Gareth growled, his chest rumbling against her ear as she bent over his lap.

She chuckled and took his cock in her mouth, her lips stretched around its girth. Emily tried to relax her throat so as not to gag on his length. She sucked him in and out, her total concentration on bringing Gareth the most pleasure—in and out, up and down in a lazy rhythm meant to prolong his ecstasy.

What Emily hadn't counted on was Gareth's lack of patience, or his strength as he tore himself first from the restraints, then from her mouth. He flipped her on her back, a wordless cry coming from her lips at the rough handling. Before she could blink or protest, Gareth was embedded in her, balls-deep.

"Okay, then, so I wasn't moving fast enough. You should have said something." She cheekily grinned as she looked into his darkened eyes. An intensity she had never seen before was showing, as was the crease in his forehead as he fought to regain control. "I think I need to use better ropes next time," she added casually, but the idea of Gareth out of control sent a shiver of excitement through her body, her toes curling at the idea.

No way was she letting him recover his composure—she loved the idea that she had made Gareth crazy with lust. Emily wrapped her legs around his hips, wriggled a little down the bed so she could reach his balls. She gently rolled them between her fingers and the effect she desired came to fruition. Gareth went frantic—he dragged her legs over his shoulders, leaving her totally at his mercy, and pumped into her hard and fast.

The sheen of perspiration on Gareth's face just highlighted his features, in Emily's opinion. The raw masculinity of her man—his six-pack rippling, his biceps bulging as he took her masterfully—drove her towards another crescendo. With the touch of Gareth's thumb to her over-sensitive clit, Emily exploded, seeing stars and bolts of light behind her eyelids as pleasure spiked throughout her body, every nerve ending joining, combining to create wave after wave of delicious pleasure. Gareth continued to slam into her until finally, with a growl, he erupted.

They lay together, breathing laboured, hearts beating furiously. Gareth sprawled over her, the weight of his body cocooning her.

"Emily Mackenzie, you are all I've ever wanted. Thank you for giving us another chance. Now that you're here with me, I'm never letting you go."

While Gareth's words were exactly what Emily wanted to hear, the reality was that she couldn't stay. She had to go back to Gunnedah, back to the farm. Someone had to be there to oversee the running of the family business and with her father out of action and probably for a good while to come, that job fell heavily on her shoulders. There had still been no word from her brother, Dylan. Emily didn't know if he had even heard the news about their father's accident yet, and even if he had, he still had a year to serve on active duty. For Emily there was no way around her responsibility. She was all there was until her father got back on his feet.

Her heart fell. How was she going to break the news to Gareth? He was assuming she would stay in Sydney. And what was more, how would she survive without him again, now that she knew how it could be?

She decided that, at least for the moment, she would keep the disturbing reality to herself, just enjoy the moment, enjoy her time with Gareth. Their being apart would not be forever. She hoped Gareth would feel the same way.

Chapter Seventeen

Having Emily at home when he returned from training was such a gift. Gareth was so used to returning to the near empty shell of his abode and being alone. Her fragrance floated in the air, her scent lingered on the bed sheets...even her toiletries and clothes had taken up residence, turning the once barren place he slept in into a real home. Leaving her warm body in his bed as he headed off to training each morning was only made bearable by the fact that Emily would be there when he returned, usually around lunchtime.

They would share a lunch that they'd prepared together, a lunch that usually led to some form of afternoon delight. He was never able to keep his hands off her for any length of time, especially when Emily had taken to wearing one of his shirts unbuttoned at the table, her creamy skin too tantalising for Gareth to resist. They would then head together to the hospital to visit Mac, spending the rest of the day and early evening by his bedside. Gareth thought Mac looked brighter every day, even after mornings spent doing rehab with the hospital physiotherapist.

Rook and Pippa had visited Mac more than once. Pippa had demanded to consult on Mac's rehab plan with the poor, overworked hospital employee, suggesting alternative strengthening exercises and generally making a well-meaning nuisance of herself. Gareth loved the concern she'd shown for Mac and Emily. Mac had even had visits from Brodie James and JT—the two coaches had taken pleasure in hearing embarrassing stories about his childhood, both men bellowing with laughter over Mac's tale about when he had forgotten to cinch his saddle properly, resulting in his very ungraceful landing in a fresh pile of manure.

The Jets had played another home game, and Gareth—this time aware of Emily in the stands with the other wives and families—had played a blinder, everything he'd attempted, every tackle, every pass, perfect in its execution. The usual after-game celebrations had been as enjoyable, if not more so, than the week before. Emily had been more relaxed and right in the middle of the festivities, once again a hit with the kids. They had coaxed her into regaling them with stories of her life on the farm, especially interested to hear about the animals in her care.

Elaina Thomson had clamoured for Emily's attention throughout the night, even with her mother, Mandy, telling her child to give Emily a bit of space. Gareth could not help but smile at the way Elaina looked at his Emily, so in awe of her, just as so many kids had looked at Elaina's own father, JT—the man was a rugby league legend.

Mac was recovering quickly, the hospital now talking of sending him back to Tamworth hospital or some rehabilitation centre a little closer to home. Gareth hoped that didn't happen too soon, because he knew Emily would worry with her father so far away.

The rugby league season was well underway, but still had a few months to go before the end of the regular season. Then there were the additional weeks of the final series, which the Jets looked in a good position to be a part of. So Gareth was stuck in Sydney for the near future. He tried not to think about that, to put it from his mind. He didn't really want to deal with any unsettling thoughts about his and Emily's future. In his mind, she belonged with him.

So it was a double blow, after having spent so much time with Emily, when everything came to a head at once. Gareth was already trying to come to terms with being separated from Emily for the three days the Jets would be away for the North Queensland game, the next in the round. Hearing that Mac was being moved back home and Emily was going with him—all scheduled to happen while he was in North Queensland—had felt like being on the end of a head-high hit.

The reality of the situation was that his parents could not be responsible for both properties forever, and Mac was nowhere near well enough to take back the reins of his farm, likely not even out of rehab for weeks. Deep down, Gareth understood that Emily had to go back, at least for the time being, but he didn't have to like it.

"Bloody Dylan should be here. This shouldn't fall on your shoulders alone, Em. Goddamn it, your brother could only manage one phone call to Mac in all this time," he shouted. His anger was misplaced, but more out of frustration and his own selfishness at not wanting to let Emily go.

"That's not fair, Gareth. If Dyl could be here, he would. How do you think it is for him, so far away and not a thing he can do about it? It's not going to be forever. Maybe I can come back to Sydney for a weekend or something, and when the season is finished you can come home. This isn't the end. I love you, Gareth. I don't want to go, but what choice do I have? Dad needs me. I can't just abandon him. You have to understand, but if you can't, there isn't anything I can do about it."

"That's just fucking great. It's just like three years ago—you putting everything before me, before us, and now I have to deal with not having you in my life again. Being alone again. It near killed me leaving you last time. Now, after having you back, I don't think I can do it again!" Gareth's anger exploded. With the force of an erupting volcano, it burst from him, unstoppable. He spun his shuddering body away from Emily and slammed his fist through the nearest wall. Plaster and dust flew into the air around him as a ragged hole appeared where his fist had connected. The pain in his flesh and bone was nothing in comparison to the pain in his heart, his mind. He wanted to howl at the sorrow that overwhelmed him—the memory of the last three years, the unrelenting loneliness and emptiness, consumed Gareth, so that rational thought disappeared.

As he gingerly pulled his hand from the punctured wall, Gareth began to feel remorse. He had never lost control of himself that way before, and in all honesty it had shocked him. The ferociousness of his fury had made him react so uncharacteristically and brutally. But what was by far worse—worse than destroying his wall and potentially damaging his hand, which would rule him out of the up-coming game—was the fear he saw in Emily's eyes. It all but brought him to his knees.

"Emily, I'm so sorry, I don't know what got into me. Please don't look at me like that. My God, Em, I'd never hurt you. Never raise a finger to you. You must know that?"

Tears filled Emily's eyes, and it broke Gareth's heart. He had caused this. He had been a selfish prick. Gareth had to make it up to her, and he had to get some ice for his hand—he could feel his fingers swelling. But he was too scared to move, didn't want to frighten Emily any more. He ached to go to her, hold her, ease her fears and her tears, but now the terrifying thought that he had gone too far—had pushed her away for good—was a distinct threat.

"Please, baby, say something. Please, Em," he begged. Time froze as Gareth waited for a reaction from Emily.

Chapter Eighteen

Even though she understood Gareth's frustrations, his anger at the situation that had been forced on her, Emily was still shocked by his reaction. She tried not to be hurt by his accusation that she was pushing him away again—nothing could have been farther from the truth. She was sick over the thought of being away from him again. She had faced so many of her fears to prove her love for Gareth—and she loved him, that fact was beyond doubt in her mind. She had always loved Gareth, no matter what her actions had been in the past. Emily now understood that her reasons for pushing him away were foolish and cowardly, but this time she had no choice. How could she not go home? Her father needed her.

Emily had never seen Gareth lose his temper, not like this. Yes, they had fought, back when she'd told him she didn't want him anymore, back when she'd been an idiot, but he had never reacted so violently. All his life, Gareth had approached any tension calmly, trying to reason out any differences. To Emily's knowledge, he had never thrown the first punch in any physical altercation, on or off the field. Seeing him slam his fist into the wall had shocked her, damn near frightened the life out of her—not that she for one moment thought Gareth would ever turn his anger against her physically. Emily knew that would never happen, but the sheer force of his anger had shaken her.

Her hesitation to go to him was due more to shock than anything else. Emily worried that Gareth had caused himself an injury—the hole in the wall was proof enough that he had used force in his punch. He was hurting in more ways than one, she could see that in his stance and hear it in his desperate-sounding apology, the sorrow clear in his eyes. Emily wanted to go to him, to soothe him, but still her feet would not move.

"Please, Em, I'm sorry..."

Her body finally caught up to her brain and Emily slowly moved towards Gareth. She lifted his still-clenched fist to her cheek, resting his knuckles against her skin gently. The swelling had already distorted the shape of his plaster dust-coated hand.

"Gareth..." was all she could mumble as the tears rolled freely down her cheeks. She was causing him so much pain. It killed her to know that it was all her fault.

"I don't know what came over me, baby. It's...it's just I'm going to miss you so much. My life over these last few weeks has been the happiest in years. Having you here, by my side...the thought of being alone again...I don't think I can do it again."

Emily felt the moisture of Gareth's tears as they slid down his face, dripped off his jaw onto her cheek, mixing with her own. Her heart was breaking, but this wasn't going to be a permanent problem, she had to convince him of that. She would be returning to him as soon as it was practical, then she would be staying forever.

"Shhh… Cowboy, it won't be like before, I promise. I'm coming back to you — if you still want me to," she added hesitantly. "We can call each other, Skype every night if you want…I do. I'll watch every Jets game on the TV — hey, I have for the last three years anyway. At least this time the sadness I feel will be due to our temporary separation, not the thought of never having you in my life again. We can do this. Please, Gareth, tell me you understand."

Emily lifted her face to his, tried to discern by his facial features what her future held — *their* future held. She prayed that he would not give up on her, but he looked so defeated, so sad. She had never seen him cry before. Even when she had sent him away, he had remained stoic. Angry and argumentative, but he had never displayed such distraught emotion as he did now.

The sadness surrounding them both was palpable, threatening to drown them. Gareth's comment about being alone was another barb through her heart, threatening to split the battered organ in two.

She had caused his suffering, his loneliness. Gareth could have been taking advantage of the women she knew had thrown themselves at him. He could have moved on with his life, but he hadn't. Would he finally give up on her now, the thought of being alone again too hard to live with? Would he turn to another woman? If he did, could she blame him?

The longer it took Gareth to answer her, the more certain she became that he would not wait for her return. Emily let go of Gareth. She needed to get some ice for his battered hand — the last thing she wanted was to be the reason he was too injured to play this weekend. Turning her back to him, to his silence, she headed for the kitchen, her thoughts on the icepack in the freezer and getting it on his swelling knuckles quickly. She pushed all other sorrows from her mind. She would deal with them later, on her own. She had survived being without Gareth once before, and hoped she could do it again.

"Em, please don't go..."

His whispered plea—so soft, so faint—had her spinning around fast. He had thought she was leaving, and she was, after she had seen to his injuries. Gareth didn't want her to go. *What does that mean, though?* she wondered, unable to stop the flicker of hope from sparking in her heart that maybe there was still a chance for them.

"I'm getting some ice for your hand, to stop the swelling."

"Oh, yeah. It hurts like a son of a bitch. Thanks."

Gareth's voice sounded hollow, masking any pain he felt. Emily could tell he was trying not to show his emotions any further—he was probably feeling disgusted with himself that she had seen him cry in the first place. "Stupid bloody alpha males," she muttered as she hurried to the freezer.

Ice-pack at the ready, she took Gareth by the arm, the feel of his muscled limb awakening the usual response in her, igniting heat in her core. One touch of his body had her melting—the heat of his skin in one hand and the cold of the ice in the other were such a contrast. How could they possibly not make it when this was the reaction that always took place when they came together? Just a brush of skin was enough to spark such passion. Her thoughts became more resolute—she had to make him believe in them.

She herded him to the couch and coaxed him to sit by her. She placed the ice pack against the back of his hand, her smaller hands now positioned below and above his larger one, comforting him.

Emily looked at Gareth's hand, so much larger than her own. She had always loved them, the feel of them on her skin. They were so masculine—his long, thick fingers; blunt-trimmed, squared fingernails; strong, hard-working hands that had delivered so much pleasure to her. It was unthinkable that they might never bring her pleasure again.

Neither spoke for what seemed an eternity. Just when Emily thought she could stand it no longer, and was ready to make one last plea for Gareth's understanding, he beat her to it.

"I do understand, Em. I'm acting like a selfish prick. Of course you need to go home with Mac—fuck, if it was Dad I'd be doing the same thing, footy or no footy. I'm sorry I lost it like that... God, don't know what came over me. It'll never happen again. I never want to have to see a repeat of that look of fear in your eyes."

"It's okay, Gareth. I know you would never hurt me. It wasn't fear of you. It was more shock...and the worry that you might have hurt yourself. I love you. That will never change, no matter what you decide."

"Just promise me you'll come back to me, Em. As long as I know you will...I'll wait for you forever."

Chapter Nineteen

Five months later...

Mac was finally up and around, albeit slowly and with the use of a cane. For Emily, it was a godsend. Finally she could take a step back from the day-to-day running of the farm.

It had been tough at first—the jackeroos had not been comfortable with taking orders from her, but with the help of Malcolm Andrews, Gareth's father, she had finally won over their support. It was tiring work, though, not helped by the contrary Australian weather—one minute the countryside was in the grip of a drought, the next the rain had arrived and was so heavy that half the farm was underwater. It was the always the way when you lived off the land—one disaster leading into another, just when you thought maybe things were getting under control.

Even though Emily loved every bit of being a country farmer, she had missed Gareth with an intensity that hovered close to addiction. If it had not been for their regular phone calls and nightly Skype sessions—when the internet connection had not dropped out due to her isolation or the weather—she wouldn't have made it, would have ended up huddled in a corner someplace, rocking to and fro under the pressure.

There had been some hot conversations between them over the months. Emily blushed just thinking about what they had managed to achieve in the sex department, in spite of their separation. More than once Gareth had sprawled naked on his bed, his cock in hand, in front of the computer screen. She in return had spread her legs wide and masturbated for him, while he pumped his cock up and down until they both came.

There had been raunchy phone calls as well. The sound of Gareth's deep, gravelly, sensual voice— describing in detail just what he would do to her when they were reunited—had brought her to climax even without much physical stimulation on her part.

There had also been the naughty packages delivered by an unsuspecting postman. The helpful postie had taken the time to deliver to her door, rather than just leave the mail in the roadside mail box. Emily felt guilty—if the postie had known what was in the packages, he might not have been so eager to go out of his way for her. She had been shocked enough when she'd opened them, thanking the gods that she had done so alone, as various-sized vibrators and dildos had fallen from the packaging. Gareth had taken to visiting adult sex shops, had said he'd enjoyed shopping for her with the thought that he could watch her using the sexy purchases on Skype...

Emily hated to think what would happen if Gareth was recognised during any of his outrageous shopping expeditions. The Sydney press would have a field day—she had spent half a day thinking up shock headlines, her favourite being '*Secret Perverted Life of Sydney Sport Superstar*'.

Everyone in Gunnedah had done their best to rally around her and Mac, the way country townsfolk did. Since Mac had arrived back home, there had been no shortage of hearty casseroles, scones and Emily's particular weakness—lamingtons. The small pieces of plain cake, dipped in melted chocolate and sugar then coated in desiccated coconut, were nearly as good as an orgasm. *Well, maybe not that good*, she mused, but she did love a 'lamo' all the same.

The Jets had enjoyed a successful season, and Emily had watched every game she could, usually alone in the house before Mac came home. She had sweated through each game as she always did, but this time knowing that eventually she and Gareth would be together. Gareth had called her from the after-game function at the club, and she had enjoyed chatting to little Elaina Thomson, who'd begged to be able to come and visit to help her with the chores. Apparently Gareth had, at length, explained all the work that she was responsible for—including shovelling manure. Emily had chuckled when, after pledging to help her with the chores, Elaina had clarified her statement by adding, "But I don't think I can clean up the horse poo. It would make me spew…eww."

As a result of the winning run, the Jets had made it to the Grand Final. Emily had really wanted to be there to cheer Gareth on, but of course, at the last minute a horse had pulled up lame, cows had broken through a fence and become lost in the bush and Mac had been released from the convalescent home. So Emily had watched the premiership-winning game from the Gunnedah Royal Hotel, surrounded by locals all cheering on the hometown boy and his Sydney-based team. Emily didn't once worry about the fire's legacy, the scars that had caused her so much misery in the past.

On the downside of Gareth's fantastic season—or the most exciting result of it, depending on which way you looked at it—Gareth had been selected to play for Australia in the Tri-Nations Cup, a series of games between representative sides from Australia, England and New Zealand. It was the pinnacle of any rugby league player's career to be chosen to represent his country. Emily was proud enough to burst at Gareth's achievement. But it meant another month apart while he trained for the games, then travelled to New Zealand, that year's host country, to play in them. It seemed to Emily that fate was playing a cruel hand in keeping her and Gareth apart.

The Australian team, after playing a number of games, had won the Tri-Nations Series. Emily had watched every game on the television in her living room, this time with her father cheering the Aussie team on beside her. Both had been glued, with senses of familial and national pride, to the international telecast. Ultimately, they had been overcome with emotion over the successful campaign and series win. Gareth had done his bit to ensure the Australian victory, and seeing him take his turn at lifting the winner's cup had had Emily both shouting with joy and bawling at the same time.

Communication had been more difficult with Gareth out of the country, and his sharing a room with a fellow teammate had stifled their usual playful phone conversations. Emily wasn't even sure when Gareth would be coming home, or even back into the country. It had been days since they had last spoken, but she was hoping, praying for it to be sooner rather than later.

* * * *

Life had to go on, though, and until Gareth returned to her there were always chores to keep her busy. Just this morning, Malcolm Andrews had called to report one of the fences down between their properties. Not wanting the cattle to wander and mix together, which would culminate in the time-consuming job of separating the two farms' stock, he had sent a jackeroo out to mend the fence line, and had been hoping she might ride over to check on his job and see if any of her cattle were missing.

"Just what I need today. The last place I want to be is out near the dam," she moaned to her horse, Sierra, as she saddled the brown mare in preparation to head out. The horse nuzzled her shoulder as if she was consoling Emily.

"I know, girl, I just need to be patient. Gareth should be home soon. It's just that seeing the dam—our dam—will only make me miss him even more."

The horse nickered, as if in sympathy, as Emily mounted up. Taking the reins, she turned Sienna towards the barn door, ready to head out to check on the Andrews' workman, only to find her father was standing in her path. She was glad to see he was walking without the aid of a cane or crutch. Mac had nearly returned to full health, but she didn't want him to push his body too far, too soon.

"Hey, Em. You heading to the north paddock to check those fences, then?"

"Yeah, Dad, might as well get it out of the way before it gets too hot. I should be back by lunch and

I'll fix us something to eat when I get back. Don't do too much while I'm gone, okay? And Dad…listen out for the phone. I'm expecting to hear from Gareth—he must be coming home soon."

"Sure thing, Em…but I shouldn't worry too much. I reckon he'll be home before you know it."

As Mac walked away, Emily noticed he seemed to be in a happier mood than usual—not that he was usually the kind of man to sulk or moan about anything. But if anything, there was a spring in his step today, which—considering her father had nearly lost his leg in the accident—made it all the more puzzling behaviour.

Well, at least one of us is feeling chipper, she thought as she let Sierra have her head. The horse responded quickly to the freedom, galloping at speed towards the Andrews farm and the annoying fence repairs.

The wind in her hair and the power of Sierra between her legs, as horse and rider flew across the countryside, lifted Emily's spirits. Sierra needed little encouragement to find the way to the Andrews property, having been there on so many occasions, so Emily just settled in to enjoy the ride and the picturesque surroundings. The different colours of the earth below her, the scent of the eucalyptus trees and native flora of the Australian bush in the air were a constant reminder of how much of a country girl she was.

Emily's irritation was quick to return to the surface, though, when she spied the fence line that was still in need of repairs. The Andrews' jackeroo was nowhere to be found, although the tools and materials needed to complete the job had been piled on the ground in readiness for the work that still needed to be done.

"What the hell? Malcolm won't be impressed his worker is skiving off when he should be working," Emily told Sierra as she stroked the mare's neck in reward for her ride. "What's the bet the lazy so-and-so has taken himself off for a swim at the dam, or maybe catching a snooze in the sunshine? What say we go take a look, give him a bit of a wake-up call?"

As Emily headed towards the dam, she noticed a tent had been pitched not far from the bank of her and Gareth's favourite swimming hole.

"Well, what do we have here?" she whispered to her horse. "The lazy roustabout has fixed himself a little home away from home for his morning kip! Well, I never — can't wait to report this development to Malcolm. No wonder he sent me along to check it out."

The nearer Emily got, the more annoyed she became. Not only had the jackeroo pitched a tent, but he had set himself up a table and a couple of chairs, strung a few lanterns among the gum trees and had a nice campfire burning. Emily started to feel a little apprehensive at the scene laid out before her. What if this was a squatter's camp and had nothing to do with the errant Andrews farm worker? Should she investigate on her own? What if the tent's resident — or residents — were not happy to find she had discovered their setup? She was out here, a woman on her own, and not the most imposing figure.

Halting Sierra's progress about fifty metres away, Emily lifted her body higher in the saddle, standing on the stirrups to try to get a better look at the campsite, and to make a decision whether to continue or return home for some backup. There was a man swimming in the dam — she could see the sun glinting off his blond hair and broad shoulders. She blinked twice, trying to focus more clearly, because for a moment Emily had thought it was Gareth in the water.

"Wow, I must be really losing it," she continued her one-sided conversation with her horse. "For a minute there, I thought it was…"

Emily didn't finish her sentence. Her thoughts were interrupted abruptly when the male in question, the blond male in the dam, stood.

Emily urged Sienna a few strides closer, her breath caught in her throat. Even though she could only see his back, there was no doubt in her mind. It was Gareth. He was home, swimming in their dam…and he hadn't told her, hadn't called to let her know he was back.

For an instant, pain lanced Emily's heart as thoughts filled her head that Gareth might have kept his arrival home a secret from her, because he had changed his mind about them being together. No, that couldn't be true, not after all they had been through. Life couldn't be that cruel to her…could it?

Emily sat back heavily onto the saddle. Sensing her agitation, Sierra shuffled her feet, flicking her head from side to side, neighing and snorting as if in response to her rider's anguish. The sound filled the silence around Emily.

Then Emily thought about the tent, the lanterns strung about, and it all started to make sense. She had been set up. There was no missing jackeroo – she was meant to find Gareth, had been sent in this direction on purpose.

Smiling to herself as a plan formed, Emily decided that two could play at this game. She had her own surprise in store for her lover.

Chapter Twenty

It had seemed like such a good idea at the time—he'd thought of it as a perfect way to reunite.

"Romantic!" his mother had crooned, when Gareth had told his parents of his plans to surprise Emily. Even Mac had seemed chuffed at the idea, quickly assuring Gareth that he would lend his support in any way he could and encourage Emily to check the fences out near the dam, as Malcolm would request of her, putting her right where she needed to be.

Gareth had spent the morning getting everything just right—pitching the tent, stringing the lanterns. He had decked the inside of the tent out to resemble what he believed a sultan's tent would look like.

He had transported over a double-bed mattress, a table and chair, and bedding his mother had pulled from what was apparently a stash she had been saving as wedding gifts. The burgundy satin sheets and matching velvet throws added to the romantic ambience he was trying to achieve. A few cushions thrown here and there, a basketful of rose petals—courtesy of his mother again—and a bottle of champagne chilling in an ice bucket next to two champagne flutes completed the picture.

He had set up the table and chairs, dressing the table with a lace cloth and some of his mother's finest crockery and silverware. Gareth had gone to extreme lengths to make this reunion one Emily would never forget. Well, the beef stew warming in the campfire billy might not be French cuisine quality, but Gareth believed the chocolate-covered ripe strawberries and the dozen or so lamingtons — Emily's favourite cake — in the ice box would make up for that. So would the one-carat diamond solitaire ring nestled in the jewellery box on her pillow, Gareth hoped.

Gareth could think of no better place to propose to Emily than this spot. After all, this was the place that Emily had stolen his heart and become more than just his best friend. This was where Emily had become the woman he wanted to spend the rest of his life with. And this was where he was about to make that become reality.

After one last look around to make certain everything was perfect, Gareth had decided to refresh in the cool water of the dam. He had worked up quite a sweat setting everything up, and the last thing he wanted was to be blasting Emily with body odour when he took her in his arms this first time after what seemed an eternity.

After washing his body thoroughly, Gareth floated on his back in the cool water and gazed up at the sunshine-filled skies. The tops of gum trees swayed in the breeze, and a few white, fluffy-looking clouds punctuated the blue sky. It was a perfect late spring day. Now all Gareth needed was for Emily to show up. It shouldn't be too much longer, if all his calculations were correct. Gareth had left out the materials for the fence repairs—for the fence he himself had cut—for Emily to find. Knowing how her mind worked, he believed she would come snooping around to see if the missing jackeroo was shirking his work and having a swim—hey, that was what he and Emily had done on more than a few occasions. It was time for him to get dressed and wait for her.

As Gareth stood up, he heard the faint sound of a horse nickering behind him. He turned towards the sound and sure enough, there was a horse nearby—a riderless horse. It looked very much like Sierra, Emily's horse. But where was Emily? Gareth looked towards the campsite he had set up, then he saw her. She was standing on the bank of the dam. More to the point, she was standing on the bank of the dam *nude*—well, apart from the shirt she had clasped in front of her, shielding the sight of her naked breasts and mound from his view.

While Gareth was disappointed not to be able to see her beautiful breasts unhindered—he imagined her berry-coloured nipples hard and protruding, just begging to be adored—he did savour the sight of her long, toned legs. Emily had the sexiest set of legs Gareth had ever seen—her small, feminine feet and delicate ankles led to shapely calves, and even her knees were adorably perfect. She was all woman. His Emily.

Gareth was lost for words. He had missed her almost beyond endurance, constantly in a battle with himself not to just chuck the whole football life in and return to be with her. If not for Rook and Pippa, and the ability to frequently speak to Emily and see her face, albeit on a computer screen, he would not have made it. But she was here now. He was here now.

Gareth's cock had risen to attention despite the cold water. It was very reminiscent of that very first time he had gazed upon Emily as a woman and not just his childhood buddy—him in the water, her standing nervously unclad on the bank of the dam. Just like the last time, Gareth watched, mesmerised as Emily's shirt floated to the ground in front of her, only this time there were no bra and panties. This time Emily was gloriously naked to his eyes.

"I have missed you so goddamn much, baby..." Gareth strode towards her, his long legs churning through the water, eating up the space between them. "This isn't quite how I planned our reunion, but in a way it's quite fitting. But I wanted it to be perfect for you."

"It *is* perfect. You're here—what more is there?"

Without notice, Emily launched herself at him and Gareth swept her into his arms, the heat of her skin engulfing him as it touched his own. Her lips were on his, her tongue danced with his. Hunger and desperation fuelled their actions—their hands roamed, rubbed and petted skin as Emily and Gareth each tried to cover and touch as much of the other as they could. It had been a long five months.

Gareth carried Emily towards the open flap of the tent. He needed to be inside her, truly believed he needed it more than he needed oxygen at that moment. He feared he would go insane if he did not quench his desire, his hunger for her right this minute. The woman—the feel of her, her skin, her taste, her touch, her scent—drove him wild. Gareth could not get enough of her taste in his mouth, could not touch enough of her all at once. His mind, his whole body, was surrounded by Emily.

"I need..." he groaned.

"Me too," she replied into his mouth, then she sucked his lip between hers. Gareth felt the sting of her teeth as she nipped at his lip—it just made him more frenzied. He fell to his back on the mattress, pulling Emily down with him before rolling them over so she was now trapped under him. Lust and need overpowered Gareth's initial plans to take Emily slowly, romantically. It was going to be hard and fast—he could not control his desire. He parted Emily's legs with his own, felt the head of his cock nudge her pussy lips and the heat emanating from her there as he slammed inside her. One hard thrust and he was buried in her cunt. Home.

"Ahh...you're so wet for me, baby... You feel so good. I'm not going to last," he lamented. He had wanted to take his time, reacquaint himself with her body slowly, but that would have to happen later. Right now, he needed to make her come, and quickly, before he erupted.

"I'm close...just don't stop." Her breathless pleas spurred him on. He drove in and out of hot, wet velvet depths, felt the sweat from his endeavours rolling down his back. *So close to heaven...so close.*

Her orgasm was hovering within reach. Even the hard edge of whatever was pushing painfully against her neck could not stop the pleasure from building. Emily sought purchase on Gareth's broad shoulders with desperate hands, and she wrapped her legs around his waist, digging her heels into his backside as she matched his thrusts one for one.

Gareth was inside her at last, after all these lonely months—rocking her world, bringing her close to the precipice of an orgasm Emily believed would send her skyrocketing into another world.

She could feel the ripples of his back and arm muscles as he drove into her, hear his grunts and groans as he climbed towards his own release, and the thought of that sent her flying. Pleasure swamped her as she hurtled over the abyss, stars forming before her eyes from the sensual gratification Gareth had wrought on her body.

Warmth surrounded Emily as she lay, spent, beneath Gareth's body, and she finally took in her surroundings. The inside of the tent had been turned into a scene from a Bedouin-inspired love story. Lush fabrics and pillows surrounded her. A champagne bottle and pair of champagne flutes had been placed beside the makeshift bed—a bed that Emily believed to be an actual inner-spring mattress, not just the inflatable type used for camping out. If not for the hard object still pressing against her neck, she might have never moved again.

"Something is poking me in the neck," Emily groaned, not wanting to spoil the moment but unable to ignore the uncomfortable problem anymore. "I think the mattress has sprung a spring."

"Aw, shit...I forgot about that. This isn't going the way I planned, Em..." Gareth's reply was confusing, and Emily waited for him to clarify. She thought everything was just perfect.

Gareth reached behind her head, moving his hand around as if searching for something. The pressure against her neck was removed, and Gareth rolled her onto her side, facing him. It never failed to amuse her that Gareth could just move her body at will, effortlessly proving how incredibly strong he was. She stared into his eyes, moved her hand to stroke his face, felt the bristle of his whiskers just breaking through his skin. So masculine, so powerful. Gareth was all man…her man. She could see his love for her reflected in his eyes, nothing hidden or masked as he held her in his sight.

"Emily Mackenzie, I have loved you all my life, will want you all my life. Would you do me the honour of becoming my wife?"

The tears erupted before she could stop them. Gareth was holding out an open jewellery box—the culprit of her discomfort—and inside was the biggest, brightest diamond Emily had ever seen. It was an engagement ring.

"I think we've wasted enough time, don't you, Em? Our parents are getting sick and tired of waiting for us to make it official, and Mum has been giving me not-so-subtle hints about wanting to be young enough to enjoy grandkids. What do you say, Em? Will you marry me?"

It only took Emily a fraction of a second to reply to Gareth's proposal, her voice choked with emotion.

"Yes. Absolutely, positively yes. I love you, Cowboy, and there is nothing on this earth that I want more than to be your wife."

Chapter Twenty-One

They toasted their engagement with champagne, ate heartily of the beef stew and fed each other strawberries. The cold fruit was eaten from the most unconventional serving platters, since Emily and Gareth each found new places on their bodies to place the fruit for the other's indulgence.

Emily clapped her hands in glee when Gareth made the lamingtons appear, and they feasted on the chocolaty goodness, licking the chocolate smudges from each other's fingers lovingly, sensually. The erotic symbolism and imagery of their actions led to even more erotic indulgences.

Gareth confessed to Emily her father's part in the elaborate surprise he had prepared for her, reassuring her that they were not expected to return home anytime soon. He'd assured both his parents and Mac that they'd not be back until Emily had agreed to marry him. Emily was amazed to find out just how romantic Gareth was under that tough cowboy-footballer façade, and how confident he had been that he would be able to persuade her to say yes. A confidence that was well-placed, considering she had not hesitated to accept his proposal.

They spent the rest of the day swimming and making love, both inside the confines of the tent and outdoors in the afternoon sunshine. They even braved the cool water of the dam. The water's chilly temperature made it difficult to fully enjoy the experience, with both Emily and Gareth exiting the swimming hole with their teeth chattering, but full of laughter over their tenacity to succeed.

When the day's light faded, Gareth lit the lanterns and they basked in the beauty of the picturesque countryside. Stars filled the sky above. Clearer and brighter without having to compete with the artificial lights of the city, they twinkled like diamonds sprinkled on a black, satiny canvas.

Arms and legs entwined, Gareth and Emily spent the night in their romantic dwelling, making up for time spent apart, now looking forward to beginning the life they had always planned. A life together...finally.

SARAH'S
SOLDIER

Dedication

For Sass and Kiki, my favourite digi-chicks. Thanks as usual to Amy for all your help and guidance. Also, my thanks to Reg the cat for pulling through.

Chapter One

"So how goes the twittering?"

Sarah couldn't hide the smile that formed as Brodie James again used the wrong terminology. No matter how many times she had tried to explain what she did as digital media coordinator to the Jets rugby league team, Brodie—the coach, and for all intents and purposes her boss—still had no idea what she was talking about.

"That would be 'tweeting', Brodie. It goes well. We've just reached twenty thousand followers on Twitter and our fan page membership is still rising steadily. You really need to open up your own Twitter account—that way you can see the impact social media is having on the game for yourself."

Sarah had had the same conversation with Brodie before, more than once, so she was a little startled when his response was more positive than ever before.

"Yeah, I know. Cate keeps saying the same thing. She loves the whole tweet phenomenon, always has her nose stuck in her phone reading or clucking away at those tweeties."

"Twitter and tweets, Brodie," Sarah corrected again.

"Yeah, but I don't like her idea of names for me. Cate reckons 'at dinosaur' or something. That's one of the reasons I called you in, Sarah. I was hoping you could give me a lesson on using this Twitter thing and maybe help me get a more flattering name. My modern wife needs to learn that her husband is no dinosaur."

Sarah pushed away the laugh that threatened as she imagined Brodie's beautiful wife teasing her sombre husband. Not that Sarah could imagine Caitlin James would be serious — it only took one look at the couple together to realise that they were deeply in love. Brodie's affection for his wife was about the only emotion easy to read on the usually taciturn man's face. Brodie was known for his calm, disciplined ways. He could be relied upon to keep a clear head and act accordingly — it was one of the reasons he had made such a successful transition from player to coach. The players respected him and treated his words almost like gospel, which explained the Jets' winning streak over the past few seasons, in many people's opinions.

Sarah decided that she would jump all over this request. While many of the younger players in the competition tweeted regularly, Sarah could only think of a couple of coaches who used Twitter. Having Brodie join the ranks would certainly boost the Jets' followers.

"It would be my pleasure, Brodie. Glad to see you're joining the modern age, no matter what Caitlin may think." Winking, Sarah pulled her chair around to sit beside him at his desk. "Right — first things first, a name that's more befitting of you."

Sarah's fingers flew across Brodie's computer keyboard. *@CoachBJames — yes, this is perfect*, she thought as she created Brodie James' Twitter account. *Simple and straight to the point, just like Brodie James.*

Sarah spent half an hour going over the basics with Brodie, suggesting a few people he might like to follow and reminding him that what he tweeted would be available to the public. She knew Brodie wasn't an idiot, but Sarah wanted to make sure he understood everything that needed to be learnt about Twitter. By the end of the lesson, Brodie had followed his wife, @*CaitlinJ10*, and some of the players from the Jets. Sarah had used the Jets' Twitter account to welcome Brodie to Twitter.

JetsRugbyLeague: Hey, Jets fans! I have special news. I would like to welcome our illustrious leader to Twitter — @CoachBJames. Follow now, everyone.

Sarah was pleased to see that within moments Brodie's account had reached over one hundred followers. She laughed at Brodie's shock over the immediate response and helped him create a few tweets about upcoming games and the latest developments at the club. She was pleasantly surprised to see that @*CoachBJames* was taking to Twitter like a duck to water.

"Think I've created a monster." She giggled as she watched him send a private message to his wife that was just a little suggestive, and fell into a fit of full-scale laughter as he waggled his eyebrows at her, the adorable smile on his face an expression she wasn't usually privy to.

"Enough of this, Sarah. There was another reason I called you in." Brodie pushed his keyboard away, his voice becoming more businesslike, more Brodie-ish.

"Have you been filled in on the Anzac weekend game against the Hawks?"

Sarah opened her iPad and brought up her calendar. She had the information Brodie was talking about stored away in her digital lifeline. The Jets and Hawks were dedicating their game to honour Anzacs past and present. The day was going to be filled with entertainment and ceremony befitting the event, with the culmination and highlight of the day being just before kick-off when, by Black Hawk helicopter, a soldier would deliver the game day trophy and ball to the opposing teams' captains.

Sarah had already offered her assistance, in any way needed, to the Jets' publicity team. She had pieced together a few videos of the players talking about what Anzac Day meant to them, and had also received a tape from a few serving soldiers, wearing their Jets supporters gear and wishing the Jets success on their upcoming match. So she was uncertain why Brodie had asked to see her specifically.

"Yep, I've been given all the relevant info. Why, is there something you need me to do?"

"Well, Sarah, as a matter of fact, there is. This is still somewhat confidential, although not for much longer, I'm guessing." Brodie's comment caused Sarah's interest to spike. "As of this morning, Steve Clark has been sacked by the Jets' board of directors. Steve has been leaking confidential information to the media. This has left us in quite a mess, considering the amount of work involved in pulling together the Anzac Day game. We were wondering if you could step up and take over his role for the short term, until we can find a replacement for Clark."

Sarah's breath hitched as the implications of Brodie's words began to sink in. She was horrified to think that

Steve Clark had been so disloyal to the Jets club, players and fans, but in all honesty found that she was not at all surprised. Sarah had always thought Steve Clark was a bit of a jerk. He had tried, on more than one occasion, to undermine her role, telling anyone within earshot what a waste of time it was to have a dedicated social media person at the Jets, and that he was capable of coordinating all media, publicity and promotions. His opinion that Twitter and Facebook were just a fleeting fancy had been proven more wrong every day by her success.

Could she do this, though? Sarah was not really a people person—well, not face to face. She was bold and courageous towards life from the keyboard of her computer, but in reality, out in the real world, Sarah was shy and reserved. Not that it showed in her appearance.

"What we need from you, Sarah, is to oversee the day, to keep an eye on the various corporate rooms, make sure the hosts are doing their jobs, co-ordinate the television and print reporters' needs. You will also be responsible for looking after our guest of honour—make him feel welcome and show Soldier Boy around the ground. Introduce him to a few of the team members. Maybe take him up to the sponsor boxes and corporate dining rooms. Look, I know this is a big ask, but I'm confident that you can help us pull this day together. It's a bit short notice, but what do you say, Sarah? Will you help us out with this?"

What is Brodie thinking?

Sarah had decided that the coach had lost his mind. Did he not see her? She was the exact opposite of what would make a soldier feel welcome. Yes—some condescending, staid and disciplined soldier would take one look at her watermelon-coloured hair, the metal piercings on her face and through her nose, and dismiss her immediately. But how could she let Brodie down? He had been so accommodating. Even if he didn't understand much about what she actually did, Sarah owed it to him to at least try. It was one day, a few hours — surely she could pull it off.

Sarah could handle the media and reporters. She knew most of them through Twitter anyway. Trevor Hughes would probably be the television presenter and she had met him on many occasions, Trevor being married to the Jets' captain's mother, Laura. The hosts for the corporate rooms had been doing their jobs all season, so probably wouldn't need much help.

"I will do the best I can, Brodie. I just hope I can live up to your expectations."

"Great — thank you, Sarah. You are doing me a great favour and I won't forget it. I owe you big time. Let me know if you need anything. Don't hesitate…"

The relief on Brodie's face was clear. Sarah knew the man had enough on his plate already. Expectations were high for him and his team of rugby league players to keep reproducing their winning form of late. She just hoped she wouldn't let him down. It had been a long, long time since anyone had shown faith in Sarah, relied on her. Fear of failure created pterodactyl-like creatures that flapped and swooped in her gut. She excused herself from Brodie's office and hurried back to her little cubicle in the main office area.

Already the talk amongst the office staff was full of Clark's termination. *News sure did travel fast*, she thought as she sank into her swivel chair, logged into her email account and found the reason for the chatter. Brodie sure hadn't wasted any time confirming her new duties, Sarah mused as she read the email he'd sent to all the Jets' staff and team. It outlined what he expected of everyone in their support of her, and briefly touched on Clark's employment termination as well.

"Think I need to make a running sheet of what I'll need to do on the day," Sarah mumbled to her computer screen. "It's all in the preparation," she added, quoting one of the coaching staff's favourite lines. She busily opened half a dozen different screens, then began to familiarise herself with the outlined plans for the day.

Chapter Two

Dylan could just make out the outline of the circular football ground on the horizon. The comforting sounds from the Black Hawk filled his ears as it drew nearer to their destination. He was nervous—this would be the first time he had been near his family in well over two years.

When he had been given the orders by his superior to represent the army at today's proceedings—and to see his family or not bother coming back—Dylan had wanted to run the other way. But he was a soldier with close to eight years in service, and he'd responded as he should. He had said, "Yes, sir," and saluted his all too knowing superior, then turned on his booted heel and marched away.

Safely back in his own temporary quarters...well, that had been a whole different affair. Dylan had literally shaken with fear, sweat pouring from his brow as he'd tried to imagine how he would face the family he had deserted and had not been there for when they had needed him most. The family he had refused to let the military inform when he'd been injured in the line of duty.

"Corporal Mackenzie, we are reaching the designated landing area. You all good back there? You're about to become a television star, Macca!"

Dylan wasn't ready at all, and the temptation to call a halt to the whole thing was on the tip of his tongue, not that the chopper pilot would have listened to him. No, his mate Tamba—or Robert Tambour, as his mother called him—would land no matter what Dylan said, and drag him from his seat if he had to. Tamba had been given orders too, and he was going to follow through on those orders no matter what Dylan wanted.

"Just put us down gently, Tamba. Don't go embarrassing us now—the spotlight is on you too..."

"That's not going to be a problem, Corporal. I'll sit her down so gentle you won't feel a thing. Smooth and sweet, just like sliding into a tight, wet—"

"Enough chatter, Tamba...I get it."

Dylan couldn't help grinning over Tamba's comparison. The man was a player, never with one woman longer than it took for his friends to remember her name. Dylan was a bit the same, truth be known, but more because he didn't want to get emotionally involved. Letting someone into your heart just meant pain, in Dylan's opinion. That was the reason he had distanced himself from his father and sister.

Now was not the time to think about that. Dylan pushed those thoughts away as he watched the football ground's grandstands surround him through the window of the Black Hawk. Tamba was true to his word and it was a perfect set-down. Dylan unbuckled his harness and removed his headset, put his hat on his head and grabbed the trophy and football. Then he stepped out of the chopper's open door, keeping his head low until he had passed the span of the rotor blades. Wouldn't be a good endorsement for the army if he lost his head in front of such a big crowd. He chuckled to himself, surprised at his own humour in spite of what he was about to face.

The sounds of the Black Hawk's rotors drowned out any other noise as the chopper took off behind him. Dylan strode towards the waiting captains of the rugby league teams, doing his best to keep hat, trophy and ball all in his possession as the strong wind from the chopper billowed around him. Then he heard the crowd. Cheers and applause filled his ears and Dylan caught sight of the huge scoreboard. His picture and profile filled the screen, including the fact that he had been injured in the line of duty and awarded a medal for 'gallantry in action under hazardous circumstances'.

The medal was still a source of contention for Dylan — he was no hero. He, Dylan Mackenzie, was in fact a coward, a coward who had run from his family the first chance he'd got. No, in Dylan's own opinion he was far from a hero.

He reached the small stage set on the grass of the football field and placed the trophy on the parapet. Then he handed the game ball to Rook Harris, the Jets' captain, whom he had met before — Rook Harris.

"G'day, Rook."

"Well, well, would ya look at what the Black Hawk dragged in! Gareth never mentioned it was you dropping by," Rook said as he shook Dylan's hand exuberantly. "Good to see ya, Soldier Boy... This ugly bloke here is the captain of today's losing team, Blake Reynolds. Blake, this is Gareth Andrews' brother-in-law, Dylan Mackenzie."

Dylan flinched as Rook mentioned Gareth. He certainly hadn't been acting like much of a brother-in-law, or brother, for that matter—hadn't even made it to his own sister's wedding. He shook hands with the Hawks' captain, then stood to attention as the ceremonies began. The 'Ode of Remembrance' was piped through the loudspeakers around the ground. Dylan was moved by the hush of the crowd in respect to the meaningful words. Both teams of players stood side by side, just behind him, as a young girl sang the Australian national anthem. Dylan could feel Gareth's glare boring a hole in his back.

Dylan deserved it—and more. What a way for his family to finally hear about his injury and medal. Emily was probably sitting in the stands in a state of confusion and hurt. Who knew what his father would make of all this secrecy on his part? It was going to be a shock for all of them when they finally got a chance to speak.

Dylan, lost in his own thoughts, felt someone placing their hand on his arm, but it was the electrical spark that raced up that limb that got his attention. He wasn't sure if he had just been electrocuted, the shock was so great, but it was the sight of the woman who had touched him that had Dylan lost for words.

"Corporal, sir, if you will follow me now… We need to clear the field and start the game. I can take you somewhere where you'll be able to watch the game in comfort, if you'll just follow me."

The woman was pulling him towards her and Dylan was rooted to the ground. The touch of her hand on his arm was making him reel, his head spin. The effect on him was unmistakeable. God, the woman was making him burn. What was more bewildering than his reaction to her touch, though, was her appearance.

This tiny wisp of a woman, wearing a spray jacket emblazoned with the Jets' logo, had bright red hair. The colour reminded Dylan of freshly cut watermelon. Her face was pierced in a number of places, metal glinting all over, distracting him from really seeing it, and just to top it all off she had some sort of ring through her nose. She was smiling, a little too brightly, in his opinion. The quality of the smile held a tinge of nervousness to it.

"Please, sir. You need to come now," she urged again, her voice becoming slightly agitated.

Dylan finally moved his size fourteens, and let the strangely fascinating woman drag him behind her. He noticed that she had quite a nice little figure as he perused her from behind. Her lush backside wiggled as she scurried towards the players' tunnel. She was talking to someone through the microphone attached to her headset. Her colourful curls bounced around her shoulders as she walked. Her hand still firmly attached to his forearm and she was clutching an iPad in her other hand, plus various pieces of paper that flapped in the breeze.

Red stopped so quickly in front of him that Dylan ploughed right into her back. He had to catch her around the waist to stop her from taking a nosedive onto the concrete floor of the tunnel they were now standing in. If he'd thought holding her hand had been disconcerting, it was nothing to the feeling he had now with his arm wrapped around her tiny waist. A vision of him pushing her up against the wall, dropping his pants and impaling her on his cock flooded his mind, the image and the fact that he'd thought it at all both equally shocking to him.

"Sorry, Red…" Dylan sputtered out, trying to regain his composure as he reluctantly let go of her. "You stopped so suddenly, I was looking at something else…" And he had been. Dylan hadn't lied—he'd just failed to mention that it was her swaying little behind that had garnered his attention.

"Oh! That's okay, sir… I just… Apparently I have another fire to extinguish today—my staff were just explaining the problem through my headset. Oh, and the name is Sarah."

Red—Sarah—was tapping her headset as if Dylan might not have noticed she was wearing one. She looked quite flustered now that Dylan concentrated on her features, trying to look past all the metal bits attached to her face. In fact, Dylan noticed that Red had the darkest chocolaty-brown eyes he had even seen—big almond-shaped eyes that blinked in front of him, long lashes fluttering back and forth. He hissed in a breath as he felt himself falling into the depths of those eyes.

What the hell was wrong with him? This wasn't a reaction Dylan had ever had before. He really needed to get his head back on straight. It must be because of all the stress he'd been under lately, what with facing his family and all. That must be what was making him act so out of character. Or maybe he just really needed to get laid. Why else would this woman, given the way she looked, have him reacting so?

"Nice to meet you, Sarah, I'm Dylan, or Macca to my friends. No need for any formalities, and definitely not 'sir'." Dylan stuck his hand out to her in an awkward attempt at a gesture of greeting.

He watched Sarah's face, could see she was distracted and wondered if she was listening to another voice through her headpiece. Finally, just as he had decided she was going to leave his hand just hanging in mid-air, she grabbed him, her smaller hand pumping his big mitt up and down. The movements were exaggerated and would have almost been comical to Dylan, if not for that sizzle that raced up his arm again from her simple touch.

"Nice to meet you too, Corp—Dylan. Can I take you up to our corporate area and offer you some refreshment while I sort out this latest problem? Then I'll be all yours... I mean, I can spend some more time with you... I mean, introduce you around and stuff."

The embarrassed groan at the end of her stuttering was adorable. Dylan was surprisingly pleased to think she might be flustered by his presence—as flustered as he was by hers. *I'm probably just projecting, though*, he hastened to correct his overenthusiastic imagination. The girl was obviously flat out running whatever it was she was responsible for, and that had nothing to do with him.

Which really was for the best. What on earth would his superiors think if Corporal Mackenzie was to start squiring the slightly feral-looking Sarah around town? She looked like one of those anti-military types. Probably hated everything he stood for. *There's no chance of any sort of dalliance between me and Red—nope, none at all*, he told himself.

He ignored that little voice that countered, *Who you trying to convince, Macca? This is the first woman who has ever set you on fire with just a touch. Yeah, just walk away... Who needs passion, lust and fire? Not you!*

Chapter Three

Sarah burst through the door to the ladies' toilets. She had been desperate to pee for the last hour, but just hadn't found the time. Her day had gone from bad to worse by the minute. So many things had gone wrong, she was starting to get paranoid and think it was all being co-ordinated to make her fail. Media double-booked into the same room, cables mysteriously going missing or being unplugged... If not for the other Jets' staff helping her put out one fire after another, Sarah would have imploded, exploded or just had a massive meltdown.

Then, to top it off, Mr Hero-Soldier-Man — a.k.a. Corporal Mackenzie, Dylan or Macca to his friends — had completely frazzled her circuits. Just one touch and her body had come alive, the sexual response mortifying to the extreme. Sarah was not one for the lust-at-first-sight theory, No, siree — she had never lusted after anyone. Did not know the meaning of the word.

"Keep telling yourself that, Sarah, but it won't help. He has cooked your circuit board big time, girly,"

Sarah told her flushed reflection, as she dabbed a wet hand towel over her enflamed cheeks.

She had been so distracted with her own problems that, until now, Sarah had not heard the soft weeping sounds coming from one of the stalls in the bathroom. Considering this was a private room, available only to the wives, girlfriends and the Jets' female staff, Sarah stopped to listen more carefully. Most of the females around the Jets team were lovely, and the thought that one of them might be in distress moved Sarah to action.

"Hello, is something wrong in there? It's Sarah Flynn. Is there anything I can do?" she asked through the closed door.

The sobs quietened, then the door slowly opened and a tearstained face peeked out.

It was Emily Andrews. She was married to the Jets' second rower, Gareth. Sarah really liked Emily—she was a lot of fun to be around. Sarah was enjoying the new friendship developing between them, both at the Jets and away from work. Her own passion for horses had brought them closer. Emily, being a country girl— even given the nickname of Cowgirl by the boys—also loved horses. They had gone riding together on many occasions. The thought of Emily upset broke Sarah's heart.

"Emily, what is it? What's wrong? Are you sick? Hurt? Did someone upset you?" She waited anxiously for Emily to answer, forgetting all about her responsibilities and Dylan for the moment.

"It's just... It was such a shock. Why didn't you at least let me know he was coming, Sarah? I still would have been upset finding out that way, but at least the whole thing wouldn't have been such a surprise."

Emily wiped the tears from her eyes as Sarah tried to make sense of what she had said. What on earth was Sarah supposed to have warned her about? She had no idea.

"Em, I'm not following you. I've been so busy today, I think I've missed something. I'm not sure what I'm supposed to have told you about. Gosh, I know some things have gone wrong for me, like making a fool of myself in front of Corporal Mackenzie, the Jets' special guest, but none that would affect you..." Sarah stopped when she saw the grimace on Emily's face at the mention of Dylan. *God, is he an ex-boyfriend or something? I've always heard Gareth and Emily were childhood sweethearts, so that can't be it*, she thought.

"He's my brother... The brother who didn't bother to come home to see his injured father. The brother who didn't bother to come home for his only sister's wedding. The brother who didn't bother to tell his family that he was injured. I'm starting to wonder if we would've even been informed if Dylan had been killed—apparently we don't figure much in his life." Emily burst into tears again.

Sarah was dumbstruck. She didn't know what to say to make Emily feel better, could not get her head around the idea that the same man she had just met might treat his family so poorly. Not that she had any idea what type of man Dylan Mackenzie was, but... He'd seemed so nice.

"I didn't know... Emily, truly, I had no idea he was your brother. I didn't even know his name until this morning. I would have told you if I'd known. Come with me—I'll take you to him now."

"No, I don't want to see him yet. I just can't face him." Emily sobbed. "Maybe after the game when Gareth is with me, but not yet. I'm going out to watch

Gareth. Don't you tell Dylan about this. Promise me, Sarah. He doesn't deserve to know how much he has upset me."

Sarah watched Emily walk away, still reeling over the news, but she had a job to do. She was going to have to tread carefully around Dylan, so as not to let on she knew anything about his problems with his family. Her day was becoming a nightmare. As for her feelings towards the soldier, Sarah was squashing them as of now. He hadn't been a good idea in the first place—they were such complete opposites, not to mention his ties with Emily and Gareth, and just because she might have felt drawn to Dylan, it certainly didn't mean he'd felt any interest for her.

"Goodness, Sarah, look at yourself. You are not likely to turn *any* heads, let alone someone like Dylan's. Get over yourself," she scolded her reflection in the bathroom mirror.

Sarah hurried off towards the room she had left Dylan in, hoping that the rest of the day would flow more smoothly. She hadn't even sent out any tweets yet—the Jets' followers would be disappointed in her lack of updates. As she raced along the corridors of the stadium she typed frantically on her iPad.

JetsRugbyLeague: Hope you're all enjoying today's game. Jets are set for a victory over the Hawks.#jetsgameday

JetsRugbyLeague: Don't forget to send pics & tweets to #jetsgameday. One lucky tweet will win free tickets to next match.

Chapter Four

Dylan was beginning to relax. The Jets had just scored and led the Hawks six-nil. He had a beer in his hand and a plate of food on his lap. Footy, beer and food—what more could a man want? *Maybe a certain redhead,* was the first thought that sprang to mind. He had wondered where she was more than once, much to his own disgust. Just as he was about to do battle with his subconscious again, the subject of his argument sat down next to him. And boom—the heat was back, his body alive at just her proximity. Dylan shook his head to try to dispel the feeling, and managed to spill his beer on her leg.

"I'm so sorry," he blurted out, too scared to move again in case he also lost control of the plate of food sitting precariously on his lap. He tried to put his drink down so he could hand Sarah a napkin to dry the spilt beer, but his coordination had completely deserted him.

Dylan was floundering around helplessly, not achieving anything, when Sarah lifted the dish from his lap. The brush of her hand on his crotch, featherlight as it was, almost not a touch at all, did him in. His cock reared to life in response. Luckily for Dylan, reaching for the napkins he had placed in his pocket also gave him the chance to reposition himself in a less painfully hard and embarrassingly obvious position.

"Here, take this. I'm so sorry... I seem to be all thumbs today," Dylan added as he handed the balled-up napkins to Sarah. She was so pretty underneath all that hardware. Dylan for the life of him couldn't understand why she would do that damage to her face.

Dylan also was having an incredibly hard time keeping himself from caressing her leg—the leg that was pressed firmly up against his. Realising that it was more to do with the seating space and the amount of room his body was taking up, rather than it being Sarah's choice, didn't stop him from enjoying the connection, though. She was so close he could hear the static coming through her headphones, and a barrage of words he couldn't quite pick up.

The groan Sarah released in response to that chatter nearly pushed Dylan's blood pressure through the roof. The little sound she'd made had him wondering what she would sound like in the throes of an orgasm—one at his hands, of course. Would she be wild like her look, fiery as her hair colour, as adventurous and uninhibited as her body piercings?

"Is everything okay, Sarah?"

"Nothing for you to worry about. Just sit back and enjoy the game. Is there anything you would like to see—maybe the players' area—or anyone you are interested in meeting?"

Sarah's voice sounded polite and businesslike, but Dylan felt that her tone had changed from their first encounter. She'd seemed friendlier, if a bit flustered before. Now, just cool professionalism shone through. He was stupidly disappointed by Sarah's demeanour, had confused his own attraction for her as reciprocal. He'd been fooling himself to think there was any chance between them, had been telling himself that very thing from the moment he'd seen her. Still, it was hard to ignore the way her presence sent his libido into overdrive.

"No, it's all good. I'm happy to just sit and watch the game," he finally managed to answer. "It's been a good match so far, not much in it. The Jets will have to keep it together to finish on top of the Hawks." Dylan's merciless mind immediately cut in with a vision of a naked Sarah on top of him. Managing to stem his errant imaginings, he continued, "If that's all right with you, Sarah. I don't want to cause you any trouble. You seem to be very busy. Is it always like this?"

"I have no idea. This is the first time I've ever had to run the show," Sarah replied, sounding exhausted. "The guy who used to oversee this sort of production was given the flick. I'm just filling in for today until the club can find a suitable replacement."

Dylan was surprised by Sarah's admission. From where he sat, the day seemed to be going fine—not that he knew what might be happening behind the scenes. But it seemed to him that Sarah felt she was not succeeding in filling the shoes of her absent predecessor.

"What do you normally do around here, then?" he added, trying to keep the conversation going so that Sarah would not disappear to fulfil another obligation. He kept his eyes on the game but could see her profile in his peripheral vision. Sarah was reading her iPad, typing every now and again.

"I'm just the digital media coordinator, usually. You know, Twitter and Facebook, fan pages and stuff." The little shrug of her shoulders sent a new flutter into Dylan's stomach. It sounded as if she didn't think her job that important, but if they had given her the job of running today, then somebody thought she was capable. He didn't know why he felt the need to bolster her opinion of herself—Dylan still couldn't figure out why the attraction to her at all—but he had to say something, that was for sure.

"Seems to me, Red, that if they put you in charge of today then someone thinks highly of you, and hey, you're doing a good job being my host."

Before Sarah had a chance to reply, their conversation was interrupted by a suit-clad grey-haired type who reached rudely past Sarah's face, shoving his hand at Dylan.

"Good to see you stick around for the game, Corporal. My name's Preston. I'm the chairman here at the Jets. I just wanted to say that we all think what you are doing over there, for those people, is admirable... Yes, admirable indeed."

Dylan didn't know what it was about this Preston guy—whether it was the way he'd rudely pushed past Sarah, or just his tone when he'd mentioned the men and women serving overseas—but something about the suit rubbed him up the wrong way. But he had to say something in response.

"Mr Preston, nice to meet you, sir. And thanks—I'll pass your message on to my superiors. But as you can see, I'm not doing much over there for anyone, 'cause I'm here watching the footy while others are putting themselves in the line of fire to help protect people in need."

Dylan shook hands with Preston, gave the man a quick salute, which of course he didn't need to do. The suit wasn't in uniform or his superior, but he figured the guy thought he was important, and if the grin that he got in return was anything to go by, Dylan had figured right. He turned back towards the game, hoping the salute would help to soften his sharp and dismissive response. The last thing Dylan needed was a reprimand for being rude.

Preston didn't stay long. Obviously taking the hint, he headed back into the enclosed section of the box. *Probably back to his drinks and canapés*, Dylan presumed, still feeling prickly and hot under the collar and not knowing why.

"Um, ya think you might have given the guy a break, soldier? He was just trying to be welcoming. Preston's okay... Bit of a stuffed shirt, but he loves the Jets, has the team and club's best interests at heart. Hey, he even talks to *me* every once in a while. Apparently the grandkids follow my tweets." Sarah was looking at him as though he had grown another head.

"I wasn't that bad, was I?" He really had to start thinking before he spoke. Lately Dylan had found that he was becoming more and more of a loose cannon when it came to behaving like a reasonable human being. Things that had never ruffled his feathers before had started to get to him—he spent so much time grinding his molars at people's comments that he figured he would need teeth implants soon.

"Well, I wouldn't say you were encouraging the chairman to make more small talk with the whole 'sitting watching footy while others serve' crap that spewed from your mouth. Sounded a bit bitter about having to be here. Sorry if it's such an imposition for you, but hey, lots of spectators came here today to show their thanks and support for the forces. Seems to me, you could be a bit more appreciative. Maybe even a hint of friendly wouldn't hurt. But hey, what would I know? I'm just the digi-chick."

Sarah's cheeks had burned as she had given him the dressing down. Even though Dylan understood what she was saying, and should have felt remorse for his actions, all he could think about was how hot she looked. He wondered if her face flamed like that in the heat of passion as well.

Dylan wanted to say something in his defence, but couldn't think of anything that would sufficiently explain all the guilt he had built up inside him. Not with the thoughts of the man that he hadn't been able to save still haunting his memory. Or those of the terrible injuries that the soldiers he had dragged to safety had sustained. Adding to the shame was the knowledge that he was home while most of his unit were still in Afghanistan, not to mention how he hadn't been there for his family when they had needed him the most.

He clenched his fists and clamped his back teeth together once again. Being reminded of these things and congratulated at the same time had just made him all the more humiliated. He should be back with his unit—there was no way someone like Sarah would understand his feelings of inadequacy. This role of public relations for the forces was not something Dylan had asked for or wanted.

He was startled when Sarah thrust a lanyard at him.

"Look, Corporal, I've got a few things to check up on before the game finishes. This pass will give you access to all areas. Why don't you head down to the changing rooms after the game and I'll catch up with you then? That is, if you're sticking around that long?" she added austerely.

Sarah stood, her gaze locked onto his. Dylan didn't want her to go, especially as she appeared to be annoyed and had gone back to calling him 'Corporal' again, but he knew she was busy. Babysitting him wasn't helping her get her job done. So he took the lanyard that she was still holding out to him and tried for a half-friendly response. "Sure, Red, that sounds fine with me. I got to catch up with a couple of people before I leave anyway. Maybe I'll see you later."

Regrettably, his voice didn't come out sounding as friendly as he had hoped—in fact, it had sounded dismissive, almost like he couldn't have cared less whether he and Sarah caught up again. The shame of it all was that seeing Red walk away was the last thing Dylan had wanted. He quickly looked at the time remaining in the game, pleased to find it would only be a few more minutes before the siren sounded and he'd have the opportunity to search out Sarah again. Unfortunately, this also meant there was not much time left until Dylan would have to face his sister and new brother-in-law.

Chapter Five

It was clear the man had issues. Sarah did not want to know, did not have time for Dylan Mackenzie or his prickly disposition... *Yeah, right, keep telling yourself that, Sarah, and maybe you'll start to believe it.* She had no idea what had caused the smart-arsed and frankly rude response to Mr Preston's welcome. It seemed good old Soldier Boy had a chip on his shoulder the size of Ayers Rock. Sarah had surmised that it had something to do with him being home and not off playing war games with his friends.

"Men!" she groaned as she raced towards the room that would hold the after-game press conference. Coaches and team captains usually made themselves available for a quick post mortem of the day's game — the room would be filled with television, newspaper and freelance journos and photographers. It would be Sarah's responsibility to regulate the 'pressa', making sure it remained polite, on topic and wrapped up in a reasonable time frame. She certainly did not have time to worry about a certain visitor or what made him tick.

Sarah had not imagined the amount of running around the day would involve. She had really chalked up some miles, and was glad she had worn comfortable shoes. The conference room, located in the bowels of the grandstand, was already half-full by the time she made it down from the top of the grandstand, where the corporate boxes were located. The number of reporters milling around was a good indication that the game was as good as over, and Sarah presumed the Jets had won, given that they'd been leading last time she'd looked.

"Hey, Sarah, hear you're running the show these days." A pretty blonde spoke as Sarah bustled her way through the crowd.

"Hey, Jen, good to see you here. Getting more assignments covering our great game, I see." Sarah was pleased to see so many female journalists now covering the footy matches, and she always made a point to say hello and make them feel welcome in the predominantly masculine world.

"Yes, and I love every minute of it," Jen replied enthusiastically. "Wow, it was quite the pre-match show today, and a little birdie tells me that you were running the gig. That Clark always made my skin crawl... Can't say I'm sorry to see him go."

"I know what you mean, but as for me, I was only helping out today. Coach James has someone in mind, but it was a bit short notice. Just quietly, I'll be happy to get back to my normal duties. I hardly had time to tweet at all today."

"So, what's the scoop on the hottie soldier? I've been hearing whispers that he's related to Gareth Andrews. Is that a fact I can quote?"

Sarah wasn't sure what to say. Was it a big secret? It wasn't as if he had hidden his name. The army had sent an extensive résumé on the hero—it just hadn't included his relationship to Gareth. But Sarah felt a bit too guilty, after seeing how upset Emily had been, to confirm anything.

"Perhaps you can ask him in person," Sarah replied, deciding that she would leave it up to Gareth, Emily or Dylan to make the call. "Corporal Mackenzie should be around. I gave him a pass to get into the changing rooms after the game," she added, hoping that would satisfy the reporter. "Anyway, have to scoot. I need to make sure Coach James and Rook are ready. See you."

* * * *

The press conference went smoothly. Brodie and Rook answered all the questions put to them politely and, in Rook's case, with plenty of humour. The captain and coach of the losing Hawks team also made brief appearances, but as was to be expected, were not as chatty. Sarah was glad when the whole show was over, but she had had time for a few tweets to update her followers.

JetsRugbyLeague: Jets pressa: @Rook_jetscap in good form, says t'day's game showed Jets have what it takes to win the comp feels like a kid again. #jetsgameday

JetsRugbyLeague: @CoachBJames congratulated Jets pup @JosephO on his debut game, said he showed sense of maturity, was destined for big things. #jetsgameday

Sarah had not had a chance to watch much of the game, and that was disappointing, considering one of her favourite Jets under twenty-ones had made his first-grade debut. She had been glad to hear that Brodie had thought Joseph Ondio had played well.

The under twenty-ones team had really gone out of their way to welcome Sarah. The younger players were probably more with it when it came to latest technology. They also had gone to incredible lengths to include her. Sarah remembered the time the boys had wanted her to judge which of them could spit the farthest. *Yuck...* The memory still caused her to dry heave.

The younger Jets players were forever asking her to feel their muscles and tell them who was the best looking, not to mention always trying to trick her into walking in on them while they were nude. To outsiders, it might have seemed like sexual harassment, but Sarah knew the boys were just playing around, that they intended no malice. They really were a lot like naughty, eager puppies, just wanting to make her feel part of the team and club. Not that the older Jets team members ever made it difficult for Sarah to do her job — it was more that they were reserved around her. Sarah figured it was probably her 'look' that scared most off. It was quite ironic that, even though she was shy and didn't particularly like being the centre of attention, her hair, dress sense and piercings tended to make her stand out.

Sarah liked her look, though. She got a piercing as a reward every time she achieved something big. She still remembered her first piercing, a stud through her tongue. She'd researched all the facts on tongue piercing, the possible problems — short-term and long.

She had listed the reasons why she'd wanted it done so badly—at the time, she'd wanted a little bit of rebellion that only she would know about. Finally, she had worked up the nerve to get it done. Sarah didn't even have that piercing anymore—she'd found the stud rubbed against her teeth. But she'd certainly had many more to make up for it.

Sometimes she thought about removing them. When an online friend, after reading some of her blogs about footy, had recommended her for the job with the Jets, Sarah had been sure that her unique appearance would probably work against her. The interview she'd had with Coach James and the club chairman had gone without a hitch. They had loved her ideas, had not even commented on her various piercings or wild hair—it just hadn't seemed an issue. Truth be told, Sarah was getting sick of them, felt like she was due a new look. She was, after all, pushing twenty-seven. It was time to grow up.

"Hey, Digi! Did you catch my game? I played awesome! Did ya see me take down that big Hawks prop? Smashed him!" Joseph Ondio had a smile a mile wide as he approached Sarah. All the Jets pups called her 'Digi'—it was their pet name for her. Guys had to have a nickname for everyone.

"Hey, Joseph. I caught bits of it. At the press conference Coach James was certainly singing your praises. Better watch out, I figure the reporters will be after a quote or two when you head out."

Joseph went pale before her eyes, making Sarah sorry she'd spoken. It was quite a feat for a Polynesian boy to look pale. "Don't look so worried, Joseph. They won't eat you. Just be sure not to swear... You'll do fine," she added, patting the large twenty-year-old on the arm, hoping to bolster his confidence.

"Maybe I'll slip out the back way." Joseph grinned. "Or you could come out with me, hold my hand, make sure I don't embarrass myself," he said as he wrapped his giant hand around Sarah's.

Chapter Six

Dylan was standing against the wall of the rowdy Jets changing room, listening to the sounds of the team song being murdered by the jubilant players. He was trying not to stand out, but seeing as he was in full dress uniform, and given that every man and his dog had walked up and shook his hand, it wasn't really working. He'd already spotted Gareth Andrews, his sister's new husband, his old neighbour from back home in Gunnedah, but they hadn't made contact. Dylan was still trying to work up the nerve to speak to him, convinced that the reception he would get from Gareth would not be a welcome one, when he spotted Sarah entering the room. She had only taken a few steps when one of the Jets players started up a conversation with her.

Dylan couldn't hear what was being said, but judging by the smile on the very large man's face, he was happy to see her. The guy took Sarah's hand into his, and Dylan felt his stomach fall to his feet. He had spent the better part of the last two hours fantasising about the little redhead, and had never once considered the idea that she was taken. What an idiot he'd been. Of course Sarah would be in a relationship—why wouldn't she be, as attractive as she was? And surrounded by men for most of her working week, it wasn't as though she wouldn't have had the opportunity to meet someone. Dylan was so focused on Sarah and her beau that he didn't notice Gareth walking up until he spoke.

"Dylan, it's good to see you, man. We were starting to think you had given us the flick. You never write, you never phone…" Gareth's words might have been friendly, but his tone was something else.

"Gareth, congratulations on the win." Dylan thought maybe a change of topic would lighten up the situation, but it didn't work.

"Seems to me, Dyl, that you owe Mac and Em an explanation. Why didn't you let us know you'd been hurt? I hate to think how Em's felt all day, after hearing the news so publicly. I gotta say, man, I don't want to think about my wife being unhappy, so you better come up with a real good excuse, and soon, 'cause *we* are just about to go and meet up with her."

Gareth looked very serious, and on one hand Dylan was relieved to know that his sister was being well cared for. On the other, if Emily didn't respond well to Dylan being back after his prolonged silence, he could be in deep trouble.

"Let's go find my sister so we can talk. I had my reasons, man. You guys had your hands full, what with Dad and Em still overcoming the fire. I just didn't want to add to their trouble," Dylan added softly, trying not to draw any undue attention their way.

"I'm not the one you need to be making excuses to, Dyl. Save it for Emily. C'mon, let's go." Gareth turned his back on Dylan and after shouting out a few goodbyes, headed towards the door. Dylan fell into step behind him, feeling a bit like he was being led to the slaughterhouse. He had been rehearsing what he would say to his family for days now, but of course, for the life of him he could not think of a single word that would make it okay.

It hadn't been till after his own injury that Dylan had heard about his father's accident. By then, his father had undergone surgery and the prognosis had been that Mac would recover, eventually, but would need some serious rehabilitation. The same had been said to Dylan about his own wounds. Knowing what a strain the farm and taking care of Mac would cause Emily, who was still trying to deal with the nasty scars that had disfigured her pretty face, Dylan had decided to keep silent.

Then, because he had not been there for his family when they had needed him, Dylan had shut himself off from them completely. Not going to his sister's wedding had been a huge mistake, but at the time Dylan had still been finding it hard to deal with his own life. He'd been sent back to active duty once his injuries had healed, only to be pulled back out of the front line after some quack had questioned his mental stability. The doctors called it PTSD—post-traumatic stress disorder. Dylan thought it was a lot of bullshit letters. So he had a few bad dreams—who wouldn't after nearly being blown to bits? But talking about it wouldn't make it go away. He just had to deal with it, and get back to the guys in his unit.

Dylan rubbed at the scar on his shoulder, the worst of his injuries the exploding IED had inflicted.

Emily was standing waiting outside the door, just as Gareth had predicted. She was surrounded by a group of women. Dylan figured they were the partners of the rest of the team.

Gareth took Emily into his embrace. The kiss he gave Em was so personal and intense that Dylan was a little uncomfortable to be watching—after all, she was still his sister, even if he hadn't been acting much like a big brother lately. Finally, the couple looked over to him.

"So, the prodigal brother returns!"

Well, at least she's speaking to me, Dylan thought before answering.

"Hi, Em, it's been a while. You're looking well." *Nice one, Dylan. That certainly was deep,* he berated himself mentally as he tried to think of what to say next. What *could* he say to the people he'd let down so badly? "I'm sorry about everything, but I can explain." *Yep, that's it, Dylan, start off with an excuse.* "Do you think we can go somewhere a bit more private to talk?" he finally managed.

"Sorry, soldier, not for a little while. Gareth is expected to show up at the Jets club, and I go where my husband goes. Feel free to tag along, and maybe we can talk later."

With that said, Emily turned her back on Dylan and returned to chatting with the other women. Gareth just shrugged.

Dylan was going to the club with his sister and brother-in-law, it would seem—that was, if he wanted to get a chance to talk to her. Well, it wasn't as if he had anything better to do tonight. And he remembered his superior's ultimatum of making peace with his family or not coming back.

"So you stayed, then?"

Sarah's voice came from behind Dylan, and when he turned to her he spotted her earlier companion hand in hand with some other girl. Well, that was interesting. *I obviously jumped to the wrong conclusion there*, he thought as his gaze locked with hers.

"Seems I did, Red. Even got myself an invite back to the Jets clubhouse with Gareth, thought I might check it out." Dylan didn't bother mentioning his relationship to Emily and Gareth—he figured that his sister might not want to own to him yet. "Will you be there? At the club, I mean," he added for clarity, unsure why he felt a so out of sorts talking to the little redhead. His attraction to her was still burning bright and Dylan still could not work out why. What was it about Sarah that sparked such an intense reaction in him?

"Course I am. It's part of my job to interview the guys and get some snaps for the fan pages and website." Sarah's snippy reply as she hurried by did nothing to quash Dylan's interest. In fact, he thought maybe it made him all the more keen. She certainly wasn't throwing herself at him because of the uniform, and that was a nice change. Now all Dylan had to do was figure out a way to make her want to stop and speak to him some more. He really was scoring low in the friendly female stakes. He watched as Sarah was swallowed up by a wall of young Jets players, all appearing to be in some sort of quest to win her attention.

"Do you have transport or do you need a lift?"

Gareth's question distracted Dylan from any further observations of Sarah and her entourage.

"A lift would be appreciated, Gareth, if that's all right with you, Emily?" Dylan thought he should at least give his sister the opportunity to decide if she was ready to spend time with him. She was still a little prickly and had not paid him any attention, or introduced him to any of the women she stood amongst.

"Of course we will give you a lift. You're still my brother…and anyway, how would it look to the Jets' board and the army if we just left you standing here, abandoned? We don't abandon our friends and family!"

Well, he certainly had just been told. Dylan stifled the grin that threatened. His little sis had definitely become a formidable woman in his absence, full of confidence and attitude, and it was great to see. He knew that the fire that had hurt Emily had damaged more than just her body—it had crushed her spirit for a while. That had obviously passed, judging by the put-down she had just delivered to him publicly. Dylan thought that Gareth had probably played a big hand in getting Emily whole again, and he would be forever grateful to the man for that. Dylan certainly hadn't done anything to help, hiding away, using the army as a convenient excuse.

"Well, little sister, I graciously accept your offer. Yes, the army would look dimly at their representative being dumped beside the road. Best to keep me with you."

"C'mon, you two, play nice." Gareth laughed as he put one arm around his wife's waist and the other around Dylan's shoulders. "Let's go celebrate and maybe peace shall reign… Isn't that what the army wants? Peace on earth?"

Dylan shrugged off Gareth's arm but followed close on the heels of his family. Maybe his superior was right—maybe this was just what he needed. He really did love his sister, and the thought of spending some time with her was starting to become more and more attractive. No longer a young girl who would annoy him by getting underfoot, Emily was her own person, a person who had stood by their father when he was injured—unlike him. A person who had managed to move past the death of their mother and find some happiness in life. Dylan only wished he could be that strong.

Chapter Seven

JetsRugbyLeague: The club is pumping tonight after our victory! Remember to tweet your messages of support so I can pass them on. #jetsfanmessages

The club really was filled to capacity with fans eager to show their appreciation to the players for another great win. It never failed to surprise Sarah how seriously some fans took their support for the Jets. Luckily, most of the tweets and posts these days were positive, but it only took one loss for all the creeps to float to the surface. Some of the comments in the past after a loss had reduced Sarah to tears. Obsessed fans could be as cruel as they were kind, never hesitant to place blame on a particular player, acting as if that player had made a mistake on purpose.

'Fickle' was what Brodie had called it one day, when he'd stumbled upon her trying to regain her composure after reading a particularly hateful and racist remark from a so-called Jets fan.

"It comes with the territory, Sarah," Brodie had said as he'd handed her a clean handkerchief. Just the knowledge that Brodie was the sort of guy who carried a clean *hanky* to rescue damsels in distress had cheered Sarah immensely. "Supporters are fickle—for some fans, whether we win or lose will affect their whole week, sad as that seems. We do charge admission, so when we don't perform we have to take the knocks. After all, we are showered with support when we win. Don't take it personally."

It was nights like tonight that brightened Sarah's heart. She felt proud to be associated with all the talented men at the Jets, especially the younger players, her babies—even though she was only a handful of years older than them.

Sarah had also noticed Dylan enter with Gareth and Emily. In fact, Sarah was well aware of every move Dylan made, much to her disgust. The more she'd tried to not look for him, the more she'd seemed to find her eyes drawn back to the tall, good-looking soldier. Still in full uniform, he did stand out, after all, but it was more than that. It was also extremely annoying to Sarah that Dylan was attracting plenty of attention from the Jets' female fan contingent.

"He is supposed to be reconnecting with his sister," she'd grumbled to herself on more than one occasion.

To her dismay, Mandy Thomson—wife of JT, the assistant coach—didn't hesitate to call her out on it. "Anyone would think that you were a bit smitten with our special guest," Mandy teased Sarah good-naturedly.

"None of my business what Corporal Mackenzie chooses to do in his own time!" she replied a little too quickly, not even convincing herself, let alone her smirking friend.

"You keep telling yourself that, Sarah, but I know that look you have on your face. I've seen it many times—on Caitlin, Pippa, Emily, and in my own mirror. You're interested...and there is nothing wrong with that. But what I'd like to know is what you intend to do about it."

Sarah was shocked to think that her attraction for Dylan was so noticeable, but she had to remain realistic, and told Mandy as much.

"I can't see that someone like Dylan would be attracted to the likes of me... I've got a feeling that Mr Soldier Boy would prefer a more traditional type of woman—you know, blonde, big-boobed, someone more befitting his profession. Not a feral like me."

"Oh, Sarah! What a load of garbage, and a bit judgemental of yourself, too. You're a very attractive woman, one who is brave enough to be an individual. Not to mention that the man in question has hardly taken his eyes off you all night. Hey, I notice these things, honey! Take some advice from an old married woman—don't let superficial appearances stop you from acting on your feelings. Look at JT and me! We're as different as night and day, but our love is fierce. You could be missing out on the chance to find that special someone... And if it's not meant to last, hey, I reckon the man can at least hold his own in the bedroom department. He's rockin' a pretty hot bod." Mandy winked.

"I hope you're discussing *my* body, wife?" JT's deep voice came from behind Sarah. "Otherwise I will have to have a serious conversation with some poor bloke." JT's voice held enough amusement for Sarah to realise that he was teasing. "Is my wife doing a bit of matchmaking again? Let me guess... You and Dylan Mackenzie, right?"

"Oh, husband, you know me too well." Mandy laughed as she snuggled up to her enormous man. It made Sarah smile to watch as JT—whom many players, old and new, feared beyond measure—become a giant teddy bear under his wife's spell.

"Sarah, you had better beware. Mandy certainly has a high success rate in the matchmaking department, or at least with knowing who is attracted to whom. Mandy was right about Laura and Trev, Pippa and Rook, and she also was right on the money when she told me Gareth was pining for a girl back home. Look at those two—you couldn't find a better match..." JT pointed in Gareth and Emily's direction. He kissed Mandy on the forehead before continuing, "Well, not counting me and Mandy, of course. But a man would have to be blind to not notice the looks our soldier visitor has been sending your way. Take it from a man—this bloke is interested in you, honey."

JT's observation nearly caused Sarah to choke on her drink. Could it be true? Did Dylan Mackenzie, smoking hot in his dress uniform, find her attractive? It was ludicrous to even go down that path of thought.

"Don't be silly! What on earth would someone like him see in someone like me?"

"Here we go again..." Mandy sighed as she pulled Sarah in for a friendly hug, nearly causing Sarah to crash into JT as well. "Tell her, JT. Sarah is sexy, and smart to boot. Of course men are attracted to her! Tell her I'm right."

The uncomfortable look on JT's face was adorable, Sarah thought. The poor man had been put well and truly on the spot by his wife. Sarah would have loved to know JT's answer, if he could have been honest without the pressure of his wife expecting him to agree with her. Before JT had time to answer, though, he was saved by just the person they had been talking about. Sarah heard Dylan's sexy voice as he joined the conversation.

Chapter Eight

"I didn't mean to eavesdrop, but I did happen to hear what your lovely wife just said, JT, and I would like to put in my two cents, for what it's worth." Dylan shook hands with JT, then took a position beside the man and turned his attention to Sarah, noticing that her cheeks had flamed red. "Well, as I've only met Sarah today, I can only go on my first impressions, and they would have to be just as your wife already said. 'Sexy' is certainly a good way to describe Sarah, and I had the opportunity to see her in action, pulling all of today's events together while babysitting me. She must be capable and intelligent as well."

He hadn't meant to be so forward, but Dylan couldn't seem to help himself. Sarah was looking a bit uncomfortable under all the scrutiny and it just made her all the more attractive to him. He just wanted to scoop her up and take her somewhere private so he could get to know her better. That thought alone should have had Dylan fleeing in terror—he could have coped with the idea of ravishing her body, taking her over and over in varying positions, sharing some wild, uninhibited sex...but what was he thinking, wanting to get to know her?

He was so caught up in his own thoughts that he nearly missed JT's reply. "Is that right, Dylan? So you agree our Sarah is sexy and smart... Dylan, this is my wife, Mandy."

Dylan made the necessary response to his introduction and shook Mandy Thomson's hand, noticing the happy, knowing grin on the curvy, dark-haired woman's face. *Uh-oh*, he thought.

Feeling as much under the spotlight as Sarah had just been, Dylan tried to think of a way to escape. He didn't have to think for too long, though, as Mandy grabbed her husband's hand and made some excuse about having to catch up with Caitlin and Brodie. In a blink the couple were gone, leaving Dylan standing alone — well, as alone as you could be in a packed club auditorium — with Sarah Flynn.

"Wow, was it something I said?" Dylan grinned as he turned his full attention back to the woman who had his stomach wrapped up in knots. "Guess it's just you and me then, and the couple hundred other people milling around."

It felt to Dylan like an age until Sarah answered, but finally she rewarded him with a look that had his cock waking with renewed vigour. "Yes, handsome, we seem to have been left to our own devices."

It wasn't the words she'd said as much as the expression in Sarah's eyes and the way she'd spoken the words that had Dylan responding so immediately. There seemed to be fire burning under Sarah's skin — power and energy sparked, just waiting to be released, and Dylan found himself wondering what it would be like if all that force let loose while he was buried balls-deep in her wet pussy. He struggled to find a coherent way to reply.

"So, sexy, what sort of devices are we talking here? I'm burning up just thinking about the two of us together...and considering we are standing in a room full of men who would probably beat me senseless if they could read my thoughts, it is quite a problem."

Dylan had made the split-second decision to go for what he wanted, and he wanted Sarah—that was an understatement. His life was so filled with planning and waiting and deciding on the most effective outcome that he had forgotten what it was like to act spontaneously. He was not going to miss out on a possible night with this sexy, unique woman by letting the moment slip by. No—Dylan was going to go for broke, even if it was incredibly forward and fast.

"I'd really like to get the chance to spend some time with you tonight, Sarah. Is that a possibility?"

"Technically speaking, I'm still on the clock," Sarah replied. Her smile lit up the room as far as Dylan was concerned, even more so when she took a step closer to him so their bodies were aligned, with just a breath of air between them. "The night here is all but over, then we usually head over to Rook's nightclub, Jetstream. I'd be happy to give you a lift. Maybe we could have a dance or something..."

"Well, that's the best news I've heard all night. I'd be happy to accept that lift, the dance and definitely the 'something'!" He knew he was being blunt, but Dylan was sure he was reading Sarah right. She was interested in him, and he was going to find out just how interested. All he had to do was smooth things over with his sister and Gareth, and the night would be perfect. "Just let me fill Emily and Gareth in on the plans, and when you're ready we can head off."

"Are you sure you wouldn't rather get a lift with them? I didn't think—you probably wanted to spend some time with your family. We can still meet up…"

Sarah sounded a bit hesitant all of a sudden. Clearly she knew of the connection between him and Emily, so Dylan wasted no time reassuring her that a lift from Sarah was what he wanted. The smile she favoured him with, a sexy seduction in itself, sent his already awoken libido into overdrive.

"You keep smiling at me like that, Red, and I may get beat up by the blokes in the room after all!" he replied. He took her hand and led her over to where his sister was sitting, surrounded by children.

It was a nice picture for Dylan, seeing Emily deep in conversation with the kids. He hadn't thought about her as a mother before, but seeing her so comfortable, with the children looking so full of awe over whatever she was saying, had him imagining her with children of her own. Where had the time gone? Here he was, considering the possibility of his kid sister as a mother—that same kid sister who used to annoy the crap out of him. She was all grown up and married, living her life in the big city and dealing with her husband's fame.

"The kids love her—Emily, your sister. She tells them about life on the farm, about all the farm animals and the bush animals. The children hang off every word she says. Just about every child she speaks to wants a horse of their own, or to go horse-riding with her. Emily and I are riding buddies, you know."

Dylan had not realised he had stopped moving until Sarah spoke. She was watching him, had clearly read his reaction to seeing his sister and the children around her. Sarah was obviously quite perceptive—he would have to be careful, make sure he hid his own self-doubt and regrets when she was around. The last thing he needed, or wanted, was some touchy-feely advice from her, or to have her running back to Emily with stories about him. No—what he wanted, Dylan reminded himself quickly, was some good, old-fashioned fun. Sweaty, blood-pumping sex was what he needed.

"So you ride horses, then?" he said, trying to turn the conversation away from his sister. Dylan really didn't want Sarah in the middle of his problems with Emily. He needed to sort them out with his sister first, anyway. He moved to within earshot of Gareth and spoke, without waiting for a reply from Sarah. "Hey, Gareth, Sarah has offered to give me a lift to this nightclub you guys all go to. Are you and Em going?"

"Yep. If I can ever get Em away from the kids, that is." Gareth was smiling so broadly that it was clear he enjoyed watching Emily with the children.

"Sarah was just telling me how much the kids love her."

"Hi, Sarah, how's it going? See you met Em's big brother." Gareth leaned in conspiratorially towards Sarah. "I've known Dyl all my life, Sarah. Anything you want to know, just ask me. I'll be happy to tell you all about him. Well, all about him up until about two years ago, that is. Dyl's been keeping secrets lately."

"Ouch, that hurt, mate." Dylan clasped his chest comically, trying to lighten the mood but well aware of the barb Gareth had just thrown. "Don't listen to him, Red. Gareth has been waiting for a chance to get back at me for years... I may have given him a hard time or two about his fondness for my baby sister."

"Really, is that right? Well, seeing as I've known Gareth and Emily for a lot longer than I've known you, Soldier Boy, I think I might have to go with what they tell me about you. So you were one of *those* big brothers — overprotective with a leaning towards bullying, then?" Sarah replied, a gleam in her eye telling Dylan she was enjoying the fact that they were ganging up on him.

"Oh, I see how it is. You all join forces against the poor returning soldier—"

Dylan was interrupted by his sister's voice. "Who is ganging up on you, brother? Not my darling husband and good friend Sarah. I don't believe it for a minute, but I'm here now. I'll protect you. What's going on?"

"Nothing much, Em, just your husband threatening to tell Sarah all about me and how mean I was to him growing up. And all the time I was just trying to protect you, my darling sister." Dylan put extra sugar into his voice as he pulled Emily to his side.

"Is that so, Dylan Mackenzie? Well, lucky for me, Gareth ignored you." Emily pulled away from Dylan's side and moved to stand in Gareth's embrace before she continued, "Sarah, just ignore these two. They have been competing against each other from the first time they could walk. Gareth was always the better footy player. Dyl never got over that," she added with a wink at Sarah.

"Yeah, but I was better at rodeo. Gareth couldn't stick a ride to save his life, and I hear they call him Cowboy — it's a disgrace. What say we continue this assassination of my character somewhere else? Sarah has offered to give me a lift to this club she goes to. Are you old married couple still up to a night out?"

Dylan was enjoying the banter. Emily was teasing him and that was a good thing. He hoped she was open to forgiving him for shutting her out for the last few years, and he still wanted to get in some private time with Sarah. The longer she stood next to him, the more he wanted to wrap her up in his arms. Watching Sarah react to the conversation around her — and he had watched her, could not keep his eyes from her — drew her to him even more. There was a sexy sparkle to her big brown eyes and the way her mouth curved up at the edges when she was trying to stifle a laugh was captivating. The fact that throughout the whole family exchange she had still held his hand in hers, not caring what Gareth or Emily thought, had him experiencing sensations he didn't want to. Feelings of belonging, of stability. He'd not felt this relaxed and happy for months.

It was confusing him. Was it being around his sister that had Dylan confronting these new emotions, or was it the presence of this intriguing redhead? This unbelievable attraction to her was making his head spin. He had spent years trying to convince himself he was better off alone, keeping those who could cause him sorrow at bay. Dylan knew through bitter experience that if you let people into your life, you opened yourself up for heartache when they were taken away. Dylan did not want to be that source of pain for others if something happened to him, either. But within a matter of a few hours, Dylan had found he wanted to connect again, wanted his family back, wanted to be as happy as Emily and Gareth. Wanted Sarah to look at him the way Emily looked at Gareth, or as Mandy had looked at her husband, JT.

And that, for a soldier like him, was heading into dangerous territory. He remembered the desolation on the face of the young widow of the soldier he hadn't been able to save. The baby in the widow's arms, at the funeral, who would never know its father. Dylan didn't know if the baby was a girl or a boy—he didn't want to know. It was bad enough seeing the pain of the woman's loss, so clear, so raw. Knowing he'd had a hand in that pain, Dylan had promised himself he would never put anyone through that. Yet here he was, letting people get close.

"Sounds like a good plan, big brother. Nice of Sarah to offer to drive you. We would have taken you, but now we might offer Caitlin and Brodie a lift. Cate usually has to drive—it will be nice for her to let her hair down and have a few bubbles for a change. Do you mind, Gareth? Maybe I can share a bottle with her and you can be the designated driver. I'll make it worth your while—you know I can!"

The giggle Emily finished with and her not-so-subtle innuendo almost floored Dylan. He did *not* need the mental image of his sister making it worth Gareth's while. Dylan's imagination went rampant, much to his disgust.

"Please, Em, I didn't need to hear that. C'mon, Sarah, save me. Let's get out of here."

"Gee, Dylan, maybe I should take a leaf out of your sister's book," Sarah replied. "You do have a driving licence, right? Maybe you should drive and we can make it a girls' night. Emily, Caitlin, Mandy and Pippa really know how to have a good time."

It was the words "…and drinking champagne makes me horny" that Sarah whispered in his ear that made up Dylan's mind.

"Fuck, yeah," was his reaction as he snatched the keys from her hand. "The first bottle's on me."

Chapter Nine

She was drunk, but having a blast. A night at Jetstream had never been so much fun. Being with Dylan up close and personal was making Sarah extremely happy—and horny. Dancing with him had been exquisite torture, with their bodies melded together, her breasts pressed into his chest and his warm breath whispering against her neck. She usually never danced—it wasn't really Sarah's thing—but with Dylan holding her in his arms it had been so effortless. Well, apart from trying to rein in her lust-fuelled thoughts.

He was just so attentive and goddamn attractive. Sarah couldn't believe that Dylan had spent the entire night with her—buying her drinks, dancing, chatting and just sitting next to her. The signals he was sending left no doubt in Sarah's mind that Dylan was definitely interested in taking this night further, but she had consumed way too much bubbly. It wasn't at all her style to let her hair down in front of her co-workers. Until now, she had always kept a clear head so she could remain professional. It was never a good idea to mix business with pleasure, especially as a woman in a male-dominated environment like footy.

Dylan had gone to her head. Joining in on the conversation with him, his sister and brother-in-law, listening to them talk about childhood adventures and growing up together had made her feel a part of something. Not that she had been involved in any of the Mackenzie-Andrews adventures, but from listening to them she could almost imagine she had. She wished she'd had a childhood like theirs.

Being around Dylan was as easy as breathing. It was hard to reconcile that they had only met a few hours ago. Sarah felt like she'd known him forever. Maybe in a past life — if she'd actually believed in that sort of thing. Her body seemed to know his, moved towards him so naturally and subconsciously that half the time Sarah hardly realised how much physical contact they'd shared. Arm against arm, leg against leg. The way Dylan played with her hair, twisting it in his fingers… It all just felt so comfortable, so normal.

But the night was drawing to an end, the nightclub closing. Sarah sat with Dylan's arm draped casually around her shoulders, as if it was meant to be there. But she wanted more. She wanted to take him back to her place, strip him naked and fuck him. Wanted to crawl all over his skin, kiss and taste every inch of him, feel him thrust into her as she clung to his sweat-slicked back. Problem was, she wasn't sure how much of her newfound mental bravado was in direct correlation to her alcohol intake.

It's now or never, though, she thought, summoning up the courage to bring her wants and needs to fruition and invite Dylan home with her.

"Dylan," she whispered in his ear, "Do you want to get out of here? I do, but I've had too much to drink to try and drive. Seeing as how you still have my car keys, it looks like you have to take me home to bed."

Sarah tried for a seductive smile, a sexy purr to her voice, but wasn't sure if she'd managed to pull it off. What she *was* sure about was that Dylan was very keen on her idea. He immediately stood, grabbed her by the hand and half dragged her out of the club, shouting goodbyes over his shoulder.

* * * *

The drive home had been a quiet affair. Sarah had only spoken when she'd needed to give Dylan directions or tell him where to park when they'd finally reached her apartment block. But the atmosphere in the car had been tangible. Having Dylan seated next to her in the confines of her small car had meant she'd felt the heat emanating from his body, smelt the maleness of his scent. She had felt the wetness coating her own underwear as a result.

Sarah had been so flustered that she had even begun searching for her keys, in preparation to open her front door, when she'd heard Dylan chuckle, followed by a jingling sound. *Crap, he's got my keys, that's right… I gave them to him to drive. Way to act cool,* she'd thought as she'd retrieved them from his grasp with an awkward smile. They'd walked side by side up the stairs to her apartment. Sarah had unlocked the door and gestured for Dylan to enter.

Now that they were inside and the bubbles were wearing off, reality was starting to hit home. But oh, Dylan was hot and her libido was raring to go—she just didn't quite know how to get the ball rolling…so to speak. She fussed around, putting down her bag and keys on the side table, trying to work up the courage to say something—anything.

"Red, come here. I want to kiss you, have been dying to all night."

That was all it took. At those few simple words Sarah all but threw herself at him. When their lips met for the first time, it was as if the world shifted on its axis. Sarah had felt nothing like it before. Kissing him, his lips on hers, his tongue parrying with hers was so all-consuming that she didn't know if she could ever pull away. There were no bells or whistles—it was more like a wave of emotion swept her up and floated her away. A sense of complete serenity stilled her mind. It was as if Dylan was interlacing with her soul. And she was letting it happen without hesitation.

Dylan's hands roamed her body. Warmth spread wherever he touched. Sarah threaded her arms around his neck and caressed his shoulders—they were so broad. She wanted to see him naked, but was enjoying the kissing and his roving hands so much that she couldn't move. When Dylan broke their lip-lock, it was near painful.

"So, now that we know we can kiss, Red—and boy, we surely can—I want more. Tell me now if we aren't on the same page and I'll slow down."

Sarah could hardly articulate what she wanted, her mouth still tingling from Dylan's kiss, but she had to speak up or miss out on what she believed—*knew*—would be the best sex she'd ever had.

"Same page entirely, Soldier Boy... In fact, same paragraph, line and letter. Fuck me, Dylan, make me come."

Chapter Ten

Sarah's answer was the single best thing Dylan had heard in months, and he wasn't about to waste any time in giving her what she'd asked for. Just hearing her say the word 'fuck' had nearly made him cream his trousers.

He pulled Sarah's shirt free from her skirt and lifted it over her head. Her breasts were encased in a sheer, bright red bra. The pattern on the filmy material framed her nipples. Dark and round, they stood out invitingly. Dylan latched onto one and sucked it hard into his mouth, bra and all. He felt the metal balls on either side of her nipple and laved them with his tongue, nipping the hard bud and piercing with his teeth. Her gasp caused him a brief moment of panic as he thought he might have hurt her. The moan that followed and the way Sarah thrust her breasts further into his face quelled his fear.

"That feels so good, Dylan, but I can't stand it any longer. My pussy is so wet, it's throbbing. Please, Dylan, touch me there."

Sarah pleading was the next best thing Dylan had heard, and her gasps and sighs as he pushed her skirt up around her waist and found her very wet pussy with his fingers rated right up there too.

She was so ready for him that Dylan moaned right along with her. After letting go of her nipple, Dylan took her mouth again, walking her backwards to the nearest wall, their lips enmeshed as he thrust his fingers into her tight, soaking pussy. When Sarah stopped moving, backed up against the wall for support, Dylan fell to his knees. He pulled her red panties down and past her feet, then spread her legs.

"Let me taste you, feel you come as I tongue-fuck you."

"Please be my guest, Soldier Boy, but I've got to warn you I don't usually get off this way. But you're welcome to try — very welcome." She spoke the words with so much need in her voice, and just a hint of challenge that set Dylan on a mission he desperately wanted to accomplish.

Spreading her swollen pink lips with one hand, Dylan set to work with the other. He was surprised at his own slight disappointment to find Sarah's pussy and clit piercing-free, but that disappointment quickly disappeared as he pushed in two fingers, then three, and drove into Sarah's heat. Moisture covered his hand, and he couldn't wait a second longer to taste her. Dylan sank his tongue into her, holding her open to him with his fingers while he lapped at her juice. Finally he touched her clit with the tip of his tongue and pressed down, up and down, listening to her sweet little moans, feeling for the spasm or contraction of her pussy walls that would let him know she was close. He pumped his fingers and thrust his tongue and loved every second of it, wanted to keep doing it all night if that was what it took to pleasure her.

"Don't stop... Yes, there! Oh, Dylan, I'm...going...to..."

The way her body trembled and shook as the orgasm took hold had Dylan's cock hard as a rock and ready for action. He didn't care—he let her ride his face, trying to extend her pleasure for as long as he could.

"No more, Dylan...I can't take it anymore," she whimpered. "I need to feel you inside me, filling me, stretching me. Get your pants off, Soldier. I want you naked and in my bed pronto...and that's an order."

Sarah's giggle and salute did something to Dylan. Something inside his chest fluttered—it was all he could do not to rub at the feeling. She was so sexy—standing in front of him, her cheeks high with colour, her skirt bunched around her waist with her pussy in full view and her breasts only covered by that sheer bra. He wanted to be inside her more than his next breath.

"Yes, ma'am... At once, ma'am," Dylan replied as he started to shuck his clothes. That was one thing about being in the army—you learnt to dress and undress quickly. Combat didn't wait for you to get ready. So Dylan was standing naked in no time, waiting for Sarah to show him the way to her bed. Just the thought of Sarah and bed had his cock pulsating.

"What about you, Red? Seems to me you're still wearing way too much clothing yourself."

"Follow me, Soldier. We'll lose it on the way," Sarah purred, her voice soft and sultry as she started unzipping her skirt and kicking her shoes off. "You'll be pleased to know that while my apartment is small,

I splurged on the bed… It's a king size. Plenty of room for fun and games."

Dylan nearly missed Sarah's last comment, he was so focused on watching her naked arse as he followed her. The heart-shaped cheeks gently swayed as she walked. Thoughts of taking that arse were already overloading his brain, even without her comment about fun and games. *Thank you, universe – thank you.*

* * * *

I know he's checking out my butt, but I have to keep walking, Sarah thought as she tried to act confident and sexy, leading Dylan to her bed. Her behind had always been a bit big for her liking. As she was quite short, it made Sarah feel a bit like a pear, and finding jeans to fit her was always a nightmare. Small waist, big butt and short legs – not easy to find that combination in pants, which was why she usually stuck to skirts and tops. So parading around in front of Dylan was taking a toll on her assuredness and self-esteem. She was also amazed at the way she had sounded so raunchy, asking Dylan to 'fuck' her – the word was so foreign to her, not usually a part of her vocabulary.

The other, more disturbing reason Sarah was determined to not turn around just yet was that while Dylan had quickly and efficiently undressed, she had seen the scarring on his shoulder. It was hard to miss. She had completely forgotten about the fact that he'd been injured in Afghanistan, had not heard him or his sister discuss it at any time throughout the night. So now she was trying to stifle the overwhelming grief that had assaulted her on seeing proof of how badly he had been hurt, how much he must have suffered.

Judging by all the puckered, silver scarring on his skin, his injuries had been extensive. The last thing Dylan would want, she was sure, was her fawning over him or getting all teary. So she was doing her best to push the emotions she now felt down and lock them away, at least for the moment.

She hadn't even had the chance to admire his physique, she had been so taken aback by his injuries. Reaching her bedroom, she took a deep calming breath and turned towards him. Reaching out, she took his hand in hers and led him to her bed, then pushed him backwards onto the mattress with a gentle shove.

"This is exactly where I want you. Here, in my bed, and by the look of you, ready and primed," she said as she climbed on top of him, dragging her hand over his hard cock. Not exactly a stroke — more of a tease, and a promise of things to come.

"I'm not complaining, Red. Go for it," Dylan replied as he dragged her down to lie over him.

He was warm and firm beneath her, his cock pushing against her stomach.

"Hmm, you feel nice under me, Dylan Mackenzie, but I think you'll feel even better in me."

"I hope so, Red, I really do. Don't suppose you have a condom handy? I left mine in my other pants." Dylan's voice was a sexy drawl, hypnotic, so close to her ear that it took Sarah a moment to decipher what he'd said and answer.

"Bedside drawer, top one, should be a packet in there…for emergency use." She giggled.

"Well, I class this as an emergency, Red, 'cause if I don't get inside you soon I'll be making a fool of myself and coming on your sheets." Sarah watched as Dylan stretched out his long arm and opened the drawer, his biceps and muscles bulging and rippling, so masculine and drool-worthy that she had to lick her lips to make sure she wasn't making a fool of herself

"Found them." Dylan placed the box between their chests. "Not opened yet, then... So is it a new purchase, or you don't have many emergencies?" he asked, a grin on his face as he tapped her lightly on the nose.

"I'm not sure if I should answer that question. If I say 'new purchase' you'll think I bring men to my bed all the time, but if I say 'no emergencies', maybe you'll think I bring men to my bed who are prepared. When the truth of the matter is, I don't usually bring men to my bed at all." Sarah felt her face heat at her blatant admission. But it was the truth. The way she lived her life — either behind a computer screen designing websites or working with the Jets as their digi-chick — she just didn't meet available men. Not counting with her trusty vibrator, Sarah could hardly remember the last time she'd orgasmed — before tonight, that was.

Sarah caught sight of an emotion that flickered over Dylan's face, but wasn't sure what it was. There was a definite change in the way he looked at her — the smile he had been wearing had suddenly disappeared. She hoped he hadn't found something wrong with her admission. Dylan's next words stilled her worry.

"Oh, baby, that is such a turn-on. You have no idea how pleased I am you thought enough of me to bring me here. Makes a soldier feel blessed." Dylan kissed her, taking his time to explore her mouth, the condom box crushed between them.

Sarah moved her hands to Dylan's shoulder and froze as she felt the welted skin beneath her fingertips. Her breath hitched and as they were still lip-locked, Dylan obviously noticed. She felt him shake his head because their lips did a little dance with the movement, but he resumed his delicious assault on her mouth.

Her head was swimming. *Just ignore it, move your hand away, get back in the game, Sarah*, she mentally admonished herself. But it was too late. Dylan had felt the change in her, her distraction from their kiss, and he pulled his mouth away.

"Is it a turn-off, Red—my shoulder? I know it's not pretty, and feels even worse. I'll understand if it's too much. Why don't I put my shirt back on so…?"

Sarah was mortified at herself, at her reactions. The sadness in Dylan's voice, his acceptance that she might even consider his war wounds a turn-off had her reeling.

"No, it's nothing like that, Dylan. I'm sorry. I got distracted thinking more about what you had gone through to have such a scar, thinking of you being hurt. Honestly, there is nothing about you that I find a turn-off—in fact, I'd go out on a limb and say you are the sexiest man I've ever seen. Does it hurt when I touch the scar?"

Sarah paused for a moment, wondering if she should ask the next question, finding it impossible not to. "What happened to you, Dylan?"

As soon as the question had fallen from her lips, Sarah knew she shouldn't have gone there. She felt Dylan's whole body tense beneath hers, actually saw him withdrawing from her, his once hungry, passion-filled eyes turning glassy, distant. It was as if he was staring right through her, did not see her lying naked on top of him. Their faces were mere inches from one another, but at that moment Dylan was someplace else. She had to do something to bring him back to her, could have slapped herself for speaking the words and for being sidetracked by the injury. There was something about this man that did things to her heart and body. Sarah had no clue what it was, or why she felt so close to him, a man who was not much more than a stranger to her, but she did and she was blowing it big time with her untimely curiosity.

"Dylan, you don't have to answer that. It's none of my business," she stammered. "Just forget I asked anything. Let me assure you, mister, I am totally hot and aching for you. That hasn't changed." Sarah cupped Dylan's cheek with her hand, trying to regain his attention. "Can we please just rewind and go back to the kissing, and the talking about condoms and you inside me?" Sarah now sounded desperate — she could hear it in her own voice, so she had no doubt Dylan would notice as well.

She hoped they could move on, prayed for it and waited, hesitant to even take a breath until he answered.

Chapter Eleven

He could have coped with putting his shirt back on if that was what had been distracting Sarah — hey, his shoulder was an ugly mess — but it was the sympathy that got him.

Fuck, he hated that look. He didn't deserve it or want it, especially not from the woman he was just about to fuck. That pitying, teary look was wasted on him. He had seen too much, got off lightly compared to others. The others were the ones who needed sympathy, not him. The widow left alone because he hadn't seen the IED buried in the road. The child who would grow up without a father. He deserved no pity. He'd fucked up with the explosion and he'd fucked up by not getting home in time to save his own mother, for not being around for his own father or for his sister. He deserved no one's misdirected sympathy.

Dylan could hear the plea in Sarah's voice for him to ignore her question, hear that she'd realised she had crossed a line he was not willing to go over. But it was too late. The memories had invaded, stolen into his thoughts. He had to get out—he could feel the sense of unease, almost panic building in his chest, knew that he had to just have a minute to himself to sort it all out in his head. *Push the memories back... Get a grip.* He lifted Sarah from his body, heard her little cry of dismay as he placed her beside him on the bed.

"Red, I need a minute. I just gotta get some air..." he said as he threw his long legs over the edge of the mattress and sat up, his back to Sarah. By now she was probably equally appalled to see the damage that had been left there, as well, by the shrapnel. He was rubbing at his shoulder again, and that annoyed the fuck out of him. *Leave it alone,* he thought as he began to stand. It was then he felt the warmth cover his back. She had put her arms around his neck—he could feel her breasts pushing against his skin.

"Please, Dylan... Don't go. Tell me what I did that was so wrong. What upset you the most? What made you want to leave?" Her mouth was next to his ear, and as she spoke he could feel the softness of her lips moving against his earlobe, the faint whisper of air against his neck as she spoke.

Sarah was caressing his pecs as she draped herself over his back. It caused an immediate reaction to his waning libido. Just for a moment, the panic subsided—his nipples were responding to her touch and his cock stirred, the feel of her skin on his overriding his anguish. Dylan had thought that speech would be impossible, his throat was so constricted, his chest so tight, but before he knew it sounds were coming from his lips.

"I can't talk about it, Red. Not now... Not ever. Too much... I'm not whole. Something inside me just doesn't work anymore. Remembering...I just can't—"

Sarah cut him off. "Well, why didn't you just say so from the beginning, Soldier? So a girl's not allowed to get a bit of a shock at a war wound she was not prepared for. If ya *hadda* said something I would've known not to ask. But no, I broke your code book, the Dylan Mackenzie 'don't ask me that question' list, and so now you're going to run away and leave me all hot and bothered." The moment she let go of him, peeled herself away, Dylan missed her touch and the heat of her body against his back. "Fine—just go, then. I can use my vibrator to fulfil my needs."

Having been instantly disgusted with himself for saying anything, let alone showing such weakness, Dylan had been expecting to be assaulted by more empathy, so he was shocked when Sarah got stuck into him. He was so taken aback that she was giving him a hard time about leaving her hot and bothered, adding the image of her satisfying her own needs with a vibrator to her tirade, that he turned back to face her.

Metal glistened from different parts of her skin—lip, nose, eyebrow, even the space between her bottom lip and chin. Her fiery red hair was tousled. She looked so vibrant and alive, and she was staring him down, wide-eyed, her cheeks full of colour. His heart flipped over, the heaviness in his chest eased and his cock rose to full attention. She was breath-taking. An angry Sarah Flynn was one hell of a thing. Dylan could not help himself as he reached for her. Damn her—he couldn't leave.

With his hands either side of her face, he dragged her back to his mouth. When their lips connected, heat and passion filled him again. He made love to her mouth, got lost in the taste of her, the touch of her tongue on his. He pushed her gently onto her back and covered her body with his own. Her frame was so small. Using his elbows to brace himself over her, he disengaged their mouths and looked into her eyes. Big and brown, they were a window to her needs, pupils dilated by her passion. She moved her legs from under his hips and wrapped them around him, and his cock made contact with the heat from her pussy.

"Good to have you back, Dylan. Please, I need you in me now. As nice as my vibrator is, I think you will be *so* much better. "

Her words sent another shiver of anticipation racing up his spine. Dylan took a few minutes to search around for the forgotten condom box. Finally finding it, he tore the package open with his teeth. Condom packets flew everywhere. The sound of Sarah giggling filled the room and Dylan realised that, just that quickly, the tension was gone. All he wanted to do was roll the latex cover over his dick and plunge deeply into Sarah, feel her pussy walls clutching his rigid cock.

Getting the condom objective accomplished ended up being a much more difficult and awkward thing to achieve with Sarah's legs trapping him against her body. "Sarah, you need to give me some room to get this rubber on before it's too late," he groaned, trying to break the hold her legs had on him.

"I don't want to let go. You feel so good against my skin, Dylan."

"C'mon, Red, just a second and I promise you'll feel more than just my skin, you'll feel me stretching you, filling you, a part of you."

When she released her grip around his waist, Dylan didn't waste a second and rolled the condom down his shaft. Holding his cock in his hand, Dylan rested it against the entrance to Sarah's pussy. With his eyes locked on hers, he slowly entered her.

Dylan watched Sarah's dilated pupils, watched the dreamy expression appear on her face as he filled her. The hiss that escaped from him could not be helped. She was so wet and tight. His cock glided into her folds, stretching and filling her as he had promised. Balls-deep, he stopped and took time to enjoy the sensation.

"Don't stop now, Dylan, move...I need you to move." Sarah wriggled beneath him.

Again Dylan was unable to refuse her direction, so he began a slow rhythm of thrusts and retreats. He could feel the bite of Sarah's fingernails digging into his back as their movements became as one, more hurried, more desperate. Placing his hands under her backside, he lifted her slightly, changing the angle of his entry so his shaft would drag against her clit as he pumped and thrust.

"That's...so...good... Yes... There... Don't stop!" Her words were disjointed and he knew exactly how she felt, answering with his own gibberish.

"Feel... Fuck... Not going to last..."

Their movements intensified. Sweat was dripping down Dylan's brow, but he couldn't find his release until after he'd fulfilled Sarah's needs. Grinding his back teeth he hung on. Sarah's body strained, lifted, and he felt the first quivers of her pussy as it greedily clasped his cock. It pushed him over the edge.

"Dylan!" Sarah called his name as he did hers. Their climaxes hit simultaneously. The pleasure was immeasurable. Dylan was caught in a vortex of pure, mind-blowing sensation. He felt it from his toes through his tight balls, right down his shaft as his cum exploded from his cock. Even the tips of his fingers tingled with satisfaction.

"Holy fucking hell, when can we do that again?" Sarah sighed in his ear, sounding sated, serene as far as Dylan could tell. It was exactly what he had been thinking — she'd plucked the words from his brain.

"Red, that was just the appetiser. Just wait till I really get going."

Chapter Twelve

"Three sugars, really?" Sarah was shocked that Dylan took his coffee so sweet. "I thought you'd be a straight-up black sort of man for sure."

"What can I say? I like my coffee like I like my women—hot and sweet." Dylan's grin reflected his terrible attempt at humour. It was such an old line. Sarah could not help but add her own retort.

"Well, maybe I should add some milk to mine...'cause I usually take mine strong and black..." When Dylan's grin turned into a knowing smirk, Sarah felt herself melt. He had such a beautiful smile—one of those toothy, brimming ones that lit up his face, caused little creases around his eyes, seemed to brighten the whole room around him. She was in deep trouble. She was falling for him too fast, too soon. One night and she was smitten. Sarah understood that when Dylan left—and he was going to do that soon—she'd be heartbroken.

It was stupid, irresponsible of her to be feeling like this, letting herself get caught up in the moment. She didn't know Dylan at all—it wasn't as if they'd shared any meaningful conversation. God, she didn't even know what sort of music he listened to—if any—or what movies he enjoyed. The only personal information Sarah had gleaned about Dylan had come from listening in on last night's conversations between him, Emily and Gareth, and he didn't want to talk about his scars. So why did she feel so close to him? Enthralled and captivated by him?

Why did she want something more with him?

The feel of his hand on her arm brought her back to the moment. Dylan was standing in her kitchen with a towel hanging loosely around his hips, the only covering on his sculpted body. It reminded her of the shower they had just shared and the three orgasms Dylan had wrung from her before she had returned the favour. She should be making the most of this moment and not worrying about the future. If this was all she would get of Dylan Mackenzie, she was not going to waste a moment.

"Sorry, Dylan. I was daydreaming—got lost in thought, and why wouldn't I? You're standing there in just a towel... You are such a temptation. I've spent a lot of time around half-naked, fit men with my job at the Jets', but Soldier, your body is one prime specimen. Sin on legs, as my friends would say. If you ever give up your day job, I reckon you'd make one hell of a living as a stripper. Women would pay big bucks for a glimpse of your bod!"

She'd done it again—said something wrong.

Dylan wasn't smiling anymore. Sarah would have kicked herself, if she'd had any idea what she'd said to distance him again.

As the silence stretched on and the moment became more awkward, Sarah decided it was time to make breakfast. She left Dylan leaning against the kitchen counter, his eyes blank. He'd gone back to whatever place it was he went, just as he had done last night. She hid her head in the fridge, pretending to be gathering food, but really trying to figure out what to say to bring Dylan back to her — again.

When he crowded her with his warm body, startling her, causing her to nearly fall into the cold fridge, Sarah used her ample behind to try to regain her balance, pushing it back into him in an attempt to give herself the space to stand. As she turned her body to him, Dylan took her face in his hands and kissed her.

The kiss was sweet, tender. Different than others they had shared. It made her heart swell, her pulse race. Her mouth automatically opened to allow Dylan to deepen the kiss. Cold air assaulted her back while the heat of Dylan's torso warmed her breasts. It was a heady combination of sensations.

Heaven — this is what heaven must feel like, she thought as she arched her body closer to his, savouring the kiss, glad for it, relieved to have him back. When Dylan pulled her forward, then shut the fridge door behind her, she went with it. When he pushed her up against the hard metal surface, she opened her legs in anticipation. Hoping that he would touch her, ease the throbbing that had begun between her thighs.

Sarah didn't have to wait long before she felt the exquisite contact of his probing fingers as he parted her robe and pushed them into her swollen folds.

Dylan moved his lips from her mouth, reattaching them to her breast, his teeth pulling at her nipple bar. The slight bite of pain was replaced with sweet pleasure as he laved at the rigid nipple with his tongue. Sarah's stomach clenched, her pussy walls contracting from the intensity of his attentions, her desire sweeping her up and out of control. She writhed under his ministrations, couldn't have stopped herself from moving even if she'd tried as the momentum of her orgasm built. With his fingers, he plundered, stroked, probed, then moved to her clit. Thumb, finger—she didn't know or care. All Sarah wanted was for Dylan to continue. The pleasure raced from her nipple to her clit and back again.

She was making noises—half mewls, half cries—as the crescendo built. She'd put her arms above her head, wrists turned, palms against the fridge door, fingers wrapped over the top edge for support—or to stop her from floating away. Sarah pressed her breast farther into Dylan's mouth, impaled her pussy on his finger, grinding herself against his wrist. Needing to come.

Dylan was mumbling, the words smothered by her breasts. "Red, what you do to me... The way you make me want you...too much..."

She shattered, her climax rushing and consuming her, releasing so much pleasure Sarah thought she would die from it. Her hold on the fridge forgotten, her arms fell to grasp Dylan's shoulders. Her head felt so light she rested it there, too. She could feel her legs giving way, started to slide, probably would've ended up on the floor in a mushy puddle of contentment had it not been for Dylan lifting her up and hugging her to his body. Unfortunately, the contentment she was feeling was very short-lived.

"That, Red, was a thank you—a reward for comparing me so favourably to the Jets guys. But honey, if you think any woman would pay to see these scars, you're kidding yourself. But I appreciate the sentiment all the same."

What the...? Sarah didn't think she could have heard correctly, 'cause it had sure sounded as if Dylan had just given her an orgasm as a reward for being an idiot. Sarah didn't know whether to laugh, cry, scream or beat the living shit out of him. *How dare he*? She'd thought he'd wanted her, wanted to make love... Love? What a stupid word to think. Maybe Dylan was right—she was an idiot. Not for finding him attractive. No, Sarah was an idiot for expecting that he would find her worthy of such a strong emotion in return, for even letting the word 'love' enter her thoughts.

Last night had been a one-night stand. She needed to keep that straight in her head. It had been a fuck— well, a couple of fucks, but who was counting? But that was all it had been—no confusion or emotional delusion about it, just two people finding sexual gratification. Not the romantic fantasy she had begun to create in her mind.

Sarah struggled from Dylan's grasp, not daring to look at him for fear her irresponsible, imaginative heart would crumble.

"So do you still want breakfast, or have you somewhere else you need to be?" Sarah was trying for an even, light, maybe even controlled tone, and would have pulled it off, if not for the tear that had escaped her eye and rolled slowly down her cheek. She felt the wet drop track its way down and drip off her jaw. She didn't swipe at that traitorous tear or try to hide it, hoping that by doing nothing she would not draw attention to it.

Chapter Thirteen

Of course he still wanted to stay for breakfast. Actually, the food part was of little consequence — Dylan just wasn't in any hurry to leave. He was enjoying being with Sarah, wanted to get to know her better, wanted to ask her about her favourite movie, music, book. Wanted to know why she had covered her gorgeous face with all those metal protuberances. What she was doing for the rest of her day, week, month, life. He was shocked at himself for thinking those things, but not as shocked as when he saw that tear tumble down her face.

What had he done? Was she upset with him? The idea that he had made Sarah cry was detestable, joining the list of things he had done wrong at a very high level.

"Sarah, what's wrong? Why the tears? Did I hurt you? Say something to hurt you? I swear, honey, that was never my intention. Yes to breakfast, yes to spending more time with you... If that's okay?"

Dylan was holding his breath, waiting for Sarah to answer him. Ready and willing to grovel if he was the cause of her sorrow. Thankfully, there had been only one teardrop. That one had affected him so deeply, he shuddered to think what he would do if Sarah really cried. He lifted her face so he could look into her eyes, wondering if he could find any answers in their brown depths.

"You finger-fuck me, then thank me like it's some kind of reward. I try not to kid myself, Dylan, but I obviously did when I thought we'd shared more than just a quick fuck."

"I don't understand, Sarah. I just said I want to spend more time with you. This was never just about getting my rocks off. We have a connection—as much as I don't want one, it's there."

Holy shit. It was what he'd said after watching her fall apart in his arms, after enjoying, revelling in the fact that he could make this woman come so hard, that she was so responsive to his touch, so magnificent in the throes of climax.

When she had complimented him, the idea that she believed his body was worth looking at, let alone paying to see, had made him so overwhelmed. He'd hardly been able to keep his hands off her. Just standing there, thinking that this amazing woman thought him attractive after seeing the battle scars that marred his skin, had given him pause to think of what his life would be like if he had her love to keep him warm. To keep the nightmares that often intruded into his mind from appearing. He had slept soundly for the first night in forever. Not that they had gone to sleep early—no, they had explored each other long into the early hours of the morning. But when he had fallen asleep he'd slept soundly, her leg thrown over his own, her body nestled into his larger frame. Peace had descended and he had rested, then awoken more refreshed than he had in months.

"I didn't say what I meant right..." Dylan fell over his own words as he tried to explain how much she had done for him, meant to him in such a short time. "I'm stuffing this up, Sarah... Spoiling what we had... Have... *Could* have." Dylan rubbed at his shoulder. "Forget what I said before. Listen to what I'm saying now. I want more. I want to see more of you, make some memories with you. Be with you."

The words were still wrong, but the emotion was clear to Sarah. Dylan wanted to keep seeing her. Spend time with her. And from what he'd said, he wanted a relationship with her but it still felt, to Sarah, that he didn't think he should want that — or at least didn't think it could be long-term. He wanted to be loved. He just didn't think he deserved happiness for some reason. Sarah wondered if after spending more time with Dylan, getting to know him, she would become privy to his reasoning. Perhaps she could change his mind, given time and patience.

And hopefully, if she couldn't find those reasons or change his mind and Dylan eventually left her, she would be able to put her heart back together. Because Sarah knew that if she let Dylan become even a tiny part of her life, she would fall in love with him.

Chapter Fourteen

For the next eight days, Sarah and Dylan spent all their free time together.

Dylan had reported to base every weekday to do whatever it was he did there. Sarah never pried. He would meet her at the Jets headquarters in the afternoon, sometimes training alongside the players. Sarah was pleased that Brodie James had extended that offer to Dylan. It made him seem part of the Jets family.

One day, she walked in on Dylan deep in conversation with Pippa Harris. The way he was moving his shoulder and the intensity on Pippa's face led Sarah to the conclusion that Dylan was discussing his shoulder injury. Sarah was shocked by the sudden jolt of jealousy she experienced when the Jets' physiotherapist moved her hands over Dylan's bare torso and along his arm. Pippa was happily married to the Jets' captain, Rook Harris. The devotion the couple shared was clear for all to see. Pippa was always professional in her dealings with the Jets players— Sarah knew all that—but still, that little green-eyed monster reared its ugly head at the sight before her. She had to shake it off quickly when they noticed her, and she forced a smile onto her face.

"Hiya, Sarah." Pippa waved at her, her voice full of the welcome and friendship that she'd always shown, making Sarah feel even more pathetic over her silly, jealous reaction. "Dylan was just asking for some advice on strengthening exercises."

"Looking for some free advice from the best physio in town, is he?" Sarah replied, pleased that she could keep her insecurities from her voice, hoping that Dylan hadn't noticed her discomfort. So far, Dylan had made no promises to Sarah, so she really had no right to feel the way she did. That, of course, was easier said than done.

"Hey, I'm not stupid, Sarah. I take advantage of a good opportunity when I see one. Army medical is great, but getting a second opinion from someone as well-respected as Pippa is a bonus I'm not about to deny. In fact, some of her suggestions… Well, I can already see how they would benefit me."

The worm of fear that burrowed into Sarah's heart at Dylan's admission that he took advantage of good opportunities was hard to fight. Was she just that? A good opportunity to spend some time in bed with an all-too-willing woman? Because that was exactly what she had been, falling into his arms the first night she'd met him. Dylan hadn't had to work hard at getting her, that was for sure—Sarah had served herself up on a platter.

She tried to brush the worry away—she was becoming a neurotic mess. Jealousy and all this insecurity were things Sarah was not used to feeling. She wished she could just focus on the happiness she felt in Dylan's arms or just in his presence, but in the back of her mind Sarah knew she wasn't winning the battle to gain Dylan's trust. To have him open up to her more about his life, his thoughts, the nightmares that woke him in the night.

He seemed to think she'd not noticed, but Sarah had. It was hard not to when she heard his cries, his pleas to 'watch out', the anguish in his voice as he shouted while still deep in the grip of his dreams. The night he had sat bolt upright in bed had scared the life out of her, but Sarah had resisted her desire to reach out and soothe Dylan. She'd just had the sense that Dylan was not ready to accept her comfort. Perhaps he would never be.

"You ready to go, Sarah?" Dylan's question shook Sarah from her inner turmoil. Again she plastered on the best smile she could muster.

"Sure am, Soldier Boy, if you're ready. I don't mind waiting if you and Pippa aren't finished, though."

"Nope, Sarah, I think Dylan and I are good. Rook will be waiting for me by now anyway." Pippa's smile was still full of warmth as she turned away from Sarah and focused back on Dylan. "Try those exercises and get back to me—let me know if they help. I'll do a bit of research on shrapnel injury and see if I can come up with something else. But my professional opinion is 'keep away from the bombs', Dylan."

So it was a bomb, Sarah immediately thought. Dylan had told Pippa that much, but not her. *Be reasonable, Sarah, she's a medical professional, needs to know all the details*, the little voice of reason in her head tried to point out. But the hurt had already quietly done its damage.

* * * *

Dylan had spent every night in her bed — nine nights, to be exact — and Sarah loved waking up next to his warm, solid body every morning, even if it was at such an ungodly hour. Dylan always made it worth her while. The way he licked her pussy or nibbled her clit with his teeth was reward enough. The feel of his cock inside her pussy, the way he took her from sleepy to dizzying heights with sexual need, desperate to fall over the precipice and quiver under the delight of yet another orgasm was a trade-off Sarah was all too willing to endure.

The Jets had played another home game, and Dylan had watched the match from the stands as she'd done her job arranging the media and promotions — Brodie had still not replaced the traitorous former media manager. Having Dylan by her side at the after-game functions had just added to her job satisfaction and enjoyment. Sarah was happier than she'd ever been, as long as she kept her fears of Dylan leaving locked away, and the Jets pups continually ribbed her about it. Joseph Ondio was the only pup who had not said anything — in fact, if she thought about it, Joseph had been a bit prickly around her of late.

Sarah decided that she would call him out on it the first chance she got. She valued Joseph's friendship, hoped that she hadn't done anything to threaten it. She was also a little protective of the young man. Joseph had been through some tough times, had been running with the wrong crowd for much of his life and had made some disappointing choices that had nearly ruined his rugby league career before it'd got started. Joseph had been lucky that JT and Brodie had stepped in and given him not just an ultimatum, but their support and guidance as well.

Dylan and Emily were deep in conversation, analysing Gareth's game, so Sarah decided it was the perfect opportunity to catch up with Joseph and headed over to where he was standing.

"Hey, Joseph, have I told you how great you played today?" Sarah thought if she started off the conversation in a friendly way she might get him to 'fess up what was bothering him.

"Hey, Digi. Thanks... Yeah, I went all right today, didn't I? Huh, sure put that international hotshot on his arse more than once, eh?" Joseph's smile was there, but not as bright as usual. Sarah was really starting to worry.

"Joseph, is something wrong? You seem to be a bit quiet of late. You know I'm here if you need to talk or anything—don't let the others know, but you are my favourite pup." Sarah gave Joseph a grin and winked.

'I'm just worried for ya, Digi. I don't trust ya soldja. I worry what will happen if he goes and breaks your heart. 'Cause if he does hurt ya, I'll be hurtin' him—so what if he's related to the Cowboy?"

Joseph seemed so serious that Sarah was taken aback. And here she had been thinking she was too protective of him... Apparently, it was reciprocal.

"Well, it's nice to know you worry about me, Joseph, but whatever happens between me and Dylan will be between us. I don't want you fighting anyone, let alone on my behalf. And anyway, Joe, what's not to say I'll break his heart first?"

"Just be careful, Digi. It's not good to give your heart away too soon."

Sarah watched, deep in thought, as Joseph ambled away. His big frame made his walk seem a bit awkward, as though he hadn't quite figured out how to move the enormous body he was still growing into.

Trying to put aside Joseph's warning, Sarah headed back to where she'd left Dylan.

Dylan and Emily seemed to have put their differences aside, or so Sarah gathered from the ease of their conversations. Whether they were reminiscing about their childhoods, catching up on what Dylan had missed while he was gone or engaging in some plain old brother-sister teasing, it was clear that Dylan, Emily and Gareth had been—and were—very close.

Their familial bond and the fond memories of childhood they shared had Sarah wishing her life could have been more like theirs. Filled with laughter and happiness instead of the long bouts of solitude and exclusion that she had been forced to deal with.

Chapter Fifteen

After their tenth night together, Sarah woke to find Dylan staring at the ceiling.

"Morning, soldier," Sarah said as she caressed his chest, playing idly with the light dusting of hair that covered his muscled torso. Dylan did not respond to her greeting or touch. He seemed lost in thought. "Is there something on my ceiling that has taken your fancy, or are you checking out the cobwebs I missed?"

"I need to pop into the base today, got to check in with one of my superiors. I was just wondering if you'd like to come with me. I can give you a tour of the base and it'd give you a chance to meet some of the guys from my unit—they're home for a few weeks."

Her heart flip-flopped in her chest at Dylan's out of the blue invitation. He had kept his work life separate until now, happy to just share in hers, and she couldn't help but feel encouraged that this was a step in the right direction. If they were to have a long-term relationship, she would need to become part of his life

as a soldier. Maybe this was the first step towards
that.

* * * *

Of course, that old adage, 'Be careful what you wish
for', struck home hard as Sarah endured an
uncomfortable hour under the unmistakeably hostile
scrutiny of his superiors, then a few more at the local
pub with some of his soldier buddies. All were
noticeably shocked or taken aback that Dylan would
find her small frame, pierced face and wild hair
attractive. To his credit, Dylan ignored their
astonished glances.

Her being the Jets' digi-chick did eventually thaw a
few of Dylan's mates, especially when she could give
them some insider knowledge. Sarah was delighted
when a good-looking, smooth-talking soldier they all
called Tamba confessed to being one of her followers
on Twitter.

"So you're behind the Jets' Twitter feed and fan
page," Tamba said, his smile warm and friendly,
which for Sarah was like finding an oasis in the desert.
"Thank you for the updates, darling. Sometimes it's
hard catching any games when you're deployed —
being able to keep up with my rugby league via your
websites and stuff is great. Between you and me,
Sarah" — Tamba winked at her — "I've won a few bets
by checking the tweet updates. Most of the guys had
no idea what time the games were on back home."

Strangely, after Tamba's conversation with her
everyone else seemed to lighten up. Dylan squeezed
her hand at about that time, letting her know that he
had noticed her not-so-friendly welcome, then her
acceptance.

* * * *

That night, in bed, Sarah brought the apparent hostility towards her up with Dylan.

"Red, you gotta understand, part of being in the army is the brotherhood. We have each other's backs. They would have been like that, reacted like that, to any new girlfriend. Of course, the fact that I've never really introduced anyone to them before—not back on home soil, at least—didn't make it any easier for you, and you have to admit you are a bit unique."

Dylan touched the piercing above Sarah's top lip—a Madonna piercing—then the ring that went through her septum, his touch gentler, then moved on to her labret piercing. She could tell he wanted to ask her about them. In fact, Sarah had been expecting the questions for a while. She wanted to answer him, wanted to take this new 'hoping-to-become-a-relationship' to a place where questions could be asked freely and answered honestly. It was imperative that they get to this stage, or they would most certainly fail as a couple.

"Go on, Dylan, just ask. I can see the words on the tip of your tongue," Sarah encouraged him.

After a few long, silent moments where Sarah could see his indecision, the mental fight Dylan had with himself to broach the subject, he finally spoke. "Did they hurt?"

While that was one of the questions she'd been expecting, it wasn't the question she had imagined Dylan would ask first. She had been sure that his first enquiry would be either why she had so many, or why she had any at all.

"Some hurt like a son of a bitch, others not really. Every piercing has a story, a reason—probably silly when you think rationally about it, but I like them. They are me. Do they make you uncomfortable or embarrass you, Dylan?"

They were scary questions to ask him. Sarah was not sure how she would react or what she would do if he answered yes to either. Truthfully, she was starting to tire of the different balls, hoops, bars and rings, had contemplated removing some, toning down her appearance as she aged. But for some reason, Dylan's acceptance of her for how she presented herself to the world was important.

"To be honest, Red, when I first saw you it was your hair that shocked me the most. I don't think I'd seen any colour quite as bright." Dylan reached out and twirled a strand of her hair around his finger. Leaning her cheek into his hand came so naturally that Sarah could not fight it. "I love the colour now, you know. It's you, Red. I have a hard time imagining you any other way. The piercings as well. I especially love the little bar through your nipple—fuck, it's hot. I guess, with or without the metal, I just love the way you look, love the way you make me so hot, the peace I feel when I'm around you."

When Dylan had said the word *love* the first time, Sarah had nearly choked on her heart, it had jumped into her throat so quickly. When he'd repeated the word, well, she'd just about exploded. Trying to contain her joy, to remain calm and consider that he might have said the words as a matter of speech and not an indication of his true feelings for her, was near impossible.

"Dylan, I don't know what to say, don't know if you realise what *you* just said, if I should read anything into the words you chose. I'm terrified that what I say to you next will push you away, but I need to let you know how I feel…"

Before Sarah could say the words that had been on her lips for days, Dylan pulled her to him. He smothered her lips with his own. Frustration that she hadn't declared her love for him was quickly replaced by passion. Desire. Need. Words now forgotten, Sarah surrendered her body and her mind to Dylan's touch.

With his large, strong hands and magical fingers, Dylan caressed her in all the right places. When he gave her a kiss that melded them together as one, she careened off into sensual delight. As Dylan's cock entered her wet and eager folds, Sarah gripped his backside, her legs wrapped around his hips. She pulled him closer, quickly finding his rhythm and matching it. She loved the feeling of his cock embedded in her as it slid in and out so perfectly, as though they had been made for each other. The sounds of their coupling, wet slaps as bodies connected, filled the room.

Dylan was more than generously endowed, his cock thick and long, just the ideal size to stretch and fill her. She had lavished attention on it with both her hands and her mouth, more than once. The feel of the shaft had been like silk, the bulbous head like satin on her tongue. Taking him deeply into her mouth, his head sliding down her throat as she'd hummed and swallowed had sent him into a frenzy. Sarah had felt powerful, sensual, sexy and wanton as she'd felt his struggle not to take control. She had loved the way Dylan had fisted her hair, needing her to quicken the pace or take him deeper, suck him harder, but he had made no demands of her, had left her in charge of the moment. She'd quickly learnt what Dylan needed when she had him in her mouth, and though Sarah liked to draw out his pleasure she knew when to bring him over the edge, his seed spurting down her throat as he shouted her name. Sometimes Sarah, sometimes Red, both voiced with such passion that it made her heart soar and her own body pulse with desire, just as it was doing now.

Chapter Sixteen

The words had come naturally. He'd heard himself say them and was expecting to panic, for his chest to tighten, his heart to race, but Dylan had felt none of this. The words 'love' and 'Sarah' fitted together — they sounded perfect.

It was at that moment that Dylan knew he was screwed. He had forgotten all the promises he'd made himself. Oaths to not care, not open his heart to anyone and flirt with the chance of more emotional pain. Where had his promise gone, to not place another soul in the same position as his mate's grieving widow? Love led to loss and ultimately pain. For him, for others. He'd loved his mother but had not been there when she had needed him. He didn't want to believe love was worth it. But after spending time with Sarah — the ease of being with her, the way she surrendered her body to him openly, honestly, holding back nothing from him — he was faltering. Losing his own battle. He loved her. It was so simple, so plain. Dylan loved Sarah against his own better judgement, but he could not hear her say the words in return. Had purposely stopped her. Once she said them there would be no going back. He would not be able to walk away — and for both their sakes, he had to.

Retreating was going to be the hardest thing Dylan had ever done, but because he loved Sarah he had no choice. Better for her to hate him now than grieve his loss later, perhaps with a child to support on her own. He made love to her fiercely, understanding it would be the last time. Had to be the last time. He would take the memory of the last two weeks with him — the time he had spent with Sarah at home curled up in front of the TV, preparing meals together, even the joy of shopping for those meals hand in hand. The time spent with Sarah and Emily, after the last game. The peace Sarah had given him, unknowingly, and also the time they had spent joined together in bed. That he would remember the most, because Dylan knew that no one would ever compare to her in terms of sensuality, sexiness and readiness to please him.

Pain was already lashing at him, already threatening to tear him apart, but Dylan held it at bay. He made love to Sarah for the last time, felt her fingernails cutting into the skin on his backside. When he felt that she was nearing her climax, he upped the pace of his deep strokes, trying to set into his memory this last poignant time together. He heard her gasp and cry as her orgasm swelled and peaked, felt her tense beneath him as she rode it to completion, and still he thrust into her until finally he couldn't hold back his own release any longer. His orgasm was a mix of both pure ecstasy and hell for what he now had to do.

Every time Dylan made love to her, it was better than the time before. This time was no exception.

Sarah could sense the change in him, the way he loved her, the passion and intent in every hard thrust of his rigid shaft. She believed beyond a shadow of a doubt that Dylan Mackenzie loved her, as he had said. She rode her orgasm with such happiness and completeness that she now floated in a haze of contentment, one she'd never experienced before. Could this be it? Had they just turned a corner in their relationship? Could she have found a person to believe in, one who would stay with her forever?

When Dylan rolled his body off her, stretched his long legs over the side of the bed and stood, Sarah thought he was just disposing of the used condom. She didn't even open her eyes, expecting him to rejoin her so she could snuggle in next to his body and drift off to sleep.

Hearing the rustle of clothing, not feeling the dip of the bed as she had been expecting, made her open her eyes. Dylan had dragged on his jeans and was in the midst of pulling a jumper over his head.

"What ya doing, sexy?" she whispered drowsily. "I want to go to sleep in your arms. Come back to bed."

Sarah waited a few moments, wondering what was taking Dylan so long, then finally, as if a light bulb had come on in her head, she became aware of the situation. It was in his eyes. Dylan was leaving.

Just waiting to say the words to her.

Sarah had failed. There was no magic corner — she hadn't managed to break through and discover Dylan's fear, what fuelled his anxiety. She'd had enough trouble getting him to talk about anything more meaningful than what he wanted to watch on TV or felt like for dinner, let alone the reason or events that had led him to the belief that he didn't deserve to be happy. Meeting his mates, going to the base… None of it had meant anything.

She didn't move, couldn't move. She was frozen, waiting and yet despising that she had to hear the words he was so close to saying. She didn't want to hear them, wished he wouldn't do this to them.

To no avail.

"Sarah, I have to go. I can't do this anymore — pretend that everything will work out. I'm a soldier. I can't have the pressure of knowing I'm leaving someone at home next time I'm deployed. I've seen how much it tears others apart. I don't want that for you. I've got to report back soon anyway — I'm being stationed in Darwin, awaiting further orders. That's what today's meeting was all about. I'm sorry. I wish it could be different…*I* could be different."

Sarah felt the exact moment her heart broke. The jagged pain was so intense, the rip so profound that she placed her hands on her chest just to make sure it hadn't torn open. The pain was so intense, so all-consuming that she could not take a breath. Perhaps she did not want to.

He was gone before she could manage to force air back into her lungs. Before she could throw herself at his feet and beg for him to give them another chance. Beg him to try to change. Tell him that she loved him, didn't think she would survive without him. But she had no chance to do any of those things — to plead and grovel with no thought for her pride — because Dylan had gone.

The sound of her front door closing was a death knell in her ears.

His words echoed in her head, bounced around inflicting wound after wound. The 'I can'ts' and the 'I won'ts'. It was all about him. *His* pain, *his* fear, *his* decision, yet she was left with her heart splintered, her soul destroyed. She should have known better. *But I love him.*

Her wail was so distraught—the sobs that racked her body so filled with grief that she thought she would never regain control of her emotions. The despair she felt sucked all the light from the room, and Sarah was afraid it would never return.

Chapter Seventeen

JetsRugbyLeague: Good to see the pups holding strong at the top of the table, another win this week will cement that position! #jetsminorpremiers #finals

Being around the under twenty-ones Jets players— her pups—was a balm to Sarah's damaged soul. The guys, perceptive of her grief and aware of her time with Dylan, of her happiness when she had been with him, tried hard to lift her spirits. Joseph tried the hardest, fussing over her like a mother hen. If she hadn't been so destroyed she would have found it amusing.

But nothing could ease her pain completely. The first time Sarah saw Gareth, he asked her what Dyl was up to and she was too upset to speak.

"Oh, God, Sarah, what's that fuckwit of a brother-in-law done this time?"

It took all of her concentration and control to eke out the simple words. "He's gone."

"Sarah…I'm so sorry. What can I do, sweetheart? Let me call Em, get her to talk with you. Maybe she can help you. If nothing else, I know she wouldn't want you to be so upset — she'd want to be here for you."

Gareth's comforting embrace was too much, and Sarah broke down again. The promises she had made to herself to shed no more tears over Dylan flew out of the window as she poured out her grief on Gareth's shoulder, while he fumbled with his phone.

"Emily, I need you to come down to the Jets ground, honey... No, babe, it's nothing about me. Sarah needs a friend, Em. Dyl's gone again."

Gareth said "Yeah" a few more times before he ended the call. He put his phone in his pocket as he led her towards a chair. She wanted to stop crying, to man up and deal with the fact that Dylan had left. They'd only been together for two weeks. It just wasn't feasible that she should be so devastated by his departure. But none of that wisdom helped. Sarah cried in Gareth's arms until she felt the gentler touch of Emily's hand on her shoulder.

"C'mon, Sarah, I'm taking you home with me," Emily told her as she helped her to her feet.

Sarah was so tired that she let Emily lead her away. She could not have made a rational decision at that moment to save her life. Irrationally, she did notice for the first time how much Emily looked like Dylan. Her colouring, her eyes — not a surprise, really, considering they were brother and sister.

"You and Dylan look a lot alike," Sarah said, her voice hoarse and croaky, most likely from all the sobbing.

"Sweetie, don't hold that against me. My brother has a lot of baggage and it seems not much of a heart, either. You're coming home with me for a while, Sarah. We can talk or not, I can pass you tissues, give you hugs, make you cups of tea. Maybe when you feel stronger we can go for a ride. Being on a horse does something for a bruised heart. I know — I spent a lot of time riding back in the day."

Emily was talking about the problems she and Gareth had had a few years ago. Sarah had heard some talk of what had happened, how Emily had pushed Gareth away because of some thought she'd had about her facial burns — a result of the bushfire she'd been caught in — making her look like a monster, and Gareth deserving a woman that was not damaged, or some such ridiculous notion. Gareth and Emily were so much in love and meant to be together, it was glaringly obvious.

* * * *

After settling Sarah down on a comfy chair in her living room, a cup of tea placed on the table beside her, Emily began to explain some of the pain that had caused Dylan to become so distant. Sarah wasn't sure she was ready for an emotion-deep and meaningful conversation with Dylan's sister, but Emily was being so supportive she couldn't really tell her to stop.

"Dylan had arrived home late. He'd promised our mother he would be home straight from school to help her with a few chores, but as usual Dylan had been out mucking around with his mates. It was awful for him, Sarah — he was the first to discover Mum. She was lying on the kitchen floor. The doctors later explained that it was a brain aneurism that took her from us," Emily told Sarah. "But Dylan blamed himself for not getting to her in time. It didn't matter that the doctors also told us that even if Mum had been in an operating room full of surgeons, the chances were she would have died. Dylan just wouldn't accept it. Could not accept that someone he loved had been taken from him."

"Oh, my God, Emily, how horrible for you all," Sarah replied, her tears flowing down her cheeks as she tried to imagine the heartbreak Dylan and Emily had faced.

"But I think there's more to it," Emily continued, her voice masking none of her pain and sorrow from Sarah. "He couldn't understand how Dad and I kept going. How we could stay on the farm and keep working. I miss Mum every day, but I had to keep going for Dad's sake as well as my own. Mum loved living on the farm, in our house, and I needed the memories of her around me. Dylan didn't. He wanted to shut them away. It was a double blow for Dad when Dylan signed up for the army. It was always assumed that he would take over the running of the place one day. My father lost his wife *and* his son when my mother died."

Sarah didn't know what to say to Emily. The Mackenzie family had had to deal with so much grief.

"Then you had to deal with the bushfire and Mr Mackenzie's accident. Oh, Emily, you really have had it hard over the past few years," Sarah added. Her words felt so inadequate, but she didn't know what else to say. "So Dylan didn't come back at all?"

"A few times over the years, but it was always uncomfortable for everyone. We—Dad and I—knew he hated being in the house, and certainly wouldn't speak of Mum or anything to do with that day. He wouldn't even go into the kitchen. So we sort of just let him go... But I still can't believe he didn't tell us when he was injured."

"And now he's left again," Sarah added sadly.

"Yes, it does look that way, doesn't it?" Emily replied with a sigh. "It seems to be Dylan's usual modus operandi these days. I'm so sorry he did this to you too, Sarah. I really don't know what is going on in that thick head of his, turning on all the people that care for him. I know you're not going to want to hear me say it, but I think you're too good for Dylan right now. You deserve much better than him, honey. Until he sorts himself out he's no good to anyone. I just hope that he does come to his senses soon, because at the rate he's going, I worry my brother will wake up one day and find he's old and all alone."

It hurt Sarah to hear Emily's words. She didn't want to think of Dylan alone—she wanted to be the one who Dylan stuck around for, as naïve as that thought might have been after such a short time together. "I think Dylan and I have a lot more in common than he thinks. Loneliness is something I understand only too well," she said, reaching for another tissue to soak up her tears.

* * * *

Speaking with Emily had been of some comfort to Sarah and over the next few days the women became even closer. In fact, Sarah could easily say that her friendship with Emily was the closest she'd ever come to having a best friend.

As the days and weeks passed, Sarah worked through her pain, focused on her work and tried to forget about Dylan Mackenzie and all the baggage he carried that had ultimately killed off any chance of them ever being a couple. She still chided herself that she'd even held the belief that she and Dylan could have a relationship.

JetsRugbyLeague: Hey, Jets fans! Introducing our new media guy @RileyW_jetsmedia. Please make him welcome & congratulate him on his new position!

The Jets first-grade team's season had been filled with ups and downs. There had been an equal number of wins and losses over the last few games of the season, but the Jets looked to be heading towards the finals series. The buzz around the club and its supporter fan base was also helping Sarah move on. Twitter was busier than ever, with the Jets trending locally most days, and the Facebook fan page was bursting with friends. Talk was mostly positive, and Sarah was happy to be part of it. Brodie and the Jets' board had appointed another media manager—after offering the position full-time to Sarah, which she had declined—Caitlin James' brother, Riley.

Riley had a degree in sports management behind him that made him more than suitable for the job. There could have been a hint of nepotism in the appointment, but 'Who cares?' was Sarah's take on the matter. She found Riley Walters to be very professional and easy to work with, and he certainly loved the Jets club. That was obvious just in the way he happily bounced around the workplace, a smile always on his face.

Emily and Gareth had offered a few times to update her on Dylan's life, but Sarah had decided it was best not to know. A clean break. That didn't stop her from missing him, though, especially at night, alone in her bed. It also didn't stop her from wearing, from time to time, one of the shirts Dylan had left behind at her place. Dylan Mackenzie might have only touched Sarah's life for a short time, but she would not easily forget the memories he'd given her. Sarah wondered if she would ever get past it. Emptiness settled inside her, a dark hole that was a constant reminder of what she had lost.

Chapter Eighteen

Going to visit the farm, and his father, had not been as bad as Dylan had expected. His guilt about not being around when his father had been injured had been lessened as soon as Daniel 'Mac' Mackenzie had wrapped his big arms around his son. Mac was not one to hide his true feelings, forever hugging his children, showing them his love. Dylan still wondered how his father could continually open up his heart the way he did, after enduring so much sorrow. He had lost his wife, Dylan's mum, so suddenly, then Dylan had abandoned them and Emily had gone through her bushfire ordeal — not to mention he had nearly died from his own tractor accident... It was amazing that Mac was still so full of life and ready to take on all it had to offer him. Farming was a hard way to grind out a living, with so many variables ready to pull the rug out from under you — drought, flood, bushfire, failed crops and stock disease, just to name a few. Dylan's dad had just taken them all head on and dealt with them as best he could.

He was what was known as a 'glass half full' kind of guy — and if ever Dylan needed his father's support, it was now.

"Dad, I think I've made a huge mistake. Actually, heaps of 'em."

Dylan and Mac were taking an early morning ride around the farm when Dylan decided to seek his father's advice. As was usually the case with Mac, he took his time to acknowledge Dylan's statement.

"Well, son, the fact that you can identify that you may have made a mistake means you are aware of what needs to be fixed." Mac's voice was calm. He sounded just like the country-born farmer he was, his words spoken slowly — no need to rush through them, there was plenty of time in the day to get the sentence out there. As kids, Emily and Dylan had cracked up every time Mac had used words like 'crikey' and 'fair-dinkum' in his day-to-day speech. It was such old-country Aussie slang.

"That's the problem, Dad. I'm not sure I can fix them. Not sure if I can fix myself enough, to begin with." Dylan realised that he sounded melodramatic, cringed as he spoke the defeatist words. He pulled his horse to a stop gently and dismounted. It had been a long time since Dylan had appreciated the beauty of the Australian countryside — the tall, lean gum trees gently blowing in the wind, filling the air with the scent of eucalyptus, the native plants and grasses struggling to survive the harsh climates, growing unevenly across the land.

"Son, you have to let it go, mate. There was nothing you could have done. She wouldn't have wanted you to beat yourself up over it. Your mother loved you, would want you to be happy. I've wanted to have a go at you about it for ages, but I hoped you'd come 'round. I understand that the house has bad memories for ya, but for me it reminds me of everything I loved about ya mother. She loved this farm, you kids, and she loved me. I'm forever grateful for her love, if a little surprised that I was that lucky. Did I ever tell you how we met?"

Dylan had heard the story before. As a youngster, he had rolled his eyes when his father had started on again with the tale, but this time Dylan was glad to hear it. To see the happiness on his father's face, the brightness in Mac's eyes as he retold his love-at-first-sight tale of the day Mac and Sally had met.

"It was Anzac Day. Me and a few mates had gone into town to play a few games of two-up at the local pub. As you know, son, two-up's illegal on any other day of the year, but Anzac Day, the constabulary turn a blind eye as a way for ya to celebrate the good old Aussie digger spirit. The place was pretty crowded. People circled around the 'spinner', betting on which way the two coins he tossed in the air would land, tails up or heads or one of each. I'd been on a lucky streak that day, more wins than losses.

"As I headed to the bloke that I'd bet against — hand out, ready to collect my win — another hand, one more delicate-looking, nearly beat me to the cash. As her hand reached for the dollar notes my hand covered it. Well, bugger me dead, son, if I'd hadn't known it was a bright, sunny day outside I would have thought I'd been hit by a bolt of lightning. Just the touch of her skin under my own had enough power to stop me dead in my tracks. Our eyes met, and hers were the biggest brown eyes I'd ever seen, eyelashes long and batting back at me. Her painted red lips were set in a cute little pout. It was then I knew I'd met the woman I wanted to spend my life with.

"Of course, we had a little dispute over who'd won the cash. You have to remember, Dylan, things were different back in the old days. Women weren't even supposed to be in the public bar. They had the ladies' parlour or lounge to sit in and sip a sherry or lemon squash. But your mother was having none of that discrimination, loved a bet, so had snuck into the public bar. In the end I offered to use the winnings to buy us both a beer. Classy, right, mate, offer your mother a beer? But she was a beaut, sport, and the rest, as they say, is history. I courted her, took her to the movies and dance halls, and finally she agreed to marry me.

"Money was always tight but your mother stood by me, next to me through all the tough times and the good. We were a team, and I'm a better man for it, Dylan. I never placed another bet after that day, figured I'd used up my portion of luck on finding Sal. The love of a good woman is what gives you strength, and even if she's gone to heaven now, her love is still living strong in my heart. Having you and Emily was the greatest gift she could have given me, a part of us both. You need to live your life as if she were here to be part of it, make her proud, Dylan. Live and love the way she did, the way she'd want you to. Sally and I looked forward to grandkids, spoiling them, watching them grow and give you and Emily grief, just like the kind of mischief-making you both put us through. We used to laugh that it would be our sweet revenge. Don't let that dream disappear. It'd break your mother's heart. Mine too."

Mac was a talker, loved to tell a tale about the good old days, Dylan knew that, but this time the words had been so profound that they'd brought him close to tears. There was a lump lodged in his throat that threatened to choke off his air supply. Dylan had never looked at it from this angle. He'd been so quick to bury his memories, shut himself off from any kind of relationship or connection that could bring the kind of emotional turmoil he had felt with his mother's passing. That desolation and deep sorrow at having his heart savagely torn from his chest over the loss of someone he had needed, loved beyond all control—he'd never once thought he would bring it all down on himself.

Dylan understood now that he could not protect himself from loving. He did love his father and sister and distancing himself from them had not helped in any way—it had made it worse. Now he also carried a truckload of guilt. Of course he would have been devastated if his father had not survived the tractor accident—it mattered little how much time or space he'd put between them. He would have been unable to stop his own grief at such a loss just as he had been unable to foresee the IED that had caused so much destruction and harm to his unit.

The sheer lunacy of trying to protect his own heart could have now cost him the special kind of connection that people spent a lifetime trying to find. Like the love between his parents that even death had not diminished, or the love shared by Emily and Gareth. A love that made you stronger, gave you the courage to build dreams and the tenacity to achieve them.

His dad was right, though—if she had still been alive, his mother would have kicked his butt by now, told him to stop sulking and cowboy up. He had been blessed with the most caring, loving parents a child could want. Dylan's childhood had been filled with happy, carefree days and good memories that both his mother and his father had orchestrated. They had always been there for him, and he needed to step up and deal with his grief. It was time to stop blaming everyone—himself for what had happened, and his father and sister for continuing to live on the farm. No one could have helped Sally Mackenzie the day she'd died. His father was still alive, and Dylan needed to start returning the unconditional love and support his father was still showing him, even after the way Dylan had treated him recently.

When Mac had mentioned the way touching his mum had felt like being struck by lightning, an image of Sarah had sprung to Dylan's mind. The memory of her hand on his arm, out there on the footy field. How he had felt that same sensation—one that had nearly knocked him off his feet. God, he missed her—Sarah. Missed her with every fibre of his being. The sound of her laughter, the way her eyebrows drew together and she chewed on the ring through her lip when she was concentrating, focused on some keyboard—be it computer, iPad or phone—as she clicked away. Her fingers flashing at the speed of light as she posted some thought or titbit of information to her masses of followers. He had signed up with Twitter just to follow her, read her tweets about the Jets just so he could feel some connection to her.

Dylan also missed her body, the way it felt under his. The way he felt inside her, buried balls-deep in her warmth. The way her nails scraped his skin as he brought her pleasure. The memory of her lips on his, or wrapped around his cock, had given him many a sleepless night. He wanted to hear again the little murmurs of contentment she made just before she curled into him and drifted off to sleep. The fact was he hadn't slept properly since he'd left Sarah. It was obvious that the petite, flaming redhead had found a place deep inside his heart, no matter how hard Dylan had tried to fight it.

He had some serious decisions to make about his future. Being back on the family land, acknowledging the beauty of the place, the open spaces and clean air, was starting to tempt him not to re-up with the army. The idea of working beside his father, working the land and with the cattle, being on horseback... Dylan realised he had missed it after all, deep down in his soul. His superiors had known—probably why they had ordered him home. He belonged here. It was in his blood. He had been hiding in the army, hiding his true self behind the uniform and regulations that had stopped him from thinking or being who he was. What he was. Just the idea of another tour in Afghanistan made him shudder—at having to deal with the constant threat of danger that he knew to be only too real. He had the scars to prove it, had got them in the heat and the dust of the desert battlefield. Maybe it was time to call it quits. He had done his duty for the country he loved—it was time to get back to living his life, making a future for himself. And hopefully he could persuade Sarah to forgive him and become part of that future.

Dylan was so caught up in his own thoughts that he forgot all about his father, standing there in front of him, until he heard Mac's deep voice and the remorse in his father's tone.

"Son, are you okay? I'm sorry, Dyl, you're a grown man—I shouldn't be tellin' ya how to live your life. It's not my place. Just...I needed to get it off my chest, and there's something about you now, son, whereas before when you came home you had this wall up between us, like you were angry at me and didn't want to be here, itching to pack up your kit the minute you'd unpacked it. Yet this time... I don't know how to explain it, all this emotional mumbo-jumbo..." Mac scratched at the stubble on his chin with his leathery, work-worn fingers, as he struggled to find the right words. "You seem, I dunno, sad—plain, downright miserable would be my guess. Is it something I can help you with, son?"

If only his father knew how much he'd needed that sermon, Dylan thought, amused that his father felt the need to apologise for stating the bleeding obvious. *I've been such an idiot*, Dylan thought.

"Dad, you're wrong. If it isn't your place to give me a kick in the pants when I get it wrong, then I can't think of anyone else who comes close to that. You are, and have always been, the best man I've ever known. I'm sorry for acting like such a self-pitying fool. I love you, Dad."

"And I love you too, son. I'm glad to hear you're not too old to listen to some advice every now and again from your old man. Sometimes a nudge in the right direction is all a reasonable man needs... So, can I assume it's some filly who has broken through the fenced corral you set up around your heart?"

Just like his old man to put it in those words and be spot on at the same time. Dylan mused. 'Corral around his heart'—yep, that was pretty much what he had done, built a fence so high, added a barren field of emptiness around his emotions, for his own protection, that had been impossible for anyone to breach. Up till now.

"'Filly'... That's an interesting way to describe Sarah Flynn." Dylan laughed, thinking about how his dad would react to seeing Sarah—her bright hair and her piercings—for the first time. Not a lot of people looked like that around Gunnedah, he was sure. The look on Mac's face would be a sight worth seeing. "Dunno, Dad, think I may have blown that one. Using an analogy to suit, I'd say it's too late to shut the barn gate—the horse has bolted."

"Now, son, if she's worth having, she's worth fighting for... Right back at ya with the sayings, kiddo." Mac's face held a broad grin as he grabbed Dylan.

Mac gave the best hugs. Dylan had always compared it to being hugged by a big bear, not that he'd ever had the experience. But Mac was so large-limbed and strong that even now, though Dylan stood probably a head taller, he still worried that his ribs would be broken.

"Go easy on the ribs, Dad! Geez, even as old as you are, you still got the strength of a bull." Dylan groaned.

"Enough of the old talk, son. Reckon I can still leave you in my dust. Race you back home—loser makes lunch." Mac didn't wait for Dylan to answer. He put a foot in the stirrup, threw a leg over his horse with unbelievable agility for a man his age and took off at a full gallop.

Dylan was happy to lose and make lunch. Seeing his dad in such good shape again after that accident was reward enough. He grabbed the reins of his own mare and mounted. Turning the horse for home, Dylan happily followed in his father's dust.

* * * *

Dylan made good on the bet, rustling up some Vegemite sandwiches for lunch. Nothing said 'Australian' like a good ol' Vegemite 'sanga'. When he'd been deployed overseas, the taste of it had always reminded Dylan of home, and there had always been the bonus of watching a Yank give it a go. That black, yeast-based spread nearly always made them puke—probably not helped by the fact that no one had bothered to tell the unsuspecting victim that you only used a smear and didn't slather it on like jam.

"Dad, what do you say about me moving back home, giving you a hand to run this place?" Dylan was a little uneasy about his father's reply. Wasn't sure what Mac had already arranged with Emily. Gareth would retire from footy one day—maybe Mac had already promised Emily the farm. After all, Dylan had once made it only too clear that he wasn't interested in taking over the reins...so to speak.

"Well, Dylan, what did you think I'd say?" Mac stood up, took two strides around the kitchen table, then dragged Dylan to his feet before embracing him and delivering a hearty thump of his palm to Dylan's back. "I'd say welcome bloody home, son—welcome bloody home."

Chapter Nineteen

Waking up early had never been a problem for Dylan. It was probably the fact that he'd been doing it all his life. It had never caused him any grief in the army, and he'd never made a song or dance about it. Other guys had grumbled and groaned every morning, but Dylan had just got on with his day. The last few weeks had given him an even greater incentive to get up, and the Australian countryside was a sight worth waking up for—nearly as good as waking up beside Sarah.

Temperatures were low and frosty, and his exhaled breath came out like little bursts of fog into the clean, fresh air. Dylan loved it all. The icy twinkle on the fields, grasses and newly sown crops, the sounds of the kookaburras laughing and the birds chirping... It was soul-cleansing. Gangs of kangaroos jumped across the open spaces, looking for a place to spend their day. The dawn's early light had caused a flurry of activity from the local wildlife.

Dylan revelled in the manual aspects of farming—feeding the cattle, fixing the fences, grooming the horses, and sowing the wheat had never felt so good. It was honest work that left him tired but satisfied at the end of the day. Working beside Mac, enjoying the man's company as an adult, an equal, was an experience Dylan would forever cherish. He had missed so much, and now he had made the decision to stay it was turning out to be the best move he'd made in a very long time. The army had accepted his decision to leave and had honourably discharged him, effective immediately.

He was still having nightmares—just this morning he had woken covered in sweat, the ringing in his ears just as real as on the day of the blast. Realising that he was safe in his boyhood room had helped ease Dylan's anxiety, but the graphic dream was still fresh in his mind, as if he had only just lived it.

The nightmare had begun like many of the others— Dylan finding himself face down in the dirt, not able to see through the haze of dust, unsure of what had occurred. The pain of his injuries had brought with it the knowledge of what had happened, as had the muffled sounds of his buddies moaning—just a whisper in his ears almost drowned out by the ringing sensation from the explosion. As he had in every vivid dream, Dylan had managed to painfully drag his body up from the hard ground and begin a frantic search for the source of the agonised groans, nearly stumbling onto the body of one soldier in the blinding dust storm the bomb had created.

Over and over, Dylan had dragged the bodies of the four soldiers who had been with him in the transport to the side of the road, and away from the torn-apart metal that had once been their vehicle. The driver's mangled remains had been the hardest to move—the sight of his mate's head, blown apart, had nearly caused Dylan to vomit. Terror of the unknown, of what could be hiding in amongst the dust and debris around him and the possibility that with each step he took he could inadvertently trigger another landmine, was very real. He didn't know when, or if, help would arrive before the insurgents came to finish the job they had started.

Only the insurmountable relief at finding himself safe and at home, and not back in amongst that horror, had stopped Dylan's heart from trying to thump through his chest. But it never changed the raw knowledge that one of his friends had been lost to him that day, while the others had suffered long-term injuries, just as he had. Dylan wondered if he would ever stop reliving that horrendous moment over and over in his sleep, but was thankful that the nightmares did appear to be lessening as time went by.

He thought it could be the combination of knowing he would not be going back into the field and the relaxing solitude of being on the farm that had helped with their frequency. The time spent in the peace and quiet of the farm gave a man a chance to evaluate things, deal with them and put them into perspective, without the burden of watching every damn step he took for fear of being blown to bits. He was finding that he was re-evaluating his priorities and he liked the new him. There was only one thing still missing in Dylan's life—Sarah.

Did he have a chance of winning back her heart? Dylan was sure she had loved him, but had he destroyed that love? It had been a month since he'd left Sarah and the army behind. The reasons for not having a relationship with her were diminishing fast. If he wasn't going back to the army then there would be no chance that he would make her a widow, or even leave her alone for lengths at a time. Could he offer her enough, being here in Gunnedah, though? What would Sarah do? Was it a lifestyle change she was prepared to make?

He'd tossed around a few ideas of what he could do in the city, run them past Mac for his input. If Sarah couldn't come to terms with living out here, he was prepared to move to Sydney for her. It was just that Dylan had fallen in love with home again. It would be a shame to leave so soon. He could now walk into the kitchen and not imagine his mother lying on the floor. He could sit on the sofa and look at the family photos adorning the wall without his chest feeling tight and heavy, his heart turning to stone. There was only one thing to do—Dylan had to go and talk to Sarah. See if there was any chance for them.

"Dyl, you do have family down there in the big smoke," Mac said one night as Dylan and he were eating dinner. "Give your sister a call, ask her advice. After all, she is a woman—maybe she can give you an idea of what's what. You did say she and your Sarah are friends. In my experience, limited as it may be, women talk to each other about stuff like this."

Dylan loved the fact that his father had said 'your Sarah'. How he wished that were true. Talking to Emily was a good idea—in fact, a trip to Sydney to visit with his dear sister and favourite brother-in-law might be just the excuse he needed to see Sarah again.

"Dad, you're a genius. I don't know how I managed to get by without you for so long. Reckon you can handle things around here on your own for a bit?"

"Think I may be able to struggle through, son." Mac laughed as he enveloped Dylan in another rib-crunching, fatherly maul.

Chapter Twenty

Something was up, she could tell. Emily was being all cagey around her, which was just not like her. Sarah was terrified that Emily was pulling away from her, growing tired of her. It also crossed her mind that something had happened to Dylan, but she was determined not to ask. If it was bad news it would only make her more upset, and if it was news that he had a woman in his life, that would be worse. *Better to stay in the dark,* she told herself, over and over. It was probably just a case of her not being enough to keep people around — as was the story of her life, she decided quite miserably.

Luckily for Sarah, her working life was keeping her busy. Both Jets teams had won their first round of semi-finals. While the ruling body of rugby league had taken over most of the arrangements for each game day from now to the grand final, Sarah and the other members of the Jets' media team were still kept busy co-ordinating all the extra attention the players were receiving, as well as keeping the fans involved and up to date. There was also planning for the after-match celebrations or commiserations, depending on the outcomes of the games played.

Twitter and Facebook were a flurry of excited tweets and messages. The Jets had run a few competitions giving away ticket packages to the games, and a fan day had been organised at the Jets' training ground as a way for the players to thank everyone for their support.

Tension was high throughout the club—players just wanting to get on the field and on with the job at hand, coaches trying to decide who to play and what players they would ultimately have to disappoint when a spot could not be found for them. Brodie James was in the unusual position, at this stage of the season, to have a full complement of players to choose from, with no one injured.

Joseph Ondio, while not finding a place in the first team, had been given the captaincy of the under twenty-ones. Sarah was so pleased for the young man. He had come such a long way since those ugly days when he had found himself the negative headline of many Sydney newspapers, owing to his excessive drinking and brawling around the nightclubs and general anti-social behaviour.

* * * *

So many fans had turned up to the fan day that Sarah had been required to help keep the crowd from becoming impatient as they joined and waited in long queues for a chance of an autograph or photo with a Jets player. She was handing out stickers, photos and banners, as well as stopping to chat with the fans who recognised her as the social media girl. The mood really was infectious—Sarah was filled with nerves and excitement right alongside the fans. It had been rumoured that Rook Harris might retire if the Jets got to the grand final, and the fans all wanted her opinion on that.

She was so caught up in the moment, making the most of the happy and optimistic atmosphere around her, that she didn't see Dylan arrive. That was, until she felt him standing behind her, her body recognising him at once, eagerly responding to his scent and heat. The sheer force of the lust that gripped Sarah caught her completely off guard.

Panic. That was the second emotion that hit. She couldn't face him yet. Hadn't hardened her heart anywhere near enough to pretend that everything was okay. That she didn't miss Dylan with every molecule of her body and mind. Dissolving into tears in front of all these people was not something Sarah wanted to do. She refused to turn around, frantically searching for an excuse to stop what she was doing and flee.

As if by magic, Joseph Ondio appeared. He reached for her through the line of fans, and taking her hand, pulled her through to the other side.

Dylan's heat and smell might have been lost to her, absorbed by the crowd now between them, but not the fevered lust that had overridden every ounce of common sense Sarah possessed. No, that had dominated her, leaving her shaking, desperate to reach out and touch him. She just wanted to feel his body against her own, bringing her the pleasure and relief that only he could deliver. Enjoy the satisfaction, the sexual connection that she had been missing. How could her body be overriding her brain this way? This man had caused her pain. She should not be feeling lust or any other emotion for him — except maybe anger.

"C'mon, Digi, let's get you away from that dickhead. What a nerve, turning up here like that. You didn't have a clue he was coming, did ya?" Joseph's voice held both anger and sympathy—the last thing Sarah needed to hear, as the memory of Joseph's threats against Dylan surfaced.

"It's okay, Joseph, it just took me by surprise. Thanks for getting me out of there. But you have to let me handle this myself. I'm a big girl, Joey, and I don't want you getting into any trouble on my behalf. Promise me. I'm so excited for you and proud that you got the captain position. Don't do anything to jeopardise that. Honestly, Dylan Mackenzie isn't worth the trouble."

Saying the words caused another stab of pain to her heart—she was lying to herself and Joseph. She would do anything to be given a second chance with Dylan, despite all her words to the contrary and the amount of time she'd spent trying to convince herself that she still had self-respect where he was concerned. The fact was Sarah ached to feel his arms around her, his lips on hers just one more time. It was torture knowing he was just on the other side of the queue of people, so close…but she needed to be strong, push away those sexual responses.

That's all it was, right? Lust, 'cause you haven't had sex since he left, she tried convincing herself. This was not the time or the place to hold any kind of reunion with the man who had destroyed her heart. *Even if he appears to still own it*, her subconscious' voice added unhelpfully.

Chapter Twenty-One

Well, that hadn't gone quite the way Dylan had imagined. When Emily and Gareth had talked about the fan day, Dylan had thought it would be a good place to catch up with Sarah, thought she wouldn't be all that busy and would have spare time for him to start the grovelling he had planned and rehearsed. Dylan had been prepared for much bowing and scraping and many apologies.

What he hadn't expected was for Sarah to ignore him. She had known he was there—he had seen it in the way her posture had changed. One second she had been laughing and joking around with the fans, the next her relaxed stance had become more rigid, tension rolling off her in waves. Then she had disappeared before his very eyes, swallowed by the swarm of fans in front of her.

Dylan's own response to Sarah had been powerful. He had all but convinced himself that he had over-fantasised the effect being around her had on him, played it up in his imagination to be more than it really was—but he had been wrong. Just standing behind her had awakened a desire for her so deep that it had taken all his control not to reach out and pull her body to his own. The time it had taken him to compose his wildly beating heart and demanding libido had given Sarah the chance to escape.

Dylan had searched for her over the heads in front of him, only to see her standing with her back to him, deep in conversation with the same Polynesian guy she'd been chatting with the first night Dylan had met her. And the guy was giving Dylan death stares. The guy held his chin out and up a little, all the while glaring at Dylan with that 'I'm going to tear off your head and feed it to you' look.

It was going to take more than grovelling to win Sarah back, Dylan realised. It looked as though it was also going to cause him some physical pain. He was prepared to accept whatever it took, even if it was not fighting back while the oversized teenager tried to rip his head off. Maybe he should check with Gareth first, though, how well Sarah's protective friend could fight. Dylan did want to live, after all.

Getting the chance to have a conversation with Gareth would be impossible. The queue in front of Dylan's brother–in–law wasn't getting any shorter. Just when Dylan was about to give up and go in search of Sarah, he caught sight of Rook Harris, noticed that Rook was beckoning him over. Dylan jumped at the chance—if he couldn't ask Gareth about the big Polynesian, then he would ask Rook.

"Hey, Rook. Quite a turnout today, the place is buzzing," Dylan said as he approached the Jets captain, trying to look calm and composed—completely the opposite of how he actually felt.

"Our fans are the best in the competition," Rook replied loudly, gaining a cheer from the crowd in response. "How ya been, Dyl? Wasn't expecting to see you 'round these parts, thought you would have shipped out again by now."

"Times change, Rook. I'm not serving anymore... Pulled the plug a few weeks ago, been back in Gunnedah with Dad."

"That right?" Rook put the pen he'd been holding down, his focus now solely on Dylan. "Well, you did your bit, mate. Glad to see you out in one piece — there's been some bad times over there lately, if you listen to the news. Too many deaths." Rook shook his head, showing his sorrow over the recent attacks on Aussie troops.

"It's true, but there's still work to do over there. I just wasn't up for it anymore. Had my mind on other things, wanted to try a different life," Dylan replied.

"So would this change of mind have anything to do with a certain redhead?"

So he and Sarah had been a source of gossip, then. Dylan shouldn't have been surprised — they had spent nearly all their time together before Dylan had stupidly run.

"Um...that's the crux of it, Rook. My only problem is that I may have realised a bit late that Sarah's the one for me. I acted like a dickhead, walking away from her — haven't even spoken to her since then. I was hoping for a chance to plead my case and throw myself at her feet to beg for mercy, but I don't think it's going to be that easy. That giant Polynesian guy that she hangs with just gave me a look that warned of significant consequences if I went near Sarah. Can you give me a heads-up on the guy? I didn't think they'd anything romantic going on, but he definitely is out to protect her... I probably deserve his wrath, but I would like to know if it's severe pain or death that I should be preparing for."

Rook chuckled, clearly amused by Dylan's predicament.

"That'd be Joseph Ondio, under twenty-ones captain. He's a good kid, had some trouble in his life, and I hate to tell ya, mate, but a lot of that strife was to do with brawling in nightclubs. I wouldn't want to be you if he really went at you. But I can't imagine Sarah would be down with him fighting... It'd cost him his captaincy. Just to be on the safe side I'd steer clear of him, though. The pups have got a training run in about thirty minutes... Maybe you should try your luck with Sarah then."

It was great advice and a timely hint that Dylan was grateful for. He didn't hesitate to show his thanks.

"Rook, you're a legend, mate. I'm going to get it right this time — if Sarah will let me, that is."

"Just as well, Mackenzie. If you hurt Sarah again, it won't be some hot-headed youngster out for your blood. It'll be me" — Rook looked Dylan straight in the eye as he made his threat — "and I got me some bloody big friends that I won't hesitate to call on to help."

Great, now I've got the threat of the whole bloody Jets team breathing down my neck if I blow it. But I'm not going to blow it a second time, so it's not a problem, Dylan told himself confidently as he headed for the Jets' offices, and his potential showdown with destiny.

He waited until he was sure that the Jets under twenty-ones had begun training — not that he was acting like a coward. He didn't want to cause Sarah any more drama. Getting into a fight with one of her friends and possibly causing that friend grief at the club would certainly not do him any favours where Sarah was concerned.

* * * *

Dylan walked the familiar route to Sarah's desk, having done it many times in that two weeks before he had abandoned her. She was sitting exactly where he had imagined she would be, but her head was down, resting on her arms as he approached. He stopped a few feet before her and after taking a steadying deep breath, Dylan stepped onto the path that hopefully, with Sarah's forgiveness, would ensure the future he so badly wanted.

"Sarah, can I talk to you, honey?" Dylan started off, his voice carrying all the uncertainty he was feeling. He waited for what seemed an eternity before Sarah moved. Dylan was starting to wonder whether she was sleeping and hadn't heard him, when finally she lifted her head. Her brown eyes, filled with anguish, bored a hole through his heart. *God, I've missed her* was Dylan's first thought. Then he noticed the dark shadows that lay beneath her eyes and cursed himself, convinced that he had been the cause. Second, Dylan noticed that Sarah was not wearing her nose ring—in fact, many of the metal adornments usually on her face were now absent.

"What do you want, Dylan?" Sarah asked.

Dylan thought her voice sounded weary, as though she was resigned to the knowledge that he was going to make her life more difficult. If Dylan had not been one hundred per cent convinced that he loved her enough to make things right for them—no matter what it took—and that he would love her forever, he would have turned and walked away immediately. That was how obviously the pain he had caused her was written on her features and in her posture. Dylan had the perverse notion that he should go and let every damn one of the Jets players take a swing at him to punish him for the damage he had done, the hurt he had caused. He would happily accept any pain just to have her in his life.

"You," he whispered, as the rollercoaster of emotions he was experiencing stole his voice.

"You had me once, and you walked away."

"It was the worst decision I've ever made, Sarah. I'm so very sorry. I was a coward, was scared to love you, give you the power to cause me pain—and yet I managed to bring about that pain all by myself, to you and to me. I'm willing to do anything to make up for it. Anything, if you'd just give me a chance to make it right, to show you how much you mean to me, how much I need you, how much I love you."

Dylan had thought that the worst thing he'd experienced had been dragging bodies from the bomb blast, not knowing if another was about to be triggered by his own foot or even the initial blast itself. But that paled in comparison to the fear that gripped his heart as Sarah's expression showed no hint of change, of her accepting his apology and letting him back into his life.

He needed a way to show Sarah that his words were true, that she was all he would ever need to live a long and happy life. Maybe in time she would begin to trust him, believe that he was going to be with her for the duration. But first she had to agree to let him try, and the longer it took for Sarah to say anything, the easier it got for Dylan to imagine the worst.

Chapter Twenty-Two

Her head was spinning, thoughts slamming through her mind one after another, confusing her. *Go to him, love him, give him a chance* — only to be overpowered by, *Don't do this to yourself, don't give him the power to hurt you again, send him away! He has too much pain and baggage. You're not strong enough* — *you only just managed to survive him last time.*

Then those negative responses were quickly replaced again with encouragement. *He said he loves you, needs you. Go to him, admit you are miserable without him. If you don't give him a chance you will regret it for the rest of your life.*

It was clear that Dylan was concerned, worried that she would send him away, from the grim way he held his lips together, his clenched jaw, the desperation in his eyes and the hand that he'd held out to her, imploring. It was that uncertainty, the fact that he appeared to understand that she was not about to fall at his feet and thank him for returning to her — even if that was a temptation she was doing her best to ignore — that gave her the courage. Confused and close to breaking point, Sarah finally managed to respond.

"I want so much to believe you, Dylan, but how can I? How can you say you need me or that you love me? You never opened up to me, shared any of your life with me. Nothing of significance, anyway. What has brought about this epiphany?"

"I think I knew from the moment I walked out of your room that I loved you, and no one else would replace you. But I couldn't make myself turn around. I had to face my own problems first. I was no good to either of us until I did. The stupid thing is that it really wasn't hard to do. I spent time with Dad, made peace with myself, really. If you let me, we can talk about it all. Let me explain why I acted like such a coward. The only thing that didn't change in all the soul searching was how I felt about you, Sarah. Now I have the courage to show you."

Her heart was thumping so hard in her chest, Sarah was sure Dylan would be able to hear it. The words he spoke and the emotion portrayed in them sounded genuine — or was that just Sarah's own hope clouding her interpretation? If she didn't give Dylan a chance Sarah knew she would live her life wondering what could have been. He had the power to really crush her, though. To give them a real chance at a future, Sarah would have to give herself to him wholly, and he to her in return. This would mean opening herself up for more heartbreak if it all turned out the same as it had before, and Dylan left her again. It didn't fill Sarah with confidence that, in her experience, the people who were supposed to love her had all, in the end, left or deserted her.

"I'd be lying to you if I said I didn't want to try, Dylan... But I'm scared, really scared to let you back into my heart, to let you close. I just don't know what to do." Sarah was close to tears, so torn between her wants and her fears. She wanted to throw her arms around Dylan and hang on for dear life, feel the warmth of his embrace as he hugged her in return, the press of his lips on hers…but her fear was paralysing.

"It's okay, Sarah. You have good reason to doubt me after how I've behaved. We can take this as slowly as you want. Knowing that you might want to try is enough… Even if it takes months or years to gain your trust again, I'll never stop trying. I'm here for you in whatever capacity you want."

"I need some time, Dylan. This isn't the place for this. I'm working. You shouldn't be here, I can't think with you standing so close. Later, yes. Later. We need to talk when I'm not at work, when I've had a chance to think about things more clearly. I wasn't expecting to see you today. No one said anything about you being here…"

"I know, honey, and I'm sorry if I've upset you even more by springing this on you, but I thought if you knew I was coming, you wouldn't see me. Hell, I probably don't deserve your forgiveness, but I had to try. Sarah, I never stopped thinking about you, so I made Em promise me she wouldn't say anything or warn you. I was desperate, honey, needed to see you, needed to witness your reaction to me being back and see if there was any hope for us."

Dylan had not moved any closer to Sarah, and she was thankful for that because deep down she knew the minute Dylan touched her she would be lost to her own desires for him—any rational thought she was struggling to cling to would evaporate. She could feel that her nipples had tightened into hard buds. Her pussy lips were swollen and wet just from hearing the sound of his voice. Her body wasn't hiding the fact that it wanted him. It was for that very reason Sarah understood she could not meet Dylan in private. If he wanted to talk and not pressure her — and she wanted that so very much, needed to know that he was genuine — they would have to meet somewhere public.

"Dinner… Can I take you for dinner, Sarah? It will give me a chance to explain, to talk to you. Can you do that for me, Sarah, come to dinner tonight?"

It was as if he had read her mind. Dinner — that would be public enough, but still give them privacy to talk. *I'll sit across from him, keep some space between us. That should help,* Sarah rationalised.

"I'll meet you at that little Italian restaurant in Ashfield, Mia's, at seven, and we will talk…but that's all, okay? I need to go slowly, Dylan. It's so busy round here at the moment I can't afford not to be on my game, or distracted by you right now."

Sarah had watched the relief show in Dylan's facial expression when she'd agreed to dinner — his jaw had relaxed a little, his eyes had brightened and he'd stopped running his fingers through his slightly longer hair. It suited him the way it was now. That reaction had changed, though, when she'd added that she couldn't afford to be distracted. That light had faded from his features as if she had flicked a switch and for a moment Sarah felt guilty, wanted to soothe Dylan's anxiety.

It's the truth — you can't afford to be worrying about anything but helping the Jets get through the next few weeks, that voice of reason piped up inside her head. *He deserves to feel a little anxiety. You know you're going to give in and forgive him, just make him sweat for a while, make him work for it. You're worth it.* Sarah was so shocked by the little pep talk that this mysterious new part of her consciousness had given her that she actually smiled.

"Seven it is, then. I'll book," Dylan replied quickly. "I'll let you get back to it then, honey…"

Even though he had said he was leaving, Dylan still hadn't moved. He just stood staring at her, and Sarah didn't know whether she should just pretend to do something on her computer or wait him out. It was unsettling—the longer he stood there the more she had to fight her body's instinct to move to him. As it was, she was hungrily eating up the sight of him, from his dirty cowboy boots up his long, jeans-clad legs, past that slight bulge in the front that reminded her how good it felt to hold his cock in her hands. She could picture it in her mind, remember the satiny feel of his shaft and the salty tang of his pre-cum on her tongue. Her mouth was watering from the memory.

Sarah dragged her eyes up away from the temptation and turned back to her monitor. Not that she could read anything displayed there—she was so feverish with need for Dylan that she couldn't think of anything.

Chapter Twenty-Three

Dinner was good. Hell, it was better than good, it was a fucking great place to start. Him and Sarah alone — well, alone at a table in a busy restaurant, but he would have her to himself. It would give him a chance to explain his feelings for her... *Yeah, I'm really an expert at that,* he thought grimly as he sat in his car, trying to recover from just being in the same room as Sarah. His cock was rock hard, threatening to burst the zipper on his pants. The once-over she had given him, especially the time it had taken Sarah to move on from staring at his groin, had not helped either. It was one of his favourite memories of Sarah — the way her eyes rounded and her pupils darkened just slightly when she was aroused. He knew that look, had rejoiced at being the man who could bring that reaction out in her, and he recognised the signs of her interest in him now as her gaze feasted on his body.

It was going to be the death of him, keeping that promise to go slow, but he would — even if he had to wank off ten times a day to keep his dick under control. He was not going to fuck this up. Sarah was his and he had to prove it to her. He had to prove to her that it wasn't just sex he wanted, it was the whole box and dice. White picket fence, kids—here in the city, back on the farm, it really didn't matter to Dylan anymore. Now that he'd seen Sarah again, all that mattered was having her by his side. *But in bed and underneath me soon would be good too,* he couldn't help thinking.

* * * *

During the whole journey home to his sister's, Dylan replayed the conversation between Sarah and him. Looked at it from every angle. Agonised over every word Sarah had spoken, every look she had given him. His mind was so full of all the *what-if*s and *but*s. Dylan was trying to predict the outcome of tonight and prepare himself in some way for the fact that it would affect the life he had been hoping to build. He was distracted, still going through it in his mind when he let himself in.

"So how did it go, mate?"

Gareth had scared Dylan half to death. He hadn't realised that his brother-in-law was home, hadn't even noticed Gareth's car out front.

"Well, Sarah agreed to have dinner with me tonight, so it's a good start," Dylan answered, then had the idea that Gareth might know more about this local Italian place Sarah had mentioned. "Do you know a place called Mia's, in Ashfield?"

"Course I do. Why you asking?"

Trust Gareth not to just answer a question directly. "It's where Sarah agreed to meet me. I think I should book. What do you reckon? Is it a busy place?" Dylan started to get agitated when Gareth began to laugh.

"What's so funny, mate? Am I missing something here?"

"Mia's is well known around the Jets. Quite a long history—goes way back. Brodie met Caitlin there, she was singing at a function he'd organised and he took her back there for their first date. JT and Mandy used to go there as well. Trevor and Laura had a first date, ended up being full of Jets guys that night. Trevor hardly got a word in all night, so the story goes. I think even Rook and Pippa have some sort of history with the place. It's been closed for a while. The original owner took ill, from what I hear. His son has just reopened. In fact, Em and I have been talking about trying it out. I think your sister would love a night out—my life has been so hectic with all this finals stuff, we could do with spending some time together."

"You wouldn't, Gareth, not tonight? Another night, maybe." Dylan was all but begging. The last thing he needed was to have Sarah invite his family to join them the same night he was preparing to bare his soul to her, talk about things that he'd never spoken of. Afghanistan, the bomb, his mother—he couldn't do it in front of them.

"No, I think tonight is exactly the right night, *mate*." The tone of Gareth's voice had changed quite dramatically, leaving Dylan in no doubt that Gareth had a problem with him.

"Spit it out, Gareth. What's got you so worked up, wanting to ruin my plans for Sarah tonight?" Dylan asked, equally pissed off.

"You hurt her again...and you won't be welcome back in my home, brother-in-law or not. Fuck you, Dylan—I don't even know whether you deserve her. I held her in my arms as she sobbed over you. She hurt for you for a long time. I think she's still hurting, just hiding it better. Did Em tell you she stayed here for a few days after you took off? What the hell's the matter with you, Dyl? You'd all but moved in with her—next thing you know, poof, you're gone. Just like the Dylan of old—when the going gets tough, Dylan Mackenzie fucks off, leaving everyone else to deal with it. But I'm warning you... No more, Dylan. No more pain for Emily, Mac or Sarah."

He deserved it—and more, probably—but it still angered him that Gareth was threatening him. Once upon a time it had been Dylan who'd ridden roughshod over Em and Gareth, bossing them around, being older. Times had changed, apparently. He now stood toe to toe, nose to nose with Gareth. Dylan hadn't even realised that Gareth had moved closer to confront him until now—he had been distracted by the disturbing image of Sarah so distraught that she'd had to be consoled by his own family. He was speechless, didn't know what to say as Gareth continued to eye him menacingly.

"You're not the only one with history here, Dylan. Do you even know anything about Sarah's past? Her life, what she's lived through, the pain she might carry? Nope, I bet you never even asked her about her life. No, Dylan, it's always been about *your* fear, hasn't it? Well, I'll be watching you. One wrong move and I'll sweep the floor with you. If Sarah wants nothing to do with you after tonight, you are going to accept her decision, 'cause I'm going to be standing in front of her making it happen. You clear on that, Soldier?"

"I'm not a soldier anymore." It was a ridiculous thing to say. Of all the things Dylan could have started off with, that was the most insignificant. He knew it, but the words had just blurted from his mouth before he'd been able to stop them. So many thoughts were going through Dylan's mind at the same time—he was thinking how good a man Gareth was to stick up for Sarah, but he was also worried about what it was in Sarah's past that had hurt her. On top of all that was the possibility Dylan now faced that he would have come to blows with Gareth—his friend, his sister's husband—over his own determination to win Sarah back, whatever it cost or however long it took. Not to mention the rest of the Jets rugby league club's players—Rook's threat was still fresh in his mind. All Dylan could do was prove to everyone that he was here for Sarah, for good. That she was his and he would spend a lifetime making sure she was never hurt again.

"I love her, Gareth. I made a mistake leaving. It took missing Sarah—and God, how I missed her—to show me how much I've been hiding out. The last thing I want to do is hurt her again. I'm thankful that she had you and Em for support. I'm going to do it right this time. I want Sarah in my life for good. Em, Dad and you, too. I want to be part of this family again, and I want to share that with Sarah."

They were just words. Dylan understood that he'd have to back them up with actions and emotions—he had to share his, as well as accept them from those he truly cared about. "I really hope you mean it, Dyl. Em has enough to deal with at the moment—I don't want her to be upset over you again."

Gareth was really protective of Emily. Dylan was glad of it, but he did wonder what it was that Emily was dealing with. He hoped it wasn't about him. He had caused his sister enough grief of late. But that would change, Dylan promised himself. He would be a better brother to her. He needed to find out what she was worried about and maybe help her through it, if she would let him. But first he had to win back Sarah's heart.

Chapter Twenty-Four

JetsRugbyLeague: What team do you think is our main threat in the finals? #jetsfinals

JetsRugbyLeague: If you can't make it to the game, what's your plan for game day? Tweet us your pics. #jetsfinals

Sarah had left the office the moment she'd been able to, had decided it would be easier to concentrate and finish all the work she needed to get done in the solitude of her own place. She also didn't really want to run into Joseph or anybody else who might have seen her talking with Dylan. She just couldn't face that sort of conversation when she had so much to think about—and decide.

Having finally finished reading through the hundreds of tweets the fans had been posting—answering some, re-tweeting others—Sarah finally looked up at the clock. *Six already! I really need to get dressed and meet Dylan.*

She hadn't thought about what to wear. Her nerves about the night ahead had been overshadowed by the amount of work she'd been doing. Her personal life might be a tragic mess, but her professional life was going gangbusters — the website, fan club and Twitter were experiencing the highest traffic they had all year. Sarah had even been interviewed recently by magazines and newspapers for her opinions, not only about social media but her thoughts on the Jets' chances this year too. It had been fun. While she was a fan of rugby league and especially the Jets, the interviews had been one of the stranger aspects of her unconventional life. Sarah really couldn't claim any in-depth knowledge of the game, not those finer points of strategy and positional play that coaches and players understood, but she knew the rules and enjoyed watching. The attention had been good for her self-esteem, though — her work being appreciated and spoken of.

Deciding on skin-tight leggings, boots and a loose-fitting jumper, Sarah locked up and made her way downstairs to the car park behind her building. She was on edge as she climbed into her car and headed towards Mia's, full of nervous anticipation about what lay ahead. She'd promised herself that she would give Dylan a chance to explain, maybe grovel a little before she ripped his clothes off and bonked him stupid. Sarah thought her outfit made her look short, but the tendency her jumper had to slip off her shoulder made her feel sexy. She hoped the glimpse of her skin — the skin that Dylan had told her during sex turned him on — would still have the desired effect on him. A little teasing on her part was the least he deserved.

It took a few trips around the block to find a parking space, and as Sarah pushed open the door to the restaurant she understood why. There was a huge table set up on one side of the busy restaurant, and every seat was taken by someone she knew. Brodie James and Caitlin sat beside JT Thomson and Mandy. Rook and Pippa sat next to Trevor and Rook's mother Laura. Riley Walters was sitting next to a blonde woman, and last but not least, Emily sat beside Gareth.

When Sarah spotted Dylan at the table set for two right beside this large group, her first instinct was to just walk right back out of the door.

This was not the night she had been mentally preparing for. Tonight was supposed to be about talking with Dylan privately, deciding if his declaration of love was genuine—learning about him on a more personal level. That wasn't going to happen under the prying eyes of her co-workers. If it hadn't been for the utter desperation on Dylan's face she would have left—turned on her heel and fled—but he looked so nervous. She could see by the way he jumped up from the table and quickly moved towards her that he was just as uncomfortable with the situation as she was.

"I'm sorry, Sarah. This isn't what I had planned for tonight. My jackass of a brother-in-law didn't trust me with you. They were all here when I arrived. I'll understand if you want to leave—we could go somewhere else, maybe."

Just hearing his voice made Sarah shiver. Dylan had a deep, husky tone that played havoc with her senses. It had been the sexiest sound she'd ever heard, and still was. It made her tingle from her toes right up to her scalp—pinpricks of pleasure raced over every nerve ending. He looked amazing, so tall, so masculine even in a room full of footy players. Dylan's body had always done it for her, and his scent was better than any aromatherapy money could buy—it turned her on and made her swoon all at once.

"You look incredible, Sarah, so sexy. That naked shoulder is going to haunt me forever. Your skin always had that effect on me, honey, so soft and smooth…"

Dylan was shuffling his feet as he stood in front of her, shielding her from the prying eyes of the table full of Jets-folk, and Sarah appreciated it. His reference to her skin also had her heart singing—it was exactly the reaction she had been hoping for—but standing here awkwardly in the doorway wasn't getting them anywhere. She made the decision easily, no mind game or mental debate needed. Sarah loved Dylan. He was worth the risk.

Placing her hands on Dylan's shoulders, Sarah stood on her toes so she could whisper in his ear, "My place… What do you say, Soldier? Do you remember the way?"

"Honey, I could find it blindfolded," was his quick response. "Are you sure? I don't want you to feel pressured. Tonight is all about you. We can—"

Sarah hushed what Dylan was about to say next by placing her finger over his lips.

"I want you to come to my place, Dylan. Let me deal with this lot first," she said as she glanced over his shoulder towards the table of her well-meaning but overprotective friends. "We can order in. You go on ahead, I'll be right behind you."

Brushing her lips over Dylan's was such a natural movement that Sarah reached up without thinking. When their mouths finally met, electricity sparked between them. She heard a moan, but wasn't sure if it was her own or Dylan's. So swift and light a connection of their bodies should not have had such a profound response. The fact that it did — still did after all that she'd gone through — should have made her shrink back in fear from the power Dylan had over her, but it was the opposite. It just proved to Sarah that he was it for her. No other man could compare, and her heart be damned, she wanted as much of Dylan as he would give her, no matter the consequences.

"I have missed those sweet lips something fierce, Red," Dylan whispered, sounding breathless and just as affected as her. "I'm going before you change your mind. See you at your place." Taking her hand in his and bringing it to his mouth, Dylan placed a kiss to the centre of her palm. Then he placed his hand and hers on his chest, over his heart. "Don't be long. I miss you already" were his last words before he turned and walked out of the door.

* * * *

Sarah stood for a moment, watching Dylan walk away, admiring the way his butt filled his jeans so perfectly. *Mmmm, I'm so looking forward to having my hands all over that,* she thought before finally turning back to face the restaurant tables. As she'd expected, all eyes at the Jets' table were on her. Judging by the look of concern on her friends' faces, they thought she had sent Dylan away. She was surprised at that — she knew she was smiling because she could feel the grin she was sporting.

"What do you all look so worried about?" she said as she reached the table edge closest to where Gareth and Emily sat. "Is it something about this weekend's game I need to know about?" she added trying to sound more serious.

Emily spoke first. "Are you okay, Sarah? We came here to show you some support. My brother doesn't really understand that his actions are often hurtful. I... We were worried. We care about you," she added, gesturing to everyone seated at the table. "I'm sorry it didn't work out for you. Dylan doesn't deserve you."

It was really poignant—Sarah had never had people to watch out for her before. The thought that all these people had come here to give her support and to show they cared nearly brought her to tears. Her eyes filled as she glanced around the table to look upon the face of each and every person who had come to be with her tonight. The men all looked furious, Gareth in particular—his jaw was clenched so tightly she thought he would start spitting out teeth any second. On the other hand, the women had so much sympathy showing for her that it did cause Sarah's tears to fall.

"That's it, Em," Gareth growled as he abruptly stood from the table, his chair crashing to the ground behind him. "I warned Dylan what would happen if he caused any more trouble. I'm going to rip his head off for this."

Sarah had jumped at the sound of the crashing chair, and the aggression in Gareth's tone was frightening. She had to stop Gareth—it wasn't like that at all, but she hadn't told them. Grabbing Gareth by the arm, Sarah began to explain.

"Wait, Gareth, stop! Everything is okay. Dylan and I are going somewhere a bit more private, that's all." Sarah's words were hurried as she tried to undo any misunderstanding. "I really appreciate you all being here, the thought is so generous and one I never expected. You guys are the ones who made me cry—

not Dylan. I've never had friends like you. Brodie, Rook, you should be focusing on the finals. Thank you for showing me, by being here"—Sarah was crying again, finding it difficult to control herself enough to continue speaking—"how much you care. Dylan and I need to sort through our problems, and we can't do that honestly with you guys breathing down our necks. Emily, I need to give Dylan a chance, for him and for me. Worst case scenario, it will give me closure."

"Aww, Sarah, I didn't even think of that. Of course you and my thick-headed brother need to talk. I give you my permission to use force if necessary," Emily said, standing up. She moved in closer and hugged Sarah.

"Hey, you could always borrow Emily's ropes. Her plan for reining Gareth in seemed to work," Rook added, followed by a hearty chuckle. It was short-lived, though. Sarah saw Pippa give Rook a nudge in the ribs that had him groaning and rubbing at his side. Sarah decided she was going to ask Emily what Rook had meant—but not right now.

An onslaught of hugs ensued. Everyone wanted to wish Sarah luck, adding their hopes that all would work out for her and Dylan. It was both wonderful and embarrassing at the same time, causing quite the spectacle in the middle of the dinner rush.

Time had passed quickly with all the hugging and crying, and Sarah just wanted to get home before Dylan thought she'd changed her mind. She rushed through another round of goodbye hugs before finally making her escape and hurrying home.

Chapter Twenty-Five

When Dylan spotted Sarah's car coming down the street he finally managed to breathe easily again. It had taken her so long to arrive that he'd convinced himself she'd changed her mind. So the sight of her black V-dub was pure relief for him, but her not slowing or stopping as she hurtled headlong towards the brick wall bordering the car park stopped his heart completely. Dylan yanked her car door open with such force, when the car finally stopped, that he was surprised it hadn't come off its hinges.

"Oh, my God, Sarah, are you okay? What happened? You nearly hit the wall, I didn't think you were going to stop... You scared the life out of me!"

Looking down at Sarah sitting behind the wheel, he was taken aback by the sight of her red-rimmed eyes—she had been crying. He was going to kill whoever had upset her... *It was probably you, stupid,* a little voice in his head interjected.

"I'm good, Dylan. Move back so I can get out."

"You've been crying."

"Just a bit, but happy tears so don't worry. I must look a mess—I'm not wearing waterproof mascara. I was distracted when I saw you standing there, that's all. It took me so long to get away from Mia's I was worried you might think I'd changed my mind about meeting you. I forgot to brake!" Sarah looked sheepishly at him as she made her admission.

She was standing so close to him as she spoke, her bare shoulder and neck enticing him. He loved this jumper—it was going to become one of his favourite pieces of Sarah's wardrobe. He needed to touch her, feel her warmth against his body, kiss that enticing piece of flesh beckoning him. Before he could stop himself, he pulled her into his arms.

"I need you, need to hold you, honey." He groaned in her ear as her body melded to his own. Having her in his arms was a pleasure he'd never thought he would feel again. The fact that Sarah had softened to his touch, had moved into him, her body pressed firmly against his own, filled him with such a sense of peace. *Home.* The word sounded loudly inside his head.

They stood motionless in each other's arms, soaking up the pleasure and warmth their bodies generated together for what seemed like hours to Dylan, but was probably just a minute or two. He could have stayed that way forever, if not for the words Sarah finally spoke.

"Inside me, Dylan. I need to feel you buried inside me so I know that this is happening, that it's not just a dream I'm about to wake up from."

"We need to talk first, honey. I promised you we would talk, take it slow—build up a relationship." Even though he had promised Sarah that very thing, it was going to be difficult for Dylan to keep his word.

He ached for the chance to be connected to her again that way, to bury his cock deep in her folds, to taste the sweet juices of her pussy on his tongue, and feel the plump softness of her breasts in his hands. *Mine*, his thoughts just kept repeating.

"And I will hold you to that promise, Soldier, but first I need you to show me how much you missed me. Actions first, then words, or the deal's off."

She was a sassy little woman, his Sarah, but what man could refuse her? Certainly not Dylan. If it was actions Sarah wanted, it was actions she would get—he would give her more pleasure than she'd ever imagined possible.

After sweeping her into his arms, he turned slightly and kicked her car door closed. Dylan carried Sarah all the way to her apartment door, only releasing her from his hold so she could find the key to let them inside. The moment she turned the lock he pushed them through the doorway, dragging her back into his arms and finding her lips with his. The kiss delivered such an impact that Dylan could have easily compared it to the force of a bomb. He was blown away by emotion and desire—his whole body shuddered with the force of it.

"Clothes... Too many..." Sarah stammered between their lips as he felt her hands grabbing at his shirt. Dylan dragged his hands away from her body for just long enough to tear his shirt from his torso. Buttons popped, fabric ripped, but he didn't care, not wanting to waste a second before he could go back to touching her. In a series of fumbled, desperate actions he and Sarah disrobed.

"You make me wild, Red—always have, always will. You are so beautiful," he said as he dropped to his knees to nuzzle against her tight curls. "Open your legs for me, let me see your pretty pussy. Let me worship you as I should have done all along."

Worshipping Sarah was no hardship at all. Dylan parted her wet pussy lips and just let himself drown in her goodness. He lost himself in the moment, the softness and warmth on his tongue as he devoured her, licked and sucked up her essence. He could not get enough of her. Sarah's sighs and moans urged him on even more. Dylan's cock was rock hard. He was so close to blowing he didn't think he had the power to stop, as he loved and laved Sarah with his mouth and fingers.

"Don't stop... Yes, there... Oh, Dylan, I'm so close."

Hearing Sarah's pleas, Dylan picked up the intensity of his actions. He circled and nipped at her clit, plunged two fingers deeper into her, hooking them slightly until he found the spot that would send her flying. He felt the quakes begin as Sarah's body neared climax — she was riding his fingers and mouth, pushing and rocking against him frantically, and as she climbed he began to tap on her clit with his thumb, then pushed down on it hard with his flattened tongue. Her body released — she shook from it. Dylan milked Sarah's orgasm from her body, wanting to bring her as much pleasure as he could, until he felt her pushing at him.

"No more, I can't take any more just yet," she whimpered as her body relaxed under his grasp.

"So we talk now?" Dylan asked as his dick throbbed in disagreement.

"You've got to be kidding me, Dylan. Talk? I can hardly think, let alone talk. Maybe a bit more action — it's my turn now!"

When Sarah wrapped her fingers around his cock, Dylan's eyes rolled back in his head. "Fuck, Sarah, stop... I won't last a minute if you keep that up," he managed to groan as he tried to not enjoy the touch quite so much, tried to hold back the pressure building in his balls, the stream of semen about to burst from him. "I want to be inside you when I come...God, you're killing me here...I can't hold on for much longer."

He tried to brush her hands from him, thought he had succeeded when her hand stilled, only for her to replace it with her mouth. In trying to regain some semblance of control, he had given Sarah the opportunity to kneel and now she was torturing him, the sweetest sort of pain a man could endure. The sight of Sarah on her knees, her lips wrapped around his cock, was the most erotic thing Dylan had ever seen. He could not take his eyes from her, from the way her cheeks hollowed as she sucked him into her mouth, her brown eyes watching him as she made him powerless to her.

Dylan let her control the pace, wanting so much to last, enjoy the moment for as long as possible, but when she grasped his butt cheeks and pulled him forward so his dick slammed into her mouth, his control snapped. He was rough with her as he grabbed her head, forcing more of himself into her than he should, but from the way Sarah was rubbing her wetness against his leg and swallowing his engorged cock, Dylan got the impression she was getting off on it as much as he was.

"Take what you need... Rub your clit... Come with me," he grunted, so close to losing his load that it was all he could do to string the words together. Sarah had understood his offer, though—the moment her fingers entered her body, as he had suggested, Dylan felt his seed explode from his cock. The sight of Sarah touching herself, with her lips stretched around his girth, had been too much, and he couldn't hold back. Spurt after spurt emptied from him and Sarah swallowed every last drop. He felt her orgasm through her mouth on his cock. At the way she sucked him harder and the vibration from her groan, all his blood rushed to his groin, leaving Dylan lightheaded and his legs only just holding him up.

The wicked smile on Sarah's face and the way she swiped her tongue over her lips was way too much for Dylan to cope with and still remain standing, so he knelt down in front of her and gently took her face in his hands. He had lost control, forced himself a little too roughly into her mouth, and he needed to make sure he hadn't hurt her before he could continue to enjoy the fact that he had just experienced possibly the best orgasm in his life.

"That was amazing. I'm really sorry I got rough, I lost control. I didn't hurt you, did I?"

Chapter Twenty-Six

The reality that Dylan had lost control and been so rough with her was what had made it so good for Sarah. He had lost it, and had let her see him that way. She loved the unrestrained Dylan Mackenzie, wanted to make him lose control all over again. He was worried he had hurt her, but the only problem she'd had was fighting off her own orgasm long enough to bring him undone—and she had done that.

"No, Dylan, you didn't hurt me. I love the way you lost control. I want to bring that man out in you, make you wild for me."

"That is not ever going to be a problem, Red. You have that effect on me. Just being near you makes me want to tear your clothes off and make love to you. That was one of the reasons you terrified me so much. You made me want those things I'd been denying myself, but around you I couldn't fight them any longer. It's why I ran. Sarah Flynn, you made me feel, and it scared the shit outta me."

"You scared me too, Dylan. I've never had anyone stay in my life for any length of time. I didn't want to fall in love with you, was so sure you would be like the rest and leave…and you did." Sarah whispered the last words, not wanting to punish Dylan, but it was the truth—he had left, as she'd believed he would.

"But I'm here now, Sarah, and I'm not going anywhere ever again. Come sit with me on the sofa, honey. I don't want you getting cold and if I don't cover you up soon, I won't be responsible for my actions…but we do need to talk first," Dylan said. He scooped Sarah into his arms just before he stood up.

Sarah couldn't help the squeak of surprise that escaped her lips at his actions. "Put me down, Dylan! I'm too heavy for you."

"Rubbish. I could carry you all day and not raise a sweat," Dylan replied with a laugh as he placed Sarah gently down on her sofa. "Wait here. I'm going to grab the doona off your bed so we can both be warm and comfy while I try and prove to you I mean what I say about us being together."

Relief and happiness had so thoroughly filled her heart and mind that Sarah was tempted to pinch herself just to make sure it had all really taken place, and wasn't some wild ride her imagination had conjured up to torment her. She had so much to be thankful for, and not just the sight of Dylan Mackenzie's totally nude body as he walked back towards her with her doona.

"Here you go. Let me tuck this around us while I tell you what made me such a fuck-up."

Sarah stayed silent, taking his hand in hers to show him some support. She appreciated that he was keeping his word about explaining to her why he'd left.

"The shrinks call it post-traumatic stress disorder, or PTSD. They reckon I've got some problems dealing with the shit that took place back in Afghanistan, the reason for these." Dylan rubbed at the scars on his shoulder as he spoke. "The part that gets me is that I can't stop reliving that day in my dreams, which inevitably leads me to going over the whole thing again when I wake up in a sweat, to see if there was something I could have done differently. It just happened so damn fast. One second I'm sitting in the transport and the next I'm being flung through the air, feeling like my body is on fire."

The pain on Dylan's face was obvious, so plain to see that Sarah could tell that whatever Dylan was about to confide in her was going to be bad — really bad. She squeezed his hand to show him some encouragement, at the same time wondering whether she was ready to hear what he had to say.

"It took a few moments of lying face down in the dirt to realise what had happened. We had been attacked with an IED — improvised explosive device. The result of the blast was actually reported as being minor, 'cause only one of my unit was killed. The brass reckon it must have misfired or been set up too far away when the initial explosion was triggered. But I gotta tell ya, Sarah, it was fucked up. There were four of us in that vehicle. None of us made it through without some sort of injury, one fatal. I started dragging my buddies off the road, worried another blast would be set off at any time. God, it was like something out of a horror movie. I knew Paul was bad. He'd been driving and I think the blast came from his side. His body shielded mine from the worst of it. Parts of his head were just mush. It was the worst sight I'd ever seen. They train you for it, tell you about the dangers, but nothing can prepare you for seeing your mate like that. Most of my own injuries were from the metal and glass flying from the truck. I was in charge. If I had been driving like I probably should have been, Paul would be alive and his kid would still have a father."

Sarah couldn't remain silent any longer. Dylan was blaming himself for the death of his friend and it wasn't his burden—it was the fault of the insurgent who had pushed the button or whatever it was they did, and she had to tell him so.

"Dylan, it was what it was, baby, a bloody terrorist bomb. I'm so sorry for your friend and his family, but I don't think you could've changed the outcome. It was the lunatic who made the decision to set off the explosion at that moment—he is the one that's to be blamed, not your choice to not drive that day. It's such a horrible thing, such a waste of human life, but I am so proud of you. You didn't hesitate to get the others out of harm's way, even with the threat of another bomb, and all while you were hurt yourself. No wonder they gave you a medal. You are so brave. I don't think I could have done that. I don't think many could put the safety of others before their own. Yet you and the soldiers serving do that over and over again, while we sit here and sip lattes and watch the footy." Sarah was on a roll. Everything she'd said to Dylan was the truth—she didn't think she would be able to recover from such a sight, such a horrific event. It was no wonder he had nightmares, and she was really glad that he was not going back.

"Thank you, Sarah. You have no idea what it means to me for you to say that. I'm trying to come to terms with the fact that I can't change what happened, but it's hard. You are in charge of these guys, feel responsible for them, listen to them talk about their lives, hopes and families. The other two guys were banged up pretty bad, but are okay now—both quit the service, though. At first I went back, but the shrinks were right to pull me back out. I just wasn't the same anymore. I was jumpy and anxious, hated making any decisions that might come back to haunt me. I just couldn't be responsible for anyone like that again."

"That is so understandable, Dylan. Just the fact you tried to go back shows you what sort of man you are—"

Dylan cut her off before she could continue. There was so much sorrow in his voice. "That's not really the case. I went back because I was too scared to come home. I didn't want to be around my family, didn't want to feel love for anyone, care about anyone. When I did care it just brought me pain and loss. After my mother died I tried to cut myself off..."

Sarah jumped in quickly to save Dylan from more heartache. "It's okay, Dylan. I know what happened— Emily told me about it. It must've been such a shock when you found your mum like that, but you know there was nothing you could have done, right?" She waited for Dylan to answer, could see the different emotions flicker across his face before he finally spoke again.

"For a long time I blamed myself. I promised her I'd come straight home from school, but like usual I was out gallivanting around with my mates while she was lying on the floor. I don't even know how long for, that's the part that gets to me the most. I guess I should at least be thankful that it wasn't Em who found her."

Sarah's heart was breaking for Dylan. He had suffered so much, held onto such misplaced blame.

"I understand that there was nothing I could have done for my mum, but when I realised that I was in love with you, I panicked. I didn't think I could cope with losing you the way my dad lost Mum, or you getting tired of me and leaving. I tried to convince myself that I was doing it for you, saving you from the loneliness of being a soldier's partner—or worse, if anything happened to me, a widow. I was kidding myself—I was scared to love you. The pain of not having you in my life was just as bad, if not worse, than what I was trying to protect myself from. Spending time with Dad on the farm, listening to him talk about Mum and the good times they shared made me wake up to myself. You can't hide from your emotions, good or bad, and cutting yourself off from the people you love is wrong. You miss out on so much and I missed you, Sarah. I want you in my life."

Hearing that Dylan had left her not because of anything she had done, but because he'd realised he was falling in love with her, left Sarah not knowing whether to slap Dylan or kiss him. As if she could have left him! She had been so far gone for him that she would have followed him to the moon and back if that was what Dylan had wanted. It was just crazy that someone brave enough to go and defend his country could be so scared of his own emotions.

"Thank you, for letting me in and for coming back to me. We can work this all out," she said as she caressed Dylan's face, trying to soothe away the pain and worry that marred his features. "I love you, Dylan, and I want you in my life as well. I was just as afraid of loving you as you were of loving me."

"Tell me why you say that, Sarah. I've told you my story—what in your past has hurt you so much?"

It was only fair that Sarah should open up to Dylan—after all, he had just bared his soul to her. But it didn't make it any easier. Talking about her own life's disappointments seemed insignificant compared to what Dylan had gone through. But she had to give him this, for both their sakes, so they could move past the events of the preceding weeks and the pain they'd caused. So, still clasping Dylan's hands tightly, she began her story.

"I think from the very beginning I expected you to leave. But after you said you loved me, twice, I started to believe that maybe you might stick around. I know what it's like to lose your mother. Maybe not as dramatically as you, but in a way I lost two. No one has ever stayed in my life.

"I grew up an only child and my parents were much older than those of my friends. They cared for me in their own way, I could see that, but they never showed me any affection, gave me hugs or praise like the parents of other kids my age did. My parents never helped out with school functions or committees—in fact, they discouraged me from joining any groups, actually going as far as forbidding it. I never got to go to birthday parties or anything like that.

"It didn't really become a major problem until I started high school. I was never allowed to do the things the other teenagers were doing, like go to the mall or the movies. I quickly found out that if you didn't fit in at school, didn't do the same as your peers, you were left behind or just left out. A social misfit. By the time I finished school I'd been labelled as a loner, even if that had been not of my own choice or making. I pleaded and argued often to be allowed to go to social outings, but to no avail. My parents never approved of any type of freedom.

"So, not surprisingly, I rebelled against them as soon as I could. The piercings, the wild hair colour, anything to fight the constraints of conservatism that had dogged my childhood. But the real shocker came on my eighteenth birthday, the day I learnt the people I'd thought were my parents...were really my grandparents. My real mother — their daughter — had dumped me on them not long after my birth, and taken off to parts unknown, never to return. They didn't even have a photo of her anymore. Told me they'd destroyed any mementos of her existence — well, apart from me, of course. There was nothing for me to see or touch. No picture of the woman who had given birth to me and then deserted me."

Sarah could feel the tears rolling down her cheeks, but didn't try to stop them. It was always the most upsetting part for her, that her grandparents had refused to talk about her mother. She'd thought about trying to track her down, but had always decided against it. After all, if her mum had wanted to see her at any time in the first eighteen years of Sarah's life, she'd known where to find her.

Dylan's clasp on her hands changed as he reversed their original positioning. His were now cradling hers. Squeezing them gently, he spoke.

"Oh, baby, that must have been a shock to you. To find out such a secret after all those years. I wonder why they waited to tell you. I was eighteen when Mum died, so I know what it's like to have that sort of shit happen to you at that age. But your parents...grandparents obviously loved you. They looked after you, even if that upbringing was a bit strange."

"That's just it, Dylan, it explained everything to me. They had loved my real mother, given her the perfect childhood. Showered her with gifts, done the ballet and piano lessons, the whole enchilada...and she had run off and got pregnant. It had devastated them. So they'd decided the same thing wouldn't happen to me. They tried to keep the outside world away from me. I think they held back some love too, probably because their daughter had caused them so much pain. Funny thing was, it didn't work. Look at me. I am an embarrassment to them. They hate my appearance, my life and job choices. We haven't really spoken in ages. I know I should be thankful, grateful that they took me in, fed me, clothed me, but..."

"They're crazy. Can't they see what a wonderful person you've become? So you look a little, um...unconventional, but that doesn't overshadow how great you are. Look at your successes—they love you at the Jets and your web design business is going well. You've achieved so much, and you and your grandparents should be proud of that."

"You didn't think that a few weeks ago. You left me too." Sarah knew she shouldn't bring it up again to Dylan, especially after he had just told her of his own emotional demons, but thinking about the past had reopened all her old wounds, leaving her feeling raw and insecure.

"That wasn't because of anything you did, it was because I was an idiot. Fuck, I'm so sorry that I did that to you, caused you any sadness," Dylan told her as he drew her into his embrace. "I won't leave you again, I promise you. You and I are perfect for each other. You make me want to be a better man. Loving you helped me find my way back to the real world and I will always remember you did that for me. You're not alone, Sarah, plenty of people care about you—just look at what happened earlier tonight."

What Dylan was saying did make sense, if she thought about it rationally. Only hours before, Sarah had discovered without a doubt that she was firmly entrenched in the extended Jets family. She had been amazed that so many had turned up at Mia's just to look out for her. "I've never had that, Dylan—people who looked out for me like that, by choice. This could end up being one of the best days of my life."

"The first of many, I hope, Red. I'm so sorry for leaving you, making you think it was your fault or something you deserved. It wasn't. You deserve love and friendship, honey. You are a beautiful person. The way you care about those young players... I can see how much they look up to you. I gotta admit, I was threatened by more than one of the Jets team, including Gareth, about what would happen if I hurt you again, and I'm glad they did it. It's good to know you have people looking out for you, and you can add me to the top of that list. I think we should both try and put the past behind us. I'm not leaving you, Sarah, not for the world."

Chapter Twenty-Seven

Emotions had been running high when Sarah and Dylan had moved to her bedroom, the excuse of needing to get some sleep before the sun came up behind their relocation, but the promise of continuing their reunion in the comfort of her bed just as enticing. They had both shed tears and consoled each other after their own personal confessions. The passion between them now contained a more personal element in its intensity. Sarah could feel it through their tender touches, and the kisses Dylan delivered, while still hungry, now held another element to them. She could feel the honesty in his touch, feel that he was open to her, holding nothing back. That was what Sarah had wished for, had hoped she could bring out in him.

Snuggled up against Dylan's chest, all Sarah wanted to do was make love again. But this new, chatty Dylan just wanted to talk some more—which was wonderful and all, but she was also very aroused at having his naked body beside her.

"Sarah, can I ask you something?"

"Mmm, yes...but I'd much prefer you touch me again soon." Sarah laughed as she continued to stroke the hard planes of Dylan's torso. "Have I mentioned how much your body turns me on, Dylan?" Sarah had stopped calling him 'Soldier'. She was still coming to terms with Dylan's declaration that he had quit the army — so he was never going away again.

"Why did you take out all the piercings? Not that they ever worried me, honey, just... Your face is so beautiful, it's nice to see it free of the distracting jewellery." The way Dylan kissed her nose, obviously referring to her absent nose ring, again made Sarah's heart flutter.

"Truth is, I'd been thinking about streamlining the metal for a while. I think I was getting tired of the look and the reasons behind wearing them. I am getting older, after all. Thought it was time to grow up and become a respectable member of society." She sighed. It was pretty much the truth — Sarah had been tiring of the shocked looks from people she met, and even though the hierarchy at the Jets had never made an issue of her unusual appearance, she could tell that they were relieved that she looked a tad more businesslike — less feral.

"So this new, respectable, grown-up outlook on life you have... Would that include maybe in the near future getting a husband and starting a family?"

He'd done it again, ignored his own promise. They'd only been back together for less than a night, and he was pushing her. The image of Sarah in a wedding gown, walking towards him, had materialised in his mind as soon as she'd made the 'respectable member of society' comment, followed quickly by equally attractive images of her with a baby in her arms. He couldn't stop his stupid mouth from asking her—not that it was an eloquent marriage proposal, but he did want to hear her answer. She was really taking her time, though, and Dylan was starting to sweat that he'd gone too far.

"In general terms, or did you have someone in mind for me?"

The little minx was teasing him, her brown eyes big and round. She was trying to look all innocent but the smirk she couldn't hide gave her away. The fact that Sarah could joke with him over his question gave Dylan the courage to keep going, this time deciding to be more specific.

"Definitely had someone in mind for you, honey."

Dylan rolled off the bed and walked around to Sarah's side, knelt down and took her hands in his. "I love you and even though I don't deserve you, have made some stupid decisions in my life, some of which have hurt those that love me...I know that this is the smartest move I will ever make. Sarah Flynn, will you marry me? I promise to love you forever, never leave you. I will do my utmost to make you happy and never regret the second chance you have so generously given me. I can offer you not only my love but the love of my family—you already have that anyway with Em and Gareth, but I can assure you my dad will adore you and treat you like another daughter. We don't have to rush if you don't want to... We can take some time to discuss it further if you like..." Dylan was starting to ramble on, nervous energy causing a fountain of words to spill, as if never-ending, from his mouth. He might have gone on forever if Sarah had not interrupted.

"Shhh, Dylan, are you going to let me answer you or not?" She laughed as she placed her hand against his mouth, smothering his next words. Dylan stopped talking and waited.

"Yes. The answer is yes… It's probably way too soon for us to be even mentioning marriage, but I don't care. I already know how much I love you… So yes."

Yes! She said yes! Dylan had to confirm Sarah's answer to his disbelieving mind. Yesterday he had been uncertain if she would even speak to him again, and today Sarah was agreeing to marry him. He was the luckiest man in the whole world.

"I may change my mind if you don't get back into this bed pronto and ravish me, Dylan."

"I did just promise to make you happy, so move over, Red, and let me at you," Dylan growled as he climbed in next to Sarah. He spread her legs and crawled between them, looking up at her. "So, my beauty, would it make you happy if I touched you here?" he asked as he caressed her knee with his open hand.

"Not really happy… I think you need to try farther up." She giggled.

Stroking farther up Sarah's leg, Dylan stopped his progress just inside her thigh. He could see the moisture glistening on her short curls. He was again thankful that he could evoke such a need in her, that he was the man she wanted to be with—despite his flaws. "What about if I touch you here? Will that make you really happy?"

As Sarah moaned, Dylan pushed two fingers into her wet opening. He teased her clit in a slow, circular pattern until she was writhing beneath him. As her pussy walls began to tighten around his fingers, Dylan withdrew. He needed to have his cock inside her, wanted to bring her to orgasm that way, wanted for

them to reach that climactic height at the same time —
together, as they would be for life.

"I need to feel your pussy wrapped around my cock,
be buried deep in your wet warmth as you come."

He was rock hard. Aligning his cock against her
pussy lips, he slid his length into Sarah slowly, her
body welcoming him eagerly. She was wet and hot for
him, and Dylan never lifted his gaze from her eyes.
Sarah was breathtaking, so responsive and open for
him, allowing him to see the depths of her emotions.
He could see her love for him in her eyes. There was a
smile on her lips, a flush in her cheeks. She wrapped
her legs around his hips and caressed his back as they
rocked together slowly. This was heaven.

"You were made for me, Sarah. Feel how perfect we
fit together, the way my cock fills your pussy, the way
we move together so easily, finding the perfect
rhythm. I love you, Sarah."

"I love you, Dylan."

Their pace increased as their passion ignited, each
urging the other nearer to completion, Dylan thrusting
and Sarah accepting him just as zealously. Their
bodies were wet from the exertion, but alive with
desire as they drove each other closer and closer to the
edge.

"Come for me, Sarah. I'm so close now. I want us to
fall together." As he spoke the words, Dylan felt
Sarah's orgasm begin. She strained, her body
becoming stiff under him, her pussy walls contracting
hungrily around his cock. As the climax swept
through her he let go, and more than just pleasure
erupted from him — love for Sarah filled Dylan's soul.
Tangled together, their arms and legs intertwined,
emotionally and physically replete, they both fell
asleep.

* * * *

The noise is so annoying. Someone needs to shut off that damn ringing... My body aches, a stabbing pain is lancing my upper arm and shoulder and I'm lying on the ground... What's happened? We were driving towards Kandahar for a routine sweep of the city. There hasn't been any new intel regarding threats from the Taliban, it should have all gone down without incident... So why am I lying on the ground with a mouthful of dust, dirt clogging my lungs, surrounded by a fog of the same shit that's filling my mouth, with fucking fire burning in my shoulder? IED – they must have triggered a roadside bomb. I've got to get up and move away, the Taliban soldiers could be nearby, but what's with all that moaning?

Briggsy, where is he? I need to find the other guys. I can't remember who was with me... My brain's all messed up. Fuck! Briggsy was halfway through telling me about some chick he had lined up for when he got leave... Where the fuck is Briggsy? The pain's getting worse but I've got to find the others, get them to safety.

Shit, what's that? A body... Blood everywhere, and dirt. I need to move the body away from the road and get help – God, I can't even tell who it is or if he's still alive... Right uniform, though. Don't look. I think his leg is still there. Don't think about it, just keep moving, drag the body, one foot after the other, ignore the pain... Keep moving. I need to find the other three. Wish the smoke haze would just fuck off so I could see. Move, Dylan, keep moving... I just want to rest for a minute, get a handle on the pain... Can't, no time. Need to find the rest before the fuckers come back to finish us off –

"Dylan, wake up. You're having a dream. It's Sarah, it's okay. You're here with me, here in bed, not over there. It's just a dream. Wake up. Come back to me, Dylan."

Dylan woke to find Sarah's arms encircling him, the sound of her voice soothing him bringing him back from the clutches of yet another nightmare. He should have been embarrassed, should have been appalled that she had witnessed one of his traumatic dreams. In the past he would have been, but Dylan felt differently now. He really wanted to share all of himself with Sarah, and his nightmares were a big part of him now, as was the occasional panic attack that affected him when he heard sudden loud noises.

Having Sarah's body next to him, bringing him back to the here and now, felt good. He was still covered in sweat and could almost taste the dirt in his mouth from the vivid recollection of the past, but Sarah's warmth and her voice gave him a pleasant distraction from his pain, gave him something much more appealing to focus on.

Dylan reached for her, his hands still shaking from the after-effects of the nightmare. Dragging her head towards his, he smothered her lips with his own and as her mouth opened for him, he replaced that cloying taste of dirt with her unique flavour. He exchanged the brutal imagery that had haunted him with the erotic vision of Sarah and him, their bodies joined as one as they brought each other the joy and pleasure that he knew they would achieve. Dylan lost himself to the beauty of Sarah's body and the symphony of her sighs, quickly forgetting what had awoken him in the first place.

Epilogue

JetsRugbyLeague: Congrats to @JosephO & team for the grand final win today. They owned the match from start to finish — Jets are looking good for the future.

JetsRugbyLeague: Commiserations to our first grade. You gave it your all & your fans are proud to be Jets supporters no matter what. Next year will be ours.

The season end had mixed results. The pups' victory had helped lift the spirits of the first grade squad over their own narrow loss. The club was filled to brimming with fans eager to celebrate a positive season, and full of hope for the coming year.

Sarah was full of hope as well. Dylan had been by her side ever since the night they'd reunited. Even Joseph had stopped glaring at him menacingly. They had not mentioned their decision to get married as yet, thought they would wait until after the last game, but secretly she and Dylan had made plans for the future.

Dylan was still having the occasional nightmare, but Sarah was relieved that they seemed to be becoming fewer and farther apart. She had convinced Dylan to do some counselling for his PTSD, and it did appear to be helping him. Those times when Sarah was awoken by the sounds of Dylan's distress, when he was again reliving those dark moments in his dreams, she would hold him and whisper soothing words in his ear until he dragged himself free from the clutches of those brutal times past. Then, together, they would make love, dispelling any lingering memories, replacing them — at least for that moment — with more pleasurable ones.

She was sad to be leaving the Jets, but moving to Gunnedah with Dylan was something she was really looking forward to. There was the possibility of expanding her website design business, which had taken a back seat to her digi duties of late. All she needed was Internet access and a phone. In truth, though, Sarah was looking forward to farm and family life.

"Thank goodness you two sorted it out." Emily's voice distracted Sarah from her own thoughts.

"You can say that again, Em. There is a lot to love about that brother of yours, and I intend to work on it forever." Sarah grinned.

"It would have made it very uncomfortable at the christening if the baby's godparents weren't on speaking terms."

Baby? Godparents? "Oh, my God, you're pregnant!" Sarah's surprised voice came out a little louder than she'd wanted, but the shock and the joy that Em and Gareth were having a baby, that Dylan was going to be an uncle and that Emily had just asked Sarah to be godmother were overwhelming. "Does Dylan know? Oh, Em, he is going to be over the moon! You really want me to be godmother?" Tears rolled freely down Sarah's cheeks. Never in her life had she felt so much a part of a family, so loved. Dylan had given her this. If she didn't love him so completely as it was, she would have loved him even more.

As if he had sensed her tears, Dylan appeared beside her.

"What's wrong, honey? Why the tears? Has Joseph been giving you a hard time again?" Dylan's concern was obvious as he took Sarah into his arms.

Emily started laughing. "You are so pussy-whipped, brother dearest. Sarah has you wrapped around her little finger." She was still chuckling as Dylan flashed an angry glance her way. It was so funny seeing the siblings taking shots at each other again that Sarah started to giggle too.

"Not helping, Emily. I hate seeing Sarah upset..." Dylan paused, finally noticing that she was laughing. "Or not upset, apparently. Okay, you two, what gives?"

Gareth had joined them. Standing behind Emily, he wrapped his arms around her and placed his hands on her belly. Sarah thought it was so moving that she nearly started to cry again. Luckily, Gareth spoke, distracting her. "So, wife, are we allowed to tell people now?"

"Yes, Cowboy. You can start with my boofhead brother—he will really need to lighten up if he is going to make a good uncle."

"U-Uncle? Y-you mean...?"Dylan stammered.

Sarah's heart was so full of love she was sure it would explode. Seeing Dylan lost for words and the way he was looking at his sister—this was what being part of a family was supposed to be about. Love, sharing joys and sadness together, each helping the others through life's journey... And hers was finally about to begin, with Dylan beside her—a man to love and be loved by in return—a friend like Emily who was soon to become her sister-in-law, and Gareth, a brother-in-law who had been so ready to protect her. Plus a father figure in Mac.

Sarah had met Mac just this past week. He had stayed with her and Dylan at the apartment. The acceptance and affection Mac had given her in that short time had done so much to heal Sarah's pain over her own family's lack of genuine love for her that Sarah had jumped at his offer that she could call him 'Dad'. It had made Dylan happy as well. She loved the smile that lit up his face when she used the paternal term in reference to his father. *Dad*—Sarah had wanted one for so long. The fact that she had found the best of them never failed to amaze her.

Sarah had everything that she'd spent her life dreaming of and missing, and she was looking forward to her new life and all it promised...

* * * *

JetsRugbyLeague: Congrats to Cowboy and Emily on the birth of baby Sally. This digi-chick is signing off to get hitched.

JetsRugbyLeague: @RileyW_jetsmedia will be taking over for a while. Thanks for all the well wishes! Jets fans are the best.

About the Author

Sydney-born Donna Gallagher decided at an early age that life needed be tackled head on. Leaving home at fifteen, she supported herself through her teen years. In her twenties she married a professional sportsman, her love of sport—especially rugby league—probably overriding her good sense.

The seven—year marriage was an adventure. There were the emotional ups and downs of having a husband with a public profile in a sometimes glamorous but always high—pressure field. There were always interesting characters to meet and observe, and even the opportunity to live for a time in the UK. Eventually Donna returned home a single woman, but she never lost her passion for watching sport, as well as the people in and around it.

Now happily re-married and with three sons, Donna loves coffee mornings with her female friends, sorting through problems from the personal to the international. But she's on even footing with the keenest man when it comes to watching and talking rugby league.

Donna considers herself something of a black sheep in a family of high achievers. Her brother has a doctorate in mathematics and her sister is a well—known Australian sports journalist. An avid reader, especially of romance, Donna finally found she couldn't stop the characters residing in her imagination from spilling onto paper. Naturally, rugby league is the backdrop to her spicy tales of hunky heroes and spunky heroines overcoming adversity to eventually find true love.

Donna Gallagher loves to hear from readers. You can find her contact information, website details and author profile page at http://www.totallybound.com.

Totally Bound Publishing